Mikey and the Chickadee

KID BOISE

To the baristas of Flying M Coffeehouse
Boise, Idaho, USA

1

In a word: stability. This man in his gray suit radiated stability, there in the rain next to a lamppost, not leaning against it as I would have done, but standing on his own two legs as he texted furiously away on his massive phone.

I stood just under the eaves of a bus shelter, on the cusp, as I was these days, of a life more adventurous.

Not the least bit troubled as his screen became flecked with water, he glanced right, south, the direction from which he, both of us, several of us, knew the bus to come.

Pathetically, this was the latest along a string of encounters acknowledged only, it seemed, within my own mind. The thread had grown lengthy enough to reach back six months to a time when a summer spent traveling clung on by one finger and I settled into my first post-grad occupation in Accounting. Yes, it's true that I had traveled, seen Europe with two friends from my college program, and it was an experience every bit as enriching as they had convinced me it would be. For nearly two months I screamed, I laughed, I became someone; I met people on the road whom I revealed my whole self to unhesitatingly. Later on, the enormity of this personal growth would serve only to enhance my disappointment and self-loathing when I slipped with alarming ease back into complacence, gasping fish into pond, at home in my new job.

Perhaps there had existed a window of time during which I

would have approached him, even with some semblance of confidence. This window began when I first assumed our shared bus route, set back down on the earth still ready to run, still willing to share myself, still holding the point of view that I was worth sharing. It ended when my mind no longer grasped so firmly the temporary perspective I had taken on, when outlines of memories were no longer in focus.

If this tiny window had existed at all, I had not taken significant notice of him from within its bounds. That happened later, on one of the last truly warm, sun-filled days, when I sat directly behind him, and he sat next to a small elderly woman. I was first exposed only to the back of his head, a shock of black-as-night hair that spiraled outward from a common center to form a structured mess that occurred to me as nest-like and effortlessly charming. Phone to his ear, he spoke with a voice that scooped up the surrounding air, in a language which, only after some time and with considerable effort, I identified as Thai. Apparently aware of his conspicuous presence on an otherwise quiet bus, his phone conversation was brief, and then he sat in silence.

In this town I would not take for granted another person's ability to speak English, however, the old woman next to him seemed to hold no such reservations.

"Do you ride this bus often?"

He turned to her and I caught one side of his face: the smooth skin of his cheek (not extremely dark but certainly darker than mine), the left eye, deep-brown and heavy-lidded, abbreviated nose, linear jaw angling cleanly upward near the neck.

"Yeah I do," he said with no particular accent that I could detect. "I ride it to work." He then smiled with such genuine compassion that the woman may as well have been his own grandmother.

"I thought so," she said. "I remember you from the last time I was on, but that was weeks ago." Her shoulders shook in quiet laughter.

"I'm sure it was me. I've been riding this route for more than a year." He then proceeded to ask her about her day and, as her answers came, regarded her with careful interest.

As I listened, forever a shameless eavesdropper, I, too, realized it wasn't the first time I'd seen him. And in the months to come I would continue to notice him. It wasn't something that happened every day. I did sustain a compelling interest in my career of choice, and I will admit that there were days when I was so engrossed in preparing for work that I couldn't have recalled whether he had ridden the bus that day at all.

So, it appeared, did he. On days when I noticed him, his gaze would often shift from papers perched on his lap to his phone's screen and then back again. Occasionally he would hold conversations in English over the phone regarding presentations and clients and many other business-related concerns, but his field never became clear to me.

And unclear it remained on this day in the rain at the bus shelter. Looking up from his phone, he seemed to think better of letting the rain soak into his suit and, in his casual manner, trudged over to stand under the eaves, next to me. Although not very broad-shouldered, he filled out his suit well. He was also tall; I had already known all of this, but our standing proximity had never permitted me the chance to size him up properly. Without looking over I could tell that he was a couple of inches taller than I was, and I stood somewhat above average.

I imagined a fantasy world in which he noticed me just for one second. What was his impression? Lighter skin, darker suit, this fledgling white boy. Younger maybe, but if so, not by much. Did he fill out his suit quite so pleasantly? Did he stand with any ounce of confidence at all? Was his compulsion to exercise regularly at the gym evident in the muscles of his neck?

In my past I had beckoned the attention of a few boys whose looks I estimated to surpass my own, and although my conceptualization of the person I projected outward was ill-defined, I lacked much of the insecurity concerning one's own appearance that I sometimes noticed in other people. I cut my dark-blond hair short, as there was a lot of it. I was dealt the fortunate hand of a clear complexion. My face was structured in a way that I believed to be pleasing. In truth, I rarely considered my physical being beyond an approximate effort to maximize what was there.

The bus arrived much more full than I'd ever seen it. I boarded directly behind him and watched him sit against the window in the last remaining open pair of seats. There were other single seats available farther down the aisle, but no matter where I chose I would be seated immediately next to someone. There was no reason not to sit next to him. I understood this then and did so.

Because neither of us was small in stature, this move immediately lacked any of the relaxed feel I'd hoped for. We were not uncomfortably close, but a brief acknowledgement of the circumstance felt inevitable. I was, however, silent for a few minutes.

Finally I said, "Busy today." I don't remember deciding expressly to speak, and yet there it was. "Must be something going on downtown."

"It's Pride," he said.

"It's what?"

"Gay Pride," he said. "Well, as in, the event. Not just the

everyday, you know, look at me, I'm gay, I'm proud."

I couldn't help but laugh at this.

"I don't mean to offend," he said, "if you're gay or something. I can be a little awkward around strangers sometimes."

I had trouble believing that. "I am, but you didn't offend me."

"Oh," he said. "Well that's good."

I felt stupid for not having remembered the winter pride event that took place every year here. Although it was smaller and by design more somber than its shimmering mid-summer counterpart, I had attended before, more than once, compelled by my own curiosity. It crossed my mind that in my haste to become a functioning adult, I had abandoned a few of my old interests (not to mention a few people I associated with them).

We kept to ourselves for the rest of my twenty-minute ride, and there was no point in my wishing we hadn't. He was still for a minute, maybe out of courtesy to me, before retrieving his phone from his coat pocket. I did not try to steal any glances at what he was up to. Already I was folding back into myself. It had finally happened, and now it was over. Nothing had come from our voices' first chance to intertwine in conversation except, I guessed, transmitting the one and only crucial fact about me that I would have wanted him to know—that I was gay.

If I stood any chance at all of gaining the particular kind of attention from him that I desired, this otherwise arbitrary detail about my life was the best thing I could have divulged. Furthermore, I hadn't said anything uninvited; in fact it was something he had all but set me up to reveal. This could have been unintentional on his part, but I refrained from wasting any more energy in analysis. At least now he knew.

Each day I left the bus behind at one of the city's busiest intersections, a two-block walk from my company's offices. I could never have known how much longer he remained on the bus, but today, as I departed, I turned back for one last glimpse of him before entering the rambling hive of pedestrian traffic. He looked directly into my eyes, and then back down at his phone. He didn't smile. He also did not seem unhappy.

I would be a liar if I said I didn't think of him on and off for the rest of the day. In all honesty, though, I believe it to be the first time thoughts of him stole more than a few seconds from each passing hour at my desk. That night I wondered cynically what situation could possibly lend itself to further interaction between us.

As it turned out, my wait for an answer was brief.

The next morning was colder, but dry. I had overslept and was walking with purpose from my transfer when I was stopped short by his approaching form, gliding above the earth, away from the bus stop.

Once within an acceptable distance he said, "The bus is down. Looks like it could be a while."

This was unfortunate timing. I had scheduled a performance review with a supervisor whose opinion I valued, and in whose hands lay the responsibility of determining wage increases. Now stomaching the idea of calling for a taxi I could not comfortably afford, I looked past him toward a handful of fellow bus riders who stood talking on their phones. "Do you think any of them would split a taxi with me?" I wondered aloud.

"Don't worry about that. My place is close and I have a car. I'll drive you."

He looked at me with such devastating concern that I very nearly needed to hug him then and there, to assure him that I felt deeply nurtured by his offering. "You really don't need to do that."

"It would make me happy if you'd say yes."

His dark eyes divulged a fleeting sadness, which I spent the next instant wondering if I'd actually seen. I had a number of reasons to say yes. "Alright," I said.

He didn't say anything but smiled and started in the direction he'd been walking, and I fell in alongside him.

"How old are you?" I asked. The question came to me out of nowhere, and sounded extremely bizarre now that it hung in the cold, clear morning air.

"Twenty-three," he said. "How old are you?"

"Twenty-two," I replied, in a casual tone that mirrored his apparent lack of sentiment for his age, and immediately struck me as idiotic, since I had obviously cared enough to ask in the first place.

"I figured we were close in age," he said.

I wanted to ask him if he had any reasoning that ventured beyond appearance, but it felt like another strange thing to ask, so we just walked in silence for a minute.

"It's not much farther," he said, "just around that corner. Do you live close to here?"

"Not really. I get off the 40A at Stratham and walk from there."

"That comes from Corbin right?"

"Yes," I said. He referred to the nearby suburb in which I rented a clean, small studio. On my street, the buildings did not crowd together and up against worn sidewalks the way they did here. I envied him a little for calling this cozy, bustling part of town his home, but the rent was out of reach for someone like me.

"I grew up in Corbin," he said. "I don't go back there too

often anymore, though."

"Oh, cool," I said. "I grew up there, too. Never quite made it out, I guess."

Cars hurried along the narrow street, shunted between endless lines of parked vehicles, punctuated only by the occasional side-street entrance or hydrant.

Suddenly he ran several feet ahead of me, whipped around, tie and coattails flying outward, and pointed at me with both hands. "Bengals."

I stopped and shook my head. "Chickadees."

"Aww, get out of here, then," he said, letting his whole frame slump down as I caught up with him. "Although I guess I would have remembered you if you were a Bengal."

I laughed. "Sorry to disappoint you." Although I had no stake in, nor had ever paid much attention to the unusually heated high school rivalries in my hometown, his impromptu display had been completely void of pretense, playful and lovable.

"My car's in here," he said, leading me off the sidewalk, through a door, and into a parking garage that occupied the first floor of his apartment building.

His silver Honda Accord sedan hunkered in a lonely stall near the back, by the alley. I sat down in the passenger seat and noted its newness in look and smell. I asked him about it as he stood removing his coat by the open driver door, and he confessed that it was still pretty much brand-new. "I bought it a few months ago, but I don't use it as much as I thought I would. Can't shake that bus."

He sat down behind the wheel, shoved his coat into the back seat, and soon we were off. He reached out to turn up the heat, and I, unable to help myself, glanced up his arm to see that his bicep stretched almost taut the upper-sleeve of his salmon button-down. I turned away quickly and looked out the passenger window.

"So besides being a brave Chickadee," he said, "what is there to know about you?"

I looked back at him. What was there to know? I became suddenly and inexplicably self-conscious. "What do you want to know?"

"Well," he said, "what do you do for work?"

I told him about the accounting job, about how it was very entry-level and still mostly administrative. I described the meeting awaiting me that morning and conceded that I was anxious about it.

The whole time he listened in silence, nodding and smiling here and there and when I was finished, said, "You'll have to let me know how it goes," with none of the gratuitous job-related reassurance that I had, ungratefully, grown a little tired of from friends and family. I rarely sought reassurance concerning my career, but often received it.

"I will," I said, excited at the thought of our interaction extending even further into the future. I folded my hands together in my lap. "So what do you do? I've noticed you look busy on the bus sometimes." This comment was a little brazen on my part.

"I work for a software development company called Pancaked. We help other software companies streamline their stuff. Make their coding more succinct, make their data take up less room, stuff like that."

"That's pretty impressive," I said. "I like the name." I found myself wishing I knew something about software and coding and data storage. "How long have you been with them?"

"About two years."

"I hope they pay you well. Sounds like pretty complicated

stuff."

"It varies, I guess."

"I see," I said, although I wasn't sure if it was the pay or the work that varied. It felt inappropriate to ask him to clarify.

He didn't say anything after that, and drove in silence for a few minutes. I found myself feeling oddly comfortable just sitting quietly beside him. I could detect, just slightly, the heat from his body, radiating across the console dividing the two seats. In a way I knew to be absurd, given what little I knew about him (and how new it all was), this made me feel safe.

Finally he cleared his throat and said, "I'm sorry. I feel like I was being a little vague. I should say that my pay isn't completely consistent because I sort of started it myself, so it's not conventional in that way."

I looked over at him. "Are you serious? That's awesome."

"Well," he said, "the thing is, I couldn't have done it without help. I have a cousin who I brought on pretty early in the game and she's made it way better than I ever could have on my own." After saying all of this he looked embarrassed, which made me feel sad.

I didn't know quite what to say in response, but because he had refrained from offering reassurance earlier, I suspected he wasn't looking for any, either. "Well, I think it sounds really cool."

"Thanks," he said. "It's a ton of fun, most days. That's about all I can ask for."

I wouldn't have described my job as a ton of fun, ever. But I found moments of enjoyment in it, which felt like enough. I considered sharing this with him, but then realized how quickly we were approaching my stop.

"Want me to get you closer?"

"No," I assured him. "This is just fine. I can't thank you

enough. Seriously."

He swung the car swiftly up to the curb and turned on the hazard lights. "What time should I pick you up?" he asked.

"What? Seriously?"

"Hurry up," he said, flashing a grin. "I'm blocking traffic. Same time you board the bus home?"

I was too selfish to tell him no, to say that he'd already done too much. I needed more time with him. "Uh, yeah sure," I replied. "That would be amazing. Thank you so much."

"No problem," he said as I stood up onto the sidewalk. "Stay out of trouble, Chickadee."

He waved and I let the door close with a muted thud. He signaled to rejoin traffic and sped away, leaving me standing there, motionless, taking this time to reflect with happiness for just one minute—time I felt I owed to myself—on what a pleasure it was to finally know this man. If today was all I should expect, if I woke up tomorrow and we never spoke again, at least I had known him once. But I was optimistic that we would see more, know more of one another in days to come.

2

Disappointment does not ask permission to enter one's life; this was the irrefutable truth with which I was comfortably familiar. What I had forgotten was its stoic disregard for any pleasantness that may have entered before it.

Later that morning I had trouble focusing on anything besides the conversation that had transpired during the meeting with my supervisor.

She had smiled continually, to the point that her face no longer appeared amiable. "We're asking you and a few others whom we have not yet chosen to be moved to the offices in Fern Hill. This branch has taken on a few new senior-level employees and we're short on room. You'll have six weeks to prepare, and relocation costs will be accommodated."

Work passed slowly today. It marked the first time in recent memory that I had even glanced at the clock before lunch. Late-morning hours normally spent careening through paperwork were chained down by the unsettling nature of our exchange.

"Thank you," I had said. "Thank you so much for finding a place for me. I appreciate this opportunity."

The thought of waking each day in a small town four hours from the city, removed from all of this fantastic mayhem, proved difficult to digest. Six weeks would allow plenty of time for digestion, but a new and strange impermanence had already crept up over the edges of my desk and anchored itself there so that my job as I knew it, my livelihood in this city, that which I had finally trusted enough to hold onto, had transformed into something only temporary.

In a sense it was not unlike my summer abroad, constrained by two dates, bollards bolted into stone, one marking the birth of an experience onto which I would tether myself, the other signaling an inevitable end. I now had another ending date, the terminus of next month, to ponder in quiet contrition during the days leading to its arrival.

I'm certain my productivity for the rest of the day could have been measured as inadequate, but I would imagine, given the circumstances, that no ruler was held up against me. I drifted through the final hours in lazy irresolution. Of course I would go. It was the natural path forward for anyone whose career was as young as mine. I realized I had yet to assert this change as necessary and valuable not just to my career, but to my personal growth and wellbeing. Maybe once I discovered how to do that, I would find peace.

I exited the building and made my way among the boundless flock of commuters, beneath cliff-like faces of stone, glass and steel, coming nearly to the bus stop before I remembered. Were my problems so immensely important that I had almost forgotten? Frustrated with myself even more than with the latest developments, I sat gloomily on a bench near where he had dropped me off and waited.

I couldn't have sat longer than a minute before his silver Honda halted at the curb just feet from where I rested. His wild-haired form and broad smile, visible through the passenger window, compelled me into motion. The whole of me desired simply to be back in the car, returned to that shared space with him.

And I was. The roar of the city died away and we were alone.

He shifted the car into first gear and turned to me. "I'm Mikey, by the way. Sorry I didn't introduce myself earlier."

Mikey—such a fantastically handsome name, and somehow it fit him perfectly.

The car began to move and he steered out into traffic, so I did not try to shake his hand. "I'm Wyatt," I said, "and don't worry; I didn't either."

"Wyatt," he said. "That's a good name. Guess I can't call you Chickadee forever."

"You can call me whatever you want. It's just a name," I said in a tone more downtrodden than I expected. In this moment, still fettered by the idea of endings, forever sounded like a beautiful, superb length of time. Feeling a bit reckless I said, "Actually, I like it when you call me that."

He was quiet for a few seconds, long enough to have me worried that what I'd said sounded strange. "That's good to know." He downshifted as we approached slower traffic. "So, how was the big meeting?"

"It was pretty good," I told him. "Anyway, it's over now, so there's no more wondering what's going to happen." I paused for a second before saying, "But I want to know what a day at work is like for you. How is it to run your own company?"

He brushed back a group of course, black strands from in front of his eyes. "I guess there are a lot of ways to answer that. But today, it was like operating some big, noisy machine that's not in very good repair. As the machine runs, it's like one component stops working, and when you fix that one, it affects another, so that becomes broken instead, and so on. It sounds awful," he said, "but it's really pretty great."

"I don't think it sounds awful," I said. "Are you talking

about fixing someone's software?"

"Yes, exactly," he said. "For me, running the company is ancillary to all of the actual work, like finding blocks of code that aren't serving a good purpose, or database structures that are poorly organized."

"Ah, okay," I said. "It sounds like you still do a lot of the hands-on work yourself."

"Yes, I still do. And I hope I always get to," he said, smiling. "That's where all the fun is, for me. It's so nerdy, I know."

I laughed. "Yeah, because accounting is so much more glamorous."

"Hey, that's right," he said. "We're not done talking about your job. What did they tell you in the meeting?"

"Well," I said, "it didn't go how I thought it would. Not at all, actually. They want to relocate me. I don't think it's permanent, but I'm pretty sure it's for a while."

"Where?"

"Fern Hill," I said.

"As in the resort town? How far away is that?"

"Four hours," I said.

"When do you go?"

"End of next month."

"You're serious?" He put a fist flat against his chest and made small seizing sounds, as if he had been physically wounded. "And just after we become friends. You're killing me, Chickadee, you know that?"

"I know, I'm sorry," I said. He had no idea how sorry I really was. And already he had called me his friend.

"I've heard it's beautiful up there," he said. "I've never been, though."

"It really is. It's a great place to visit. To live there, though, I'm just...I don't know." I stopped and looked at him. His eyes focused on the road, but I could have sworn that most of his attention had been diverted toward me. I looked away.

He turned and glanced at me for an instant before looking back at the road. "If I were in your shoes, I would be very upset right now," he said. "How do you stay so calm?"

"I'm not calm. I mean, I definitely don't feel calm," I replied. "It must just not show."

He took his time responding, staring ahead and making small adjustments to the car's path of travel as we crossed the bridge out of downtown. "You know, even though we just met and all, you don't have to hide that from me."

"I don't know if I'm hiding anything," I said, although I suspected he might be right. "I am upset, that's true."

"So," he said, "what do you think you're going to do?"

"There isn't much I can do," I replied. "This is my career. In the whole scheme of things, like, later in life, ten years down the road, I think I would look back on it as a small sacrifice. A year or two away in exchange for long-term stability. I mean, that's nothing, right?"

I sat in thought for a minute. He must have sensed that I wasn't finished, because he stayed silent.

"It's just…this doesn't feel like a small sacrifice," I said. "It feels like a massive sacrifice, if I'm honest. That's how I feel right now. I can't be me in ten years. I can't get into that head-space."

He started to say something but only a small amount of air escaped his mouth. We rode along without speaking for at least another minute before he moved his hands to the bottom of the steering wheel and said, "But the you in ten years isn't a real thing. It literally doesn't exist."

It occurred to me that Mikey might fall in among those extraordinary people who wait to speak until they can say something in which they have full confidence. "Right," I said. "Yes, that's true."

"You, sitting here, right now. That's all."

I smiled at him. "I'm not disagreeing with you."

He laughed. "Well, I'm done. That's all I have to offer you."

"You've done enough listening to this garbage." I noticed we had turned right, off the main road, and were closing in on his neighborhood.

"It isn't garbage, and I will be here as long as you need to talk. But I think it would be rash to decide anything today, so maybe we do need to change the subject."

"We're out of time, aren't we?" I asked. "I mean, you can just drop me off on Stratham. The 40 should come by soon."

"Would you be violently opposed to me driving you all the way home? It would be nice to see Corbin again."

I was beginning to feel that he enjoyed talking with me as much as I did with him.

"Not violently, no. If you're okay with it, I would be very appreciative."

"I am more than okay with it."

"Well, fuck the 40, then," I said.

He smacked the rim of the steering wheel. "Yeah, fuck the 40."

After we had turned south I said, "If I had a car I don't think I'd ever take the bus. Is that terrible?"

"No. If I had your commute, I would probably drive. I have a space in the garage under the office, so parking isn't really an issue. It's just that I live so close to the bus stop, and I don't have to transfer like you do."

"Still," I said, "it seems like it would take a lot of willpower to get on the bus every single day, especially with a shiny new car at your disposal."

He paused. "I do kind of have this thing about mass transit. Sustainability and all that. Cars may not be an option forever."

I turned and threw him a sly smile. "But Mikey, you said it yourself: All we have is right here, right now."

"Hey." His lips spread into a massive grin and then he punched me on the shoulder.

"Ouch," I said, laughing. "Was that necessary?"

"If you can't handle it, don't dish it out."

"I was dishing out words," I insisted. "The proper response to words is opposing words."

He laughed at this. "Well, I didn't have any opposing words." He attempted a pouting face, extending his bottom lip outward just a little before giving up and cracking a smile.

"Seriously, though, I get what you mean. Sustainability. That's actually really noble."

"I don't know," he said. "It feels like the right thing, most of the time. It's a shame, though, because I really do like driving."

"Is it hard to drive a manual? I never learned."

"It took me about a week to get used to it," he said. He shifted into another gear and then back again in absent demonstration. "Not on this car, but on one I had in high school. Do you want to try it?"

"No," I said. "Well, not right now."

"If you ever want to learn, tell me," he said. "You'd be good at it."

Mikey said things in a way that invoked visions of us spending time together in the future. I considered this while I watched the sun set out my window. Beyond houses, buildings and occasional fields, all of it racing by, I caught flickers of open water and the far-off levee holding it at bay. The next few miles were peppered with conversation borne, still, out of an inscrutable dose of caution and unfamiliarity. How does one coax something from a void? What kind of enigmatic force conjures a friendship between strangers? How fragile those first times together must be, yet with so much depending on them. For one covert second, I swelled with sadness, not just because a continued relationship with this beautifully unchained boy was so improbable, but for the tragedy of all friendships that died in infancy. Then with a symmetric abruptness, I deflated back down to my normal self in time for him to ask, "Do you have your own place?"

"Yeah," I said. "It's pretty small. I don't really need a lot of room, and I keep a few things at my parents. They don't live very far away."

"Same here," he said. "Well, not about my parents, but my apartment. It's just a studio."

"Did your parents move out of Corbin?"

"Actually my parents passed," he said. "It was a few years back."

"Oh," I said. "Wow, my god. I'm so sorry to hear that." I turned slightly away from him, wishing I had sounded less affected.

"It's okay," he said, then seemed to ruminate for a few seconds before adding, "It feels like a very long time ago now."

"Alright," I said. I considered letting the road leading to my apartment pass us by, but then thought better of it. "Sorry, turn right at the intersection."

"No problem," he said.

"Hey, this is a lot faster than the bus. It's still light out."

He smiled. "I'm glad. Do you have any grand plans for the evening?"

"No. In fact," I said, thinking quickly, "would you like to come up? At least I could get you a drink to say thanks."

"I would like that," he said.

I pointed out my building, and soon we left his car at the curb. I apologized for the crumbling state of the wooden stairs leading to my third-floor apartment, and their unsettling tendency to shift underfoot. He showed no sign of aversion.

"It's nice," he said as I led him through the door.

"It's small," I told him, removing my coat, "and it hasn't been updated in a long time."

"You've done a really good job making it nice, though," he said.

"You're very polite," I said, offering to place his coat on the bed with mine. "I should frame some of these posters if I really want to keep them. They look kind of tacky just pasted up on the walls like that."

"*In Rainbows*," he said, untying a dressy black pair of Vans. "I like that album."

"Yeah, I'll put it on if you want."

"What a fantastic host you are," he said, jerking at his tie and letting it hang loose around his neck.

My apartment was narrow with a cramped entryway near the bed and bathroom. It had wood floors throughout, which I'd partially obscured with two small area rugs. Past the bed lay an unceremonious living area, modular white couch on the left wall, flat television of modest dimensions to the right. I had placed a broad, very low coffee table in the center of the room, or more cosmically, at the center of the whole apartment, and so did it possess its own gravitational pull, as many small items I owned were drawn to its surface. Along the far wall stood a small, complete kitchen. It was rarely put to good use because I wasn't any good at cooking.

I told him to make himself at home. "Do you like wine at all?" I asked.

"Wine is just fine," he said.

Glasses were poured, music was set to play, and I dragged over a wooden chair from the drop-leaf table that hugged the wall of the kitchen.

"It's good," he said. "I know nothing about wine, though."

"You can't know any less than I do," I said, holding up the bottle. "Thirteen dollars. Real top-shelf stuff."

He grabbed it from me. "2013," he said in a silly, elevated tone. "A good year for grapes. I'm sensing some oaky undertones here."

"Give me that," I said, laughing and snatching back the bottle.

He'd undone the top button of his white dress shirt, just as I had. His tie was loosened even more so that it looped down over his chest like a sash. I could make out definition in the muscles of his torso underneath and then had to deliberately restrict my gaze to his face. I realized this was the most casually dressed I had ever seen him.

"If I was my own boss, I don't think I could dress as well as you do," I said.

"I like dressing up. Besides, we're always having unplanned meetings with customers. I'm never sure when I'll need to look nice," he said.

"That makes sense."

He sipped his wine and asked, "So, you're gay, right? Do you have a boyfriend?"

"No," I said, "not right now."

"Ah, okay."

I tried to detect some hint of feeling in his reaction, but came up with nothing. "What about you?" I asked. "Are you seeing anyone?"

"No. Until recently I had almost no free time. But I had to take a step back from that, or they would have found me in a ditch somewhere. These days I'm not really sure what I'm doing, in that arena, anyway."

I gathered some courage and asked, "Do you prefer guys or girls?"

"Girls. I mean, well, yeah, my girlfriend and I broke up about a year ago." He took a drink of his wine.

I forcefully suppressed all urges to read into this statement. I still did not know him very well. In fact this showed me that I hardly knew him at all. "That's cool," I said. "Yeah, relationships are hard."

"Relationships turn you completely batshit crazy."

"Right," I said, grinning. "That's what I meant to say."

"So have you ever dated a guy long-term?" he asked.

I told him I had been with someone for a little over two years in college. "He graduated," I said, "and he moved away. I asked him if he'd consider long distance until I could move to be with him and he said no. So that was that."

"It really sucks, doesn't it?" He traced the rim of his glass and stared off at some point on the surface of the coffee table. "You care for someone, and they don't feel the same way. Seems like such an uncomplicated thing. But it's not."

"That's true," I said. "It's a problem without a solution. But I spent a long time trying to find one."

"Me too," he said. "When my parents died, she was all I had. After she broke it off, I would spend hours wondering if she had only stayed with me because she felt sorry for me."

"I'm sure it was more than that."

He took another sip. "It doesn't matter anymore." He leaned forward and picked up a large piece of white sea glass from the coffee table. I watched him stare intently at it and turn it over a few times in his hand. "You have a very nice home," he said. "Some people really don't, but you do."

I laughed a little. "Thanks. Now I'm interested to know what yours is like."

He finished his glass of wine and looked around the room. "You'll have to come over sometime. You can be the judge."

"I would really like that," I told him.

"This has been nice, right?" he asked. "Us talking, I mean. There's something about it. I don't know."

"I know what you mean," I said. "I've had a really good time today."

He stood up and walked over to the kitchen. Radiohead continued to play quietly. "Would you consider hugging me right now?"

"Hugging you?"

"Yeah, is that asking a lot? Is it crazy if I think we both could use it?"

I stood up. "I'm fine with it, if you are."

He motioned me over with both hands, so I approached and pulled myself close to him. His body was very warm, even more so than I had expected, now that it was pressed against mine. He leaned slightly back against the edge of the sink and I fell into him a little, allowing him to support just the smallest amount of my weight. He drew in a quick breath and then exhaled slowly, almost imperceptibly. I felt his hands wander the expanse of my back through the fabric of my shirt, fingers exploring the tiny rifts between muscles. "If it's okay, I just need to do this," he said. His voice, barely above a whisper, nonetheless transmitted through our joined torsos, and I felt it profoundly. "It's okay," I said. His arms and chest became known to me, unmistakably now, as considerable and robust. I attempted to feel, so that it could be locked away and recalled later, when I was alone, the smooth olive skin of his neck, pressed delicately against my own.

I do not know who became erect first, but by the time I felt the bulking presence of him at my waist, I, too, had expanded significantly into the same space. He pressed himself firmly into me and I countered with equal vigor. He backed off slightly and then rebounded with even more force. Then he receded once again and became still. I felt our bodies decouple just slightly. He whispered in my ear, so that I could barely hear above the music, "I better go home now, Chickadee."

I fell away from him and stepped backward into the living room. At first, he didn't move from where he stood at the counter, and our shared arousal was still very much on display. I was not embarrassed. He didn't seem to be, either, and he stepped peacefully past me to claim his coat from the bed.

I trailed him and said with directness, to ensure that he could hear, "I hope that wasn't too much."

"It was a lot," he replied. "But it was just the right amount." His tie still hung loose under his unbuttoned coat. He smiled to himself. "I couldn't have dreamed of a day like this."

"I know," I said. "Crazy."

"Will I see you on the bus tomorrow?"

"I'll be there," I said, opening the door for him.

"Well, until then."

"Goodbye, Mikey."

After the door closed I stood next to it and listened to the quick thumping of footsteps as he made his way downward. When they had faded completely I could not withhold myself from kneeling on the couch and peering out the window behind it. The street was now dark, glimmering with a coat of rainwater. The headlights of his Honda flickered on and dimmed slightly as it started. He pulled away from the curb and was gone.

3

Before bed and after an evening spent in mostly worthless reflection, only half-interrupted by a trip to the gym and the resulting takeout meal, I made a promise to myself. I would never pressure Mikey. Whether out of fear or discretion, or some measure of both, he had arrested our quickly intensifying moment together. He'd done it with poise and certainty. His action revealed a striking ability that might have been otherwise difficult to distinguish: He knew how to look after himself. A further advance into intimacy would not have indicated the contrary; it wouldn't have proven anything other than the actuality I had already come to know (his attraction to me). But he had chosen to stop, an employment of the same deft certitude he'd used to rock us into motion. He lacked the clarity I possessed regarding my desires and certainly my orientation, but his authority eclipsed my own—which, with regard to sexual advances, I would relinquish.

With this in mind, I did not sleep poorly, and in fact felt revitalized during my walk between buses the next morning. I picked out his apartment building among the others as I passed his street. At this point our paths sometimes coincided, at which time one would follow the other while maintaining a suitable distance. I found it solacing to consider that this distance would no longer be necessary. Today, however, I saw no sign of him until I came to the bus stop.

He flashed a smile as I approached, so I smiled back and arrived to stand next to him in front of the shelter. He wore a black peacoat I had never seen before. His thick hair, blacker still, had been shaped a little more deliberately than usual, and was swept up, far away from his eyes.

"Any important meetings today?" I asked.

"No, actually. Nothing scheduled, anyway."

"Well," I said, choosing my words carefully, "you look ready, if they show up."

"Thanks." He must have known what I referred to, because he then said, "My hair's getting way too long. I can usually get by putting some gel in it and tossing it around. Today it needed extra attention."

"It looks good," I said. "I mean, it always looks good."

He smiled. "Thank you."

I leaned back against the glass wall of the shelter and after about a minute, so did he. We watched cars and pedestrians pass by for a short time, and then he turned toward me a little. Even though the roadway roared with life, he lowered his voice when he said, "I want to apologize for coming on to you last night. I shouldn't have done that."

"It didn't bother me," I told him.

"Well, it shouldn't have happened."

The bus arrived and the subject rested until we had boarded, offering me time to consider how to respond. I had not expected him to feel this way. I entered the bus before him, a fact for which I was soon grateful; I had taken it for granted that we would sit next to each other, and realized suddenly that this might not be what he wanted. I sat by the window, and was relieved when he did not ask, but simply came to rest at my side.

We did not say anything immediately. I gave a little more

thought to what he had told me, and recalled the carefree way he had smiled when I first showed up. Both his attitude and his tone seemed to dismiss what I felt had been a meaningful exchange, and this annoyed me. I asked him, "It shouldn't have happened last night, you mean? Or it shouldn't have happened at all?"

He hesitated.

I could sense that he strained to find an answer and I stopped him. "I'm sorry. I'm not sure what I'm getting at."

"You're really putting me on the spot here, Chickadee." He laughed, but he also looked very nervous.

"Really," I said, "I don't need an answer. It's not a big deal." I tried to set aside my agitation; his feelings were obviously more complicated than I had thought.

His expression vacillated between confusion and a kind of unfiltered sadness. "I don't blame you for asking," he said.

I didn't say anything for a while. I began to perceive an overarching message of apology from Mikey, apology both unfounded and misplaced. I cleared my throat. "Could you try to trust me about one thing?"

He looked at me.

"You need to know that you didn't do anything wrong."

He stared at the back of the seat in front of him. "Okay," he said in an uncertain tone. "I'm glad to know that's how you feel." His phone rang and he excused himself before answering.

I could see the call was work-related and probably important. I sat back and looked up to the front of the bus, through the gaping windshield at the path ahead. Mikey's own desires, or more appropriately his cognition respective to them, differed from mine more than I could ever have anticipated. I marveled at the dissonance between his displays of clarion confidence and these fresh moments of uncertainty. Even now his voice rang in quiet tenacity as he negotiated an exchange of money and services to occur later in the day.

His phone call persisted until my stop, at which point he said, to whomever he was speaking with, "Hold on just a minute," and covered the bottom half of his phone with his palm.

To me he said, "I'm staying downtown late tonight, so I'll see you tomorrow. We can talk then."

I told him goodbye and left the bus. It didn't occur to me until I was a block from the office that it was Friday, and I guessed he hadn't remembered, either. I resented the thought of a whole weekend spent vaguely suspended by an unfinished conversation. At least it had not been entirely unfinished; I had let him know he wasn't in the wrong, something I felt deeply, and which, I reflected, overshadowed anything else I could have said. Still, I couldn't help but sink a little into frustration after having my hopes partially dashed, and considered it a forfeiture of some of the connectedness I had felt with him the night before.

I resolved to limit my thoughts about him in general, and if I did ponder over him much further, to use other people in my life as sounding boards. I was not an especially unsocial person, and in that moment was shocked to realize that, other than Mikey and my work colleagues, I hadn't spoken to anyone in several days.

I was pleasantly surprised to find work that morning engaging in spite of lingering doubts about my approaching relocation. By some miracle, considering my penchant for frantic anticipation, I was able to put it out of mind. I had lunch at a pho place down on the street, accompanied by a work acquaintance, Jennifer, whom I had become somewhat close with, and who had very recently received the same relegation.

"I just wish they had told us this could be a possibility from the beginning," she said.

"I know. It wouldn't have made any difference for me, though," I said. "I felt pretty lucky when they hired me."

"Me too. And I mean, obviously they expected us to be versatile. It's not really asking that much. The trade-off is in how fast people rise up through this company."

"So you're going?" I asked.

"Well, it's not like I have a choice." She paused and then said, "Aren't you?"

I told her I would probably go, that the reality of it just hadn't sunk in yet.

"I feel the same way," she said. "It's going to take a little time. I'm sure I'll feel a lot better about it when the time comes."

We said nothing for the next few minutes as we ate our soup.

Eventually I sat back and said, "The thing is, I just met someone who's made a really good impression on me, and it's not that it really matters—I mean, I hardly know the guy—but just thinking about Fern Hill and how small it is…what are my chances of meeting someone like that up there?"

"If you think about it," she said, tilting her head to one side, "small winter village…people trying to stay warm…I don't know—opportunities may present themselves."

"Sounds like you've already thought about it."

"I have," she assured me through a mouthful of noodles. She finished and said, "Wyatt, with a face like yours, what could you possibly have to worry about?"

"If you're saying that for the return compliment, I'm not giving it to you."

She laughed.

Conversation turned as it usually did to our work; we discussed sources of confusion and complained about our superiors. Back at the office I labored energetically and the afternoon hours passed at a tolerable pace. I began preparing to leave for the day, contemplating a long ride home and the uneventful Friday evening ahead.

Down in the lobby I texted one of my closest friends and asked if I could catch the train with her to Celadon. Marie, who also worked in the city and became free around the same time I did, lived by herself in a high-rise condo several miles east of downtown. After many late summer nights spent together in hostels around Europe, turning sleep away as we discussed life's beautiful and ugly truths, we lately bonded over a shared perception of life back at home as nebulously unsatisfying.

"I'm already on," she texted back. "Follow me! You'll only be one or two behind."

I walked underground and bought a twenty-four hour pass, unsure whether I would be staying overnight. The eastbound car arrived after a few minutes and I sat near the front.

Two stations later the train climbed above ground and I was met with a dignified view of the harbor to the north, where colossal container ships, some languishing at the docks and some drifting glacially, were the reigning species. I attempted to imagine the lowly human effort responsible for the creation and movement of such monumental beasts, but to the discredit of shipbuilders and crew the world over, I couldn't do it; in my mind, epicenter of the childish and absurd, they had birthed themselves into existence through their own endeavors and they did not bow to human influence.

Rain had begun pouring and battered the front window of

the train car. One long wiper swept silently across the expanse of glass. Someone now sat in the seat next to me, their elbow pressed slightly, painlessly, into my side.

If Mikey were here, I wondered, what among all of this movement would he find remarkable? If, in some moment of disregard, I unmasked my thoughts about the mammoth creatures of the harbor, would he laugh, or would a part of him, either tiny or considerable, find validity in my impressions? I did not favor one hypothetical response over the other, but I longed to know which it might be.

I found Marie about fifteen minutes later waiting for me at the station.

"You could have just gone home," I said as she squeezed me tightly.

"Nonsense," she said. "I haven't been here long. Besides, you never carry an umbrella. I couldn't stand the thought of you out in the rain." She opened hers and pulled me under it. She wasn't very tall, so I had to duck a little until she laughed and handed it to me. "Here, you hold it."

Marie was an only child whose parents moved from Korea when she was very young. We met during the first week of college and had melded together over our tentatively chosen path to an accounting degree. I had been drawn to her initially because of her energetic disposition; people with that kind of unbridled verve and spontaneity often rubbed off on me. Later on she would offer undying loyalty, even during my most self-infatuated period to date, the eleventh hour of my failed relationship.

"You saved me," she said. "Another night alone streaming shows and movies—I would have died."

I laughed. "I was dreading the same thing. That's why I texted you."

"I'm so glad you did," she told me as she surged up the street to her building. Her pace was astonishing, if not unfamiliar to me. "It's been too long," she said as we entered the lobby. "Come into my home and I will tell you what has changed."

"Something's changed?"

"Shhh." She held a finger to her lips, then grabbed her umbrella from me and folded it into her cavernous purse. "Not until we have drinks."

She stamped her feet frantically as we rode to the 11th floor.

"The suspense is killing me," I said, half-sarcastically.

"I know," she said. "Me too." The door opened and she took off down the hall, towing me along with her.

Marie's parents owned the one-bedroom condo and rented it to her at a forgiving rate. She had filled it with mostly modest furnishings, but the unit itself was finished with materials that gave one the impression of lasting quality.

She told me to wait on the couch and then leapt over to the kitchen to throw together two of the strongest Vodka Collinses yet known to the world.

"Let me taste yours," I demanded as she sat next to me. After sipping it I said, "Okay, as long as we're in this together."

"I'm not trying to get you drunk, Wyatt." She slapped my thigh. "Not without me, anyway."

I laughed. "So? Big news?"

"So, I broke up with Anthony last night."

I set my drink on the table. "What? Why didn't you text me?"

"It just didn't feel text-worthy. Besides, I knew we were long overdue for a chat and, well, here you are." She grinned.

Text-worthy or not, she seemed ecstatic to be reporting the news. At the risk of sounding selfish, I had been as bored with her relationship as she was. I dreaded circumstances that would bring the three of us together, such as whenever she felt an obligation to include him on our exploits. Anthony's emotions were delicate and required a certain level of outside care and upkeep during a given evening; this ranked highly on a short list of social traits that I considered unacceptable. I kept this mostly to myself, but when Marie complained, I lamented alongside her.

"Well, you know how I feel," I said. "I'm not going to miss him."

She raised her glass and we clinked them together. After taking a drink she said, "You know what sealed it for me? I gave him an ultimatum for more sex—you know about our dry spell—and he actually couldn't bring himself to do it. He kept ducking around the issue so I just let him have it. I could have internalized it and made it into something I was doing wrong, but you and I have talked about that. If he doesn't want it, he doesn't want it. I'm not going to wait around trying to read into it."

"I'm so proud of you," I said.

"Thank you. You and my parents both. I told them this morning. Although I think for them it has more to do with the fact that he's white."

"Come on," I said. "Your parents aren't really like that."

"Well, I'm sure a good Korean boy would be the answer to their prayers, but yeah, they want me to be happy. Also, it's strange because I keep waiting to become sad, but it feels like that's not going to happen. Maybe we'd become even more distant than I thought."

I told her it had certainly appeared that way to me.

"I just can't believe I pulled this off without you," she said. "Where have you been? What have you been doing?"

"Working," I said. "Tandon and Dufresne. Got me right where they want me." Even at that moment the irony of the expression did not escape me. I wandered within inches of telling her how, in fact, they now wanted me four hours north. But I had grown very tired of the subject and resolved to tell her on the very next occasion that found us together. Instead I just sat back and took a long drink, staring out her floor-to-ceiling windows at the rain and fog cloaking downtown's distant skyline.

"Something's on your mind," she said. "I can tell."

I was certain she could. It was a matter of deciding what exactly to divulge, which suddenly had me wondering why I was being so cagey. "I think I met someone good," I said.

"Oh my god," she said, leaning into me. "Not just anyone, but someone good? Tell me everything; leave out nothing."

"Well, honestly, I only met him a couple days ago. But we've been riding the same bus for a long time."

"Thai Guy," she said. "It's Thai Guy, right? You finally talked to him?"

I had completely forgotten that a few days after Mikey had first caught my eye—months ago—I had mentioned him in passing to Marie. "How the hell do you remember that?" I asked.

"I don't know," she said. "You sounded quite taken at the time. Anyway, I figured he'd disappeared or something. You never said anything after that."

"Nope. He stuck around. I just never got brave enough to talk to him until the day before yesterday. Then, yesterday, the bus was broken down so he offered me a ride to work in his car."

"Stop it. Stop right now." Marie was enjoying her drink at least as much as I was, and there was little liquid left to spill when she gestured wildly with it still in hand. "What happened?"

"Nothing much," I said. "I mean, something did happen, but not much to confirm anything."

"What does that mean?"

I told her about the ride home and how, from the beginning, talking to him had felt special, for lack of a better word. "He really opened up to me," I said, "and he knew I was gay. It came up when we first met. It definitely didn't affect him, at least not in a bad way. I don't really want to generalize, but straight guys tend to not act that way around me. They're always really friendly, but this just felt like a little more than that."

"Oh," she said. "Would you call it flirting?"

"Well, no, not exactly," I said, suddenly observing the effects of alcohol on an otherwise empty stomach. "I mean, yeah, but not at first." I started to tell her about the hug. "He instigated it. He, like, asked me if I would come over and hug him."

"What? Just a normal hug?"

"At first, yeah, but then he definitely started feeling around, and soon we were both hard, which was interesting."

"Holy shit, Wyatt. So he's into guys for sure."

I explained the rest of it, about how he had stopped it not long after that, and then how he had clearly regretted the whole thing on the bus the next morning.

"Regretted the timing, or that it happened at all?"

"That's exactly what I asked him," I said. "But then he got pretty awkward and I felt bad for asking."

"You would," she said. "You're not always at fault, you know. He's the one who started it."

"I know," I said. "Anyway, he wants to hang out again." I told her about how I had decided not to put any pressure on him. I was, after all, satisfied just to call him a friend.

"Sure you are," she said. "Is he fit?"

"Yes," I said. "Marie, he's an exceptionally attractive man."

She squealed at this, setting down her vacant glass and closing in on me. "Could you tell how big he was down there? Don't believe what you've heard about asian guys."

I backed away playfully. "Marie, stop it. It was definitely there; that's all I need to know."

"If it was that obvious through his pants, I bet he's big."

"Oh my god, Marie," I said, cracking up.

She took my empty glass and said, "Have one more with me and let's go back downtown for the night. Dinner and dancing. I'm a newly single lady and you've just met a stunning new man. These are the things to celebrate in life."

I raised no objections and half an hour's time found us giggling our way into the train car, by which we were compelled fluidly into the violet lake of night.

I had not forgotten that Mikey stayed late in the city that evening. My imagination ventured far enough to see his face a handful of times—including once at the second club we visited, where I was so convinced that I trailed a stranger halfway across the floor before he turned around, and I quickly turned away ("You're so fucking hopeless," laughed Marie). Always, a second glance had cured me, and halfway through the night I had thankfully given up. It was not a small city and downtown carried on for miles.

Hours later we were spat out, stumbling together on legs made feeble by unrelenting movement and slack by alcohol, having shed the last of any strangers who'd temporarily shackled themselves onto us. I had missed the final southbound bus and neither of us wanted to be alone, so we boarded the train together and were towed mercifully back to her home.

4

I did not wake up until close to noon. Marie had left already to satisfy a prior obligation. I drank two brimming glasses of water, locked the door behind me and slept through much of the transit back home. By the time the 40B shuddered to a stop down the street from my apartment I no longer felt any nausea, but just a lingering and unspecific lethargy.

I willed myself up the gradient street, passing a cluster of pines that still retained some overnight rainwater and dripped steadily in the sunlight. The deep blue of my suit jacket drew in the sun's rays and my face was met with a constant, cold breeze that moaned down the hillside. Nature's dichotomy refreshed me in a moment when I had been feeling extremely unrefreshed, and would carry me through to the hot shower for which I was currently clamoring.

I stopped suddenly before unlocking the front door; a small, folded and tucked triangle of paper was wedged into the doorframe. I took care not to tear it when coaxing it open and found a message penciled in deliberate and unadorned handwriting:

"Hey, I couldn't find you through the usual technological avenues. Sorry for stalking you at your place of residence and in general. I spoke rashly on the bus yesterday. This experience is new to me and confusing. Thank you for being patient. I will be home all day tomorrow if you would still like to talk. Please come by if you have time."

The note concluded with the street address for his building and apartment number. Flipping it over, I discovered a small sketch of a chickadee, minutely cartoonish in its glowing face but otherwise precise, like the artifact of some ornithological study. It bowed slightly on needle-like legs and its tiny feet gripped the suggestion of a spindly branch.

I stood there in the breezeway staring at the drawing long enough to feel chilly in the absence of direct sunlight. It was a creation that reflected admirable artistic skill, especially because it had probably been done in haste. I refolded the paper, careful to obey the exact pattern, a relic of my childhood reeled in from the fringes of memory, and entered my apartment.

I completed a few sets of upper-body exercises on the floor between the bed and living room, then took my long-awaited shower. I ate lunch and watched two episodes of a show. Eventually I fell into a very long novel chronicling the lives of several families in 1950s India. I had been etching away at the book for the past few months. The evening carried on in much the same way, with only a brief call from my mom to break up the languid scene.

I'd hardly given any thought to whether or not I would visit Mikey. There was nothing to consider. If the sun rose in the east the next morning, if the earth had managed to heave itself one more time around, I would go see him.

On these terms, I found myself standing before his building's intercom sometime before one o'clock the following day. I pressed the button to ring his apartment, anticipating some sort of interaction, but instead the door to the stairwell emitted a metallic clack and I hurried through. I did not rush up the stairs to the fourth floor; being short of breath would certainly not calm any of the nerves now bouncing off the walls of my stomach.

His building was at least a few decades older than mine, but had been meticulously preserved, and exuded the refinement and class of something that is not of this time, but has surrendered none of its relevance to the passing years.

I waited a very short time after knocking on his door. It swung inward and there he stood, barefoot, white cotton t-shirt, slim flat-blue pants and hair restored to its wild midnight glory. His skin appeared slightly darker now that more of it was visible, especially where upper arm met soft, white sleeve.

"So glad you decided to come over," he said energetically. "Come in. Sorry it's a little warm; I don't have any control over the heat."

I followed him silently into the living area, removing my coat.

"These old radiators…they're all kind of connected," he continued. "Sometimes I even have to open a window. We should be okay today, but let me know if you're too warm."

"It feels nice," I said, looking around the room.

"Good," he said. "Please make yourself at home. Sit down if you want." He pointed to a deep, brown leather Chesterfield sofa that fit the space handsomely. He reached out to take my coat. "Do you want something to drink?"

I asked for some water. "Wow," I said. "Your place is beautiful." He had hung a few framed pieces of artwork around the room, each striking me as tasteful and distinct. His bed lay at the far end of the unit from the front door, sectioned off by a wall that reached about halfway to the ceiling. His apartment was somewhat larger, but he had not filled it with any more furniture than I had mine. The furniture itself was of much higher quality than anything I owned. It formed a space that was uncrowded and minimal, but did not feel empty. A large

TV sat on a low stand with a Playstation and cluster of controllers perched on the shelf underneath.

"Thank you," he said, handing me a glass and sitting opposite me and against the armrest, knees tucked up near his chest. "It's the first time I've been able to be kind of selective about things. I like the way it turned out."

I set down the glass and tugged my sweater over my head, now also down to just a t-shirt, prompting him to mention the heat one more time. "It's really not that bad," I assured him. "T-shirt weather, for sure, but I'm comfortable."

"Okay," he said. "If you're sure." He paused for a few seconds and then added, "Sorry for coming by unannounced yesterday. I realized later that I shouldn't have done that."

"Really," I said, "it didn't bother me at all." Suddenly I noticed a small, sloped drawing desk at the edge of the room by the kitchen. "That drawing was really cool, by the way," I added.

He flashed a slightly crooked, captivating smile. "Thanks. Kind of a creative outlet for me."

"Well, you're really good at it," I said. "It made me feel... uh, I don't know." I lingered on the edge for a second and then said, "It made me feel really good."

His chest heaved slightly and he said, "That's all I wanted. I kept thinking it was such a strange thing to do—leaving you a drawing like that."

"I didn't think it was strange," I told him.

"Okay, good." he said. "So, look, about yesterday on the bus—I feel bad for leaving you hanging like that. There's some stuff I really should have told you and I didn't. I know you don't think I did anything wrong, but hear me out on this."

"Alright," I said, pulling my feet up off the floor and onto the cushion. We now nearly mirrored one another, backs propped against opposite ends of the couch.

"So, the thing is," he started slowly, "I hooked up with a guy a few months ago. I met him at the gym and he took me to his place. It was pretty bad. I mean, I really didn't feel good about myself after. Since then it's been this weird thing for me. Like, why did I want do something that I knew wouldn't be..." he paused and I smiled to show him that I was not alarmed. He nodded vaguely to himself and said, "I wanted something even though it didn't feel right."

"It's okay, Mikey," I said.

He was still for a few seconds and then attempted to smile. "And here you are. I'm just worried that it's the same thing starting all over again."

I felt that deep down, he suspected the situation might be different now—that I might be different, but I didn't know this for sure.

"I wasn't lying when I said I prefer women. At least that's how it feels. Thinking about guys in that way...it just makes me so nervous. I don't get any of that when I picture myself with a woman."

I'm certain there were things about myself that I still did not yet know or acknowledge. But my attraction to men stared me in the face long before I ever left high school. For Mikey, it hardly showed its face at all, and only recently had begun making sounds, too loud to ignore, from some back room in his mind.

I thought for a minute and then said, "Maybe it would help not to focus on men versus women so much. I mean, if you can put that aside, what kind of person attracts you?"

He sat and stared at me for a few seconds before saying, "I guess that's a good way to think about it. I can try to start thinking that way."

"If it helps," I said, "I don't have any crazy expectations or anything. You can relax if you're worried about what I think."

"Thank you," he said. "You've been too nice. I'm honestly a little surprised you're still willing to talk, after yesterday."

I shrugged. "Thursday night, after we got close like that, did it bring back a lot of the feelings you had after you were with that guy?"

"Well, things went a lot further with him, but no. You're right, it was different. I think I just felt uneasy because I was the one who came on to you."

"I think it's a good sign that you didn't feel the same way," I said.

"Yeah, definitely," he said. "I know you might be thinking that I'm equating you with that other guy. I promise I'm not. It's just this whole mess I've built up in my mind."

"Don't worry. I wasn't thinking that," I said. I understood that he still had many thoughts left unsorted. I feared that I could not offer him anything more by way of clarity. "Let's just keep hanging out," I suggested. "We're interested in each other. Just don't do anything you're not comfortable with."

"Okay," he said. "It's just...my biggest concern is that I'm leading you on. If you're looking for romance or anything beyond just a friends-with-benefits thing...I just can't picture it."

"It's totally fine. I'm not looking for another boyfriend. Even if I was, I'm leaving at the end of March, so it wouldn't be a good idea, anyway."

"So you decided for sure?" he asked.

"I guess," I replied. Interestingly, by not making the decision—by banishing the subject, in fact, completely from my mind—my answer had fallen to a default, if not enthusiastic, affirmative.

"I like your intensity," he said.

I laughed. "It's not something I'm very excited about." I paused and then said, "Really, though, I haven't given the subject the amount of consideration it deserves."

"You still have quite a bit of time, though."

"Right. I mean, if I haven't talked myself out of it by then, it's probably the right move."

He smiled at me. "Well, I support you."

I thanked him and admired privately the nature of this statement—unladen by provision, absolute in its brevity. He had communicated his support and I felt it.

He finished his water and said, "This is the first time we've hung out. You know, just for the sake of it."

"That's true," I said. "Did you have something in mind?"

"Have you had lunch?"

I told him I'd had a small, late breakfast, and that I was starting to feel hungry again.

"Let's go somewhere for food," he said, jumping to his feet. "Then we can see what else there is to do."

I found myself swept up in his eagerness and after a few minutes we left the garage, side by side once again in his car. We settled on a Korean place, well-established but new to both of us, inexpensive and emphatically-reviewed. The parking lot, similar to many in this part of the city, was shared among several businesses, shrunken and overflowing. Mikey managed to cajole his Honda into a small space near the back. By the time we had fully emerged after extricating ourselves through doors that could not be opened more than several inches due to the proximity of neighboring cars, we held our stomachs in fits of laughter.

The restaurant teemed with people and the service was curt and brisk. We sat facing one another at a compact table crowded up against the front windows, where white daylight flooded in.

"I heard you speaking Thai a few times on the bus," I said. "Is that where your family is from?"

"Yeah," he said. "I was born in Corbin, though. They came over a few years before that. I was probably talking to my aunt—my mom's sister. She lives in the city."

"Do you have a lot of family here?" I asked.

"Her daughter Sophie is that cousin I told you about—the one I hired after I started my business. We're basically partners now. No other family in the city besides her. My uncle died when we were kids." He looked out at the passing traffic and then back at me. "What about you?"

"Just my parents and sister," I said. "She's about ten years older than I am. We weren't that close growing up, but we've been getting closer since I left home. All of my extended family is on the east coast, so I don't see them very much."

"I bet it's nice, even though you guys are just now becoming close," he said. "I always wanted a sibling. Sophie's the closest I'll ever get."

"You guys are probably closer than we are."

He shrugged. "All I know is that it's been really good having her around." He adjusted his napkin so that it sat parallel with the edge of the table. He grinned at me and said, "So, I'm sure after growing up in Corbin you could say you know your way around asian cuisine."

"I could say that," I replied. "Pretty much raised by asians." Corbin's white population hovered around ten percent; more than half of its residents were Chinese or descended from Chinese people. Furthermore, racial groups were mostly dispersed throughout the city, meaning there existed few appreciable neighborhoods, white or otherwise.

"I bet," he said. "So you're an egg, then."

"White on the outside, yellow on the inside."

We both laughed.

"Wow," I said, "I haven't been called that since high school."

He looked away and smiled. "Probably because it's kind of a dumb thing to call someone."

Our food arrived and we started quickly in on it. Mikey poked eagerly at the contents of his bibimbap and asked, "How do you feel about walking along the levee after this?"

"That sounds really nice," I said.

We ate quickly and did not remain long after our meal; people lined up along the counter waiting for tables to open up.

During our drive west Mikey confessed that he felt conflicted about work. "When I decided to limit my hours, I did it out of necessity. I really don't think we're meant to spend over forty hours a week focused on the same thing."

I nodded. "I feel the same way."

"I'm still struggling to find a balance. It's so tempting to stay into the evening working on projects. And when I don't, the work does back up. I can either hire more employees or stop taking on new clients for a while."

"One means the company grows and the other doesn't."

"Exactly, so—" he stopped himself for a few seconds. "How important do you think it is for a company to grow?"

"I'm not sure," I said. "I would imagine there are risks either way."

"That's true." He laughed. "There's never a definite answer, is there?"

"If you're looking for one, you're doing it wrong," I said.

"Did they teach you that in Accounting school?"

I laughed. "Definitely not. Formulas and protocol for everything. That's the problem with accounting. It doesn't solve any of life's real problems."

"I wouldn't say that," he said. "Anyway, it keeps people out of trouble."

"Well, that's true."

When we arrived at the northwest corner of the levee the clouds mostly kept to themselves, but Mikey grabbed an umbrella from the center console anyway. "I don't know how far you want to walk, but I'm not convinced it's gonna stay dry." Already a few fearless drops landed on the windshield, but thankfully it was now a bona fide temperate day, at least in comparison with the last few weeks. Mikey wore just a gray cardigan over his t-shirt.

We began to make our way south along a gravel path built upon the levee's ridge. Seagulls whirled around in the turbulent air above the water. The tide slowly crept in to blanket the reeds and stones and mud that tapered unhurriedly out to sea. Other than the one or two bicyclists who passed us by, and a slow-moving elderly couple whom we passed, we were alone as we trudged along under his large black umbrella.

"I'm sorry if I was insensitive about the asian thing earlier," he said. "It's not something I usually take very seriously, and it can come off the wrong way sometimes."

Mikey had made several apologies to me in the brief time we'd known each other and I considered lightheartedly pointing it out, but then thought better of it. "It didn't bother me at all," I told him. "My friends and I still joke about it sometimes."

"Well, I don't think it should matter to me," he said, "but apparently I cared enough to comment on it. I don't know why."

"I think most people are that way," I said. "It's rare that

anyone can totally forget about race, living here."

He tugged his fingers through the hair on the back of his head and said, "Hey, did you ever... Was there ever a time when you wished you were something else?"

"Well...yeah," I said. During my childhood and well into adolescence, I had occasionally wished (in a cursory way that did not affix itself to a particular country or culture) that I had been born asian. It was a delicate, personal issue that I kept almost entirely to myself, but suddenly I felt no need to hide it from Mikey. "I didn't have a lot of white friends growing up," I told him. "Most were asian. Sometimes I really wished I looked like them."

"I totally understand that," he said. "And I know how you feel. I used to wish I was white."

"I think your experience makes so much more sense, though," I said. "Movie and shows and stuff were all full of white people. It sets really unhealthy standards. As a kid, I could imagine how it would be pretty overwhelming."

"Yeah, but it doesn't take anything away from how you felt," said Mikey. "You were just a kid, too. Kids don't think about things on that kind of racial level—you just wanted to look different. It's the same feeling, either way."

"I guess," I said.

"If we had been friends back then, I would have let you know how good you looked. I would have told you that you were beautiful and made you happy to be you."

I eyed him in mock suspicion. "Really? I can't picture that."

"Seriously. What if I went to your school? What if I had been a valiant Chickadee alongside you?" At this, he motioned out ahead in an exaggerated arc with his free hand. "Think about it. I bet we would have been best friends. And if you came along one day and told me you didn't like the way you looked, I would've given it to you."

I laughed. "Excuse me?"

"You know what I mean." He reached up and ruffled my hair, and then gave my bicep a squeeze. "'Beautiful hair. Fucking hot body. How dare you think you are not attractive?' I would have said."

"Stop it," I said through a broad grin, certain my face was reddening.

"I'm just saying, you would've been doing me a favor. You would've had me asking questions about myself a lot sooner. Instead, you show up years later on a dirty bus. Thanks a lot." He beamed at me with dark, furtive eyes.

His outburst had left me with some newfound confidence. "Well, if that's all true, I would have come on to you faster than you would know what to do with. I hope you realize that."

"I would've been prepared to accept the consequences."

"Alright," I said. "If you say so."

Both of us walked in silence for a few seconds before looking at each other and bursting into laughter.

Soon after, Mikey became quiet and said, "I'm really going to work on what you said. About who I find attractive and all that. I think I've…" He paused. "I think I have to get over some things. Some mental blocks, maybe."

I gave him a chance to continue but he said nothing. "Is that something you want to talk about with me?" I asked.

"I don't know," he said. "I still don't know how I feel. It makes me nervous to really talk about it. I know, it's stupid. I can flat-out call you attractive…but I can't talk about myself."

"It's not stupid," I said.

"My dad—" he started. He collected his thoughts for a moment and said, "He was really against this kind of thing. He was a really strict guy."

"Oh," I said.

"There's not much else to say about that, though."

"That's fine," I said. "You don't have to say anything." I thought for a moment and then told him, "Mikey, I want you to know that if we had been friends back then, I would have done the same. I mean, if you were ever sad or felt bad about anything, I would have done whatever I could to make you feel better."

He walked a few more steps and said, "You're a really caring person."

I didn't say anything.

Before we had gone much farther the clouds grew angry and the breeze lay defeated by a veritable wind blowing inland from the sea. Far off in the water, where boats and ships roamed, placid blue was now disrupted with seemingly unmoving white-capped surfs. We turned back toward the car and quickened our pace.

"This is useless," he said after a few minutes, folding the umbrella. "Do you like to run?"

"Sometimes," I said.

He took off down the path and I followed. I sprinted playfully past him, and as I slowed he caught up to me in a sort of half-tackle. "You fucker," I said, breaking free and bolting ahead once again. I remained ahead of him for a minute or two, each of us fighting off laughter as we drew in restorative breaths, but soon I slowed my untenable pace slightly and he passed me. We continued like this until we reached the car, with Mikey ultimately about ten yards ahead. He smacked the taillight and raised his arms in victory, still clinging to the collapsed umbrella.

I ran to him and we laughed together, gasping for breath as rainwater streaked down our faces.

"Now we know who's in better shape," I said, breathing hard.

"It was close," he said, "I don't think this proves anything."

As we drove away from the levee Mikey said, "We should put all pretenses aside and just go for a run next time."

"We're obviously both dying to do it," I said. "When we try to suppress it, that's what happens."

He laughed. "Okay. Running. On the docket. By the way, how are you doing on time?"

"I'm going to my parents for dinner around six," I said. "We still have a couple hours if you want to keep hanging out. I don't need to get ready or anything."

"Do you want to hang out at your place? That way you don't have to bus home. Or I can just drive you home later, if you want," he offered.

"My place is fine," I said. We were already a fair distance south of his part of town.

Mikey was quiet for the first half of the drive to my apartment. At one point he turned to look at me and I thought he was going to say something, but then he looked back at the road. After another minute or two I asked if there was something on his mind.

He drew in a breath. "I don't want to be someone who fucking strings you along. That's not right."

"You aren't stringing me along," I said.

"Well, it feels that way to me. I already told you I'm not into guys beyond just sexual attraction. Since we're both attracted to each other, that establishes this whole friends-with-benefits thing, which you said you're okay with, right?"

"Right," I said. Already I found myself caring for Mikey much more than I would a person with whom I was only hooking up. But if his feelings did not extend into romance, I had no qualms about simply enjoying what was offered me.

"Then I need to get over myself," he said. "I want to see you. And I want you to see me."

"You mean like…our bodies?" I asked.

"Exactly," he said. "God, I am so lucky you can read my mind. I am terrible at talking about these things."

I laughed. "Well, the thing is, I want you to call the shots. I don't want to push you into a situation that isn't good for you."

He thought for a moment. "How about we start by jerking off together? I am so ready for it. Would you be okay with something like that?"

"Is that even a question?" I asked, grinning. "If you say you're ready, you'll have to fight me to keep my pants on."

"Not here," he said, laughing. "This is a public place. Your apartment would be suitable, though."

I cracked up. "How fast does this car go? Step on the gas."

He gave the gas pedal a playful nudge and then backed off.

We were only a few minutes away, which was fortunate because the rest of the drive undulated between nervous laughter and strange fits of excitement.

"You sure you're ready for this?" I asked as we climbed the stairs.

"Don't worry," he said. "It feels like the right time."

We burst into my apartment, quickly removing our shoes and coats. Soon we stood facing one another between the kitchen and the living room.

"If you take off your clothes," Mikey said, "I'll take mine off, too." He wore only a t-shirt and pants, as did I. When I'd seen him remove his socks along with his shoes, I had done the same.

"Shirts first," I said. "If we do it all right away, I'll be a little overwhelmed."

"Okay," he said. "That's a good idea."

We removed our shirts and dropped them to the floor. Neither one of us made any effort to hide our fascination in witnessing for the first time the other's naked torso. Mikey carried a well-balanced physique, each muscle group discernible and prominent. With some amount of bulk, but also a lean athleticism, he looked very strong, and not oversized at all. I had never before identified that exact parity in male proportion which I found to be ideally attractive, but I realized now, as Mikey looked me over (and over), that it was on display in front of me.

His nipples were small and dark. Out from under his arms peeked hints of straight, jet-black hair. There was also a thin strip of hair leading down underneath the band of his underwear and his belt. He had no hair on his chest. I myself had very little chest hair. He was slightly larger overall, a little leaner and certainly darker than I was, but on the whole, we were of the same body type and both reasonably fit.

"Looking good, Chickadee," he said with an enticing sheepishness.

"Wow," I said. "You look great, Mikey."

"You work out sometimes, huh?"

"Yeah," I said. "You obviously do, too."

"Hey, so I only trim a little down there," he said. "Hope that's okay."

"Don't worry. I'm the same way."

"Okay," he said. "Are you ready?"

I unbuckled my belt and tugged my pants downward. Mikey did the same. After we kicked them off we held ourselves through our underwear, both of us aware of our conspicuous arousal. My gaze fell to Mikey's waist and he removed his hand, revealing his hardness as it stretched the fabric down to the opening at his leg, where it nearly surfaced. I responded by removing my own hand, and he, too, looked down.

"Wow," he said, standing firm, as if anchored to the floor.

Our eyes then locked briefly, which was sufficient to communicate our willingness to complete the final step. We removed our underwear and stood boldly before one another. Mikey's cock had sprung up, straight out from his body, shadowed by a group of tidy, black hairs. It was fairly large and shielded by dark foreskin right up to where a small amount of the tip emerged through. I had no particular reaction to that detail; I was circumcised but my ex had not been. Mikey and I were otherwise very similar in shape, length and size.

"Holy fuck," I said, gaping at him.

"I'm a little concerned," he said slowly, "that if I start jerking now I'm going to come immediately."

I laughed. "You're not the only one. Let's move the couch. If it doesn't take long, I don't mind."

"Okay," he said. "If we could just watch each other, that would be best for me. I don't think I'm ready to be touched this time."

"Of course," I said. "That's all I was expecting."

We sat next to each other on the couch and I was afforded a new perspective of his body, laid out before me, closer now, intensified in its grace and candor. About one foot of open space lingered between us.

With his left hand Mikey propped his cock up at its base and then gave it a couple of solid strokes while looking over at mine. His body shuddered slightly and he looked up at me. "I'm so sorry. I don't think I'm going to last very long."

He had not realized, or rather I had not adequately communicated that I was at least as aroused, which was why I'd had yet to touch mine. "I will be right there with you," I said.

"Should we just go for it, then?" he asked.

"I kind of want to," I said.

I stroked myself a few times, testing the water. "Fuck," I said.

Mikey joined in and suddenly we jerked off furiously, side by side. Mikey's gaze remained unceasingly fixated on my cock, just as mine was on his. An utterly conquering energy gathered within me over the next several seconds.

"Fuck," Mikey was saying. "Oh, fuck." He erupted rapidly onto his chest in tangled, sinewy liquid lines.

Before he had finished I reached my threshold, jetting milky fluid immediately up under my chin, the rest quickly trailing down my stomach.

Together we ebbed gradually, both suspended for another moment in secondary, rhythmic convulsion which then gave way to several quiet seconds of warm, exulting repose.

At first Mikey did not say anything, but his satisfaction was clear, as his face glowed and he tilted his head back. "Okay," he said, staring up at the ceiling. "That was really good."

"I know," I said. "It was everything I wanted."

"I don't know why I was worried." He turned his head toward me. "I knew you were not the same." I watched his sperm-laden stomach rise up and then fall as he heaved a restorative sigh. "I'm in a very good place now."

5

I showed Mikey to the bathroom so he could clean himself up, then used my underwear to wipe down my own torso. When I finished I dropped them into the hamper and retrieved a new pair from my dresser. I waited until Mikey returned to begin dressing, since he remained naked and I did not want him to feel vulnerable.

"Still big, even when you're soft," he said, stepping over to his clothes.

"I'm not completely soft yet," I said. "And look who's talking."

"If we don't change the subject I'm going to get hard again."

As far as I was concerned, he wasn't joking. I felt my own corporeal response occurring as we spoke.

"Do you mind if I stay awhile longer?" he asked as he dressed.

"Of course not."

"Cool." He sat down on the couch and looked at his phone until I was dressed and came over to sit next to him.

"Although it would be pretty hilarious if you just left after that," I said.

He laughed. "No words. Just walked out the door." He picked up the sea glass from its perpetual home on the coffee table. "We can joke, but seriously, I'm not about that at all.

That's not what this is."

"I know." I stared blissfully ahead into the void of the powered-down television.

"What are you reading?" he asked, exchanging the sea glass for the paperback novel I'd left near the edge of the table. "Fuck, this is a long book." He flipped through the pages. "*A Suitable Boy*, huh?"

"Yeah, it's really good. If you like to read I can lend it to you when I'm done. Might be a while, though."

"I should say so," he said. "Fourteen hundred pages. Jesus. Yeah, I'll give it a try when you're done." He turned it over and skimmed the back for a few seconds. "You're sure this doesn't say something about you? I mean, I get that you're not looking for a boyfriend, but still…"

I laughed. "It's about a lot more than just that."

He set the book down. "Do you read a lot? I always feel like I don't read enough."

"Sometimes," I said. "I go through phases."

"So what do you like to do? You can't possibly just go to work and read at home and that's it."

"Well, let's see," I said, pretending to recount my activities from some mental schedule, "there's work, reading, movies, porn, listening to music, the gym… Nope. No free time after that."

"Oh, come on. You're keeping something from me. Porn only takes, what, two or three hours from your day?"

"Fine," I said, laughing. "I like to write. But I haven't done it much since I was in school. My job's been a little overwhelming."

"I knew it. You're too creative to be someone who just sits around. What do you like to write?"

"Poetry," I said. "And sometimes prose. Fiction. But it has

to be spare and important, like poetry."

"Is all poetry spare and important?"

"All good poetry is," I said.

"Whoa." Mikey raised up both of his hands. "Sit down, Emily Dickinson."

I laughed and punched him lightly on the shoulder. "You don't know anything about it."

"Hey, look who's getting violent now." He rubbed his arm in feigned injury.

Over the next several minutes we discussed combining our talents into some kind of illustrated book of poems or stories.

"What would we call it?" I asked.

"The title would come to us in the process," he said, now laying on his back with his head near my hip, hair spilling across the cushion and legs dangling over the arm of the couch. "That's where all the best titles come from."

"I'll agree with that."

Mikey's mouth unhinged into an enormous yawn and then he said, "I still like books with illustrations. Never grew out of that."

"Me too," I said.

The conversation slowly abated over the next few minutes and Mikey said softly, "The test of a true friendship: napping together."

I smiled to myself. Completely relaxed, I had also begun to feel drowsy. "Good idea," I said, curling myself into my corner of the couch. Mikey didn't say anything after that.

I woke up as my phone shook angrily in my pocket. I glanced up at the wall clock. An unfathomable hour had slipped by—it was ten minutes after six. "Mikey," I said groggily, turning toward him.

He didn't stir so I fished out my phone and read the

offending text. "If you haven't left yet," my mom wrote, "could you please bring your rice cooker with you? Something is wrong with ours."

"Mikey," I repeated.

He sat up. "What?" He looked around the room and then flashed a broad smile at me. "Oh, hey Chickadee."

"It's after six," I said. "I better go. My mom wants me to bring my rice cooker."

He still looked a little dazed as he stood up and went over to the front door.

I rummaged through a cabinet under the counter for the plastic serving scoop that went with the cooker.

"I'll drive you," he said, putting on his shoes and coat.

"Don't worry about it. It's only about a mile from here—I walk all the time."

"With a rice cooker?" he asked.

"Alright," I said, grinning. "If you insist."

By the time we sat in his car we were restored to full alertness.

"I feel bad," he said, patting down a cluster of rogue hairs that attempted to escape from orbit. "If I hadn't suggested a nap, you wouldn't be late."

"I'm not late. The fact that my mom just now asked for the rice cooker means we won't eat for an hour. Setting a meeting time with my parents is a pretty hopeless pursuit."

"Alright," he said, tossing his phone on my lap and starting the car. "Before I forget, can I get your number? I'll text you later so you have mine."

He told me his passcode and I opened up a new contact. "I guess not having each other's numbers has already been a problem," I said.

"Exactly. Now I can stalk you whenever I want."

"Yeah, whatever," I said.

I directed him to my parents' house and as we turned down their narrow street I saw both of them and my sister chatting out in the front yard. The sun had fallen down from behind the clouds in one last brilliant bid of light before disappearing completely. Their shadows sprawled across the lawn and crept up the wood siding of the house.

"Shit," I said. "Okay, when I get out, you just hit the gas, let out your clutch—whatever it is that you do—and just go. If they manage to flag you down, they will ask you every question imaginable. They live for this stuff."

Mikey laughed. "It doesn't bother me."

"You say that now," I said.

"Alright, alright," he said, still laughing. "I'll text you later, okay?"

"Perfect," I said. "Thanks again for the ride." He stopped the car and I climbed out, cooker cradled in one arm. We said goodbye, I closed the door and he drove away.

The house had been built in the 1960s and stood in various stages of remodel. The kitchen was mostly modernized, but the layout remained sectioned off into small, dedicated rooms. It had a main floor and carpeted upstairs, but was not large. Around the time I was born, the carpet in the dining room had been torn up, down to the particleboard base. It was a project that had remained unfinished my entire life. Many of the decorations were old family pictures and keepsakes, mostly from my mom's side, extending back a few generations.

My dad and sister greeted me warmly and my mom ordered me to follow her to the kitchen with the rice cooker.

"I told Dad to just pay the extra thirty dollars for the better brand," she said. My mom was small, fit and energetic with wavy, dark hair that hovered above her shoulders. Lately she unabashedly indulged in the mod-style fashion that had been popular when she was a little girl. She wore a bright orange, sleeveless dress that fell just below her knees.

"I'm glad you're here," she said. "Stephanie and your dad insisted that we get some sun before it disappears. I was so cold standing out there."

"All you're wearing is that dress, Mom. It looks kind of like summer."

"Do you mind if I hold onto your rice cooker? Are you using it?"

"Not much, lately," I said. "Keep it as long as you want."

"Who was your friend?" she asked. "He looked very cute."

"How could you even see that?"

"I looked when you had the door open," she said, transferring the half-cooked rice from one pot to the other. "Is he older? How does he pay for a fancy car like that?"

"It's just a Honda," I said, sorting through a pile of mail by the refrigerator. My parents did not buy new cars.

"Well, tell me about him," she insisted. "You never bring guys by."

"There's not much to tell. He's a new friend, around my age. I don't know him that well yet. He's a nice guy."

My dad and sister walked in, closing the front door and laughing their way toward the kitchen.

"Wyatt, Dad says you haven't been visiting enough," said Stephanie. "They're getting lonely over here." With her angled features and small nose, Stephanie very much resembled a taller, younger version of my mom, but she'd borrowed my dad's lighter hair (as had I) and she grew it out, well past her shoulders.

"Hey, I visit as often as you do," I said.

"That's not saying much," she replied, giving me a hug.

"I'm in Brickhouse. What's your excuse? You're literally right across the highway."

"You both should visit more," said my mom. "But I'm told if I pressure you, it will only push you away. So that's all I'm going to say."

"Wyatt," said my dad, "I'm disappointed you didn't introduce us to your friend. He looked very nice, from what little I could see of him."

"I gave him the business already," said my mom. She then complained that it was too crowded with all of us together in the kitchen, so my dad, Stephanie and I headed for the living room. My dad turned on the television to catch the tail end of the news and Stephanie and I talked as we waited for dinner. We covered the usual subjects, including the finalization of her divorce, which had been fairly amicable but mystifyingly drawn-out.

My dad insisted that we watch a commercial he liked, and when it was over Stephanie turned to me. "Who is he?" she hissed. "I mean, who is he really? I saw him, too. Holy shit, Wyatt."

"His name's Mikey," I whispered. "We're just messing around. He says he's not looking for anything romantic."

"Well that's not all bad, right?"

"No," I said. "It's definitely not."

My dad cracked up at another commercial and my mom yelled from the kitchen that dinner was ready.

We gathered in the dining room and sat down. My mom had separated the meat, greens and rice into different serving bowls. Wine glasses were set for all of us, each containing the same generous amount. We were quiet as we dished up our plates and began to eat.

I knew my announcement of the possibility of moving would

have to occur sooner or later, so I spoke up after a minute or two. "Tandon and Dufresne wants me to move to Fern Hill. They told me on Wednesday. I would leave in a little over five weeks."

Everyone stopped eating.

"What?" said my mom. "Isn't there plenty of work in the city?"

"They have kind of a little stronghold up there," I said. I explained about how they were short on room and some of the new hires were expected to, in essence, do their time away from the main branch. "They'll pay for relocation costs. I'm just not sure if I'm going to do it."

My dad cleared his throat. "Hold on. Are there any ramifications if you don't?"

"Well, yeah," I said. "I won't have a job with them anymore."

He frowned. "Well, what is it that you're not sure about?"

"I don't know," I said. "There's like a ninety-five percent chance I'll go. It's just hard to imagine actually doing it. There's a lot I'll miss about the city. Plus it's nice to be close to you guys again."

"Sweetie," said my mom, "we love it, too. Every minute of it. But if this is your career we're talking about, and as long as it's only temporary, I just don't think it's right to pass it up. Not if it'll cost you your job."

"I know. That's where the ninety-five percent comes from."

"Okay," she said. "Alright, that's fair. You just need some time to get used to the idea. I understand that."

Stephanie had been listening silently and began to eat again. "He'll probably go," she said with a mouthful of rice, "but if he doesn't, it's because it wasn't right for him." She swallowed. "Anyway, it's his decision, not yours."

"We know that," said my dad, "but spending, what, a year or two away? That's not a big deal. Not with a job that has so much potential for growth."

"Don't worry about it," I told them. "Stephanie's right; I'll probably go. And I could use some help with the move."

"Of course," said my mom, gesturing up to the ceiling with her fork. "We'll get the old truck out of the garage—it'll be just like when you left for school. Dad and I will come visit as often as you let us."

"I'm not eighteen anymore," I said. "You can visit whenever you want."

We continued to eat for a few minutes and then my dad said, "Stephanie's officially a single woman again. I'll drink to that." My dad had never liked my sister's marriage with her now ex-husband because he had suspected, long before any actual evidence surfaced, that Craig was closeted.

"Hide your husbands," Stephanie muttered, sipping her wine.

"You've handled it all with such poise, sweetie," said my Mom.

She sighed. "Ultimately, there's not much to contemplate. Makes things easier. That and hopefully staying friends."

"I like you better as friends," my dad announced.

"Yes, thank you, Dad," said Stephanie. "So good to finally know how you feel."

I couldn't help but laugh.

"So, Wyatt," my mom began, "I know you don't want me to ask, but you're always so quiet about your love life. If a boy spends his time driving you around, I think that could mean he's more than a little into you."

"What if he's straight, Mom?" said Stephanie. "Not every boy Wyatt hangs out with has to be gay."

My mom turned to me. "Well, is he gay?"

"He's interested in guys," I said, "but not romantically. He's only dated women. And for what it's worth, as far as the gay thing goes, I usually pick up vibes from people. I'm not getting any from him. But that doesn't really mean anything either way."

"You say he's interested?" my mom asked. "Interested in what? Friendship?"

"And sex," Stephanie added.

"Oh." My mom took a long drink from her glass. "Oh, well, I really hope you're being careful."

I laughed to myself, elbows resting on the table and hands clasped to my forehead. "Don't worry, Mom."

"What does he do for work?" asked my dad.

"He owns a software company," I said. "It's doing well."

"Sounds promising," he said, reaching out and playfully shaking my arm.

I smiled but did not say anything in response. We returned to discussing the logistics of my probable move, then wandered into the topic of what movie to watch after dinner. When we were done eating, I stepped in to complete the post-meal cleanup, and soon after, we settled into *Big Hero 6*, which only Stephanie had previously seen.

Later that night, after the movie was over and my parents had gone to bed, Stephanie and I put on our coats and sat together on the front porch swing. The yard glowed very dimly in the orange gloom of a towering lamp at the end of the street, silhouetting the ancient cherry tree that stood at the center of the lawn.

"Sorry if I embarrassed you at dinner," she said. "I was just kind of irked at Mom and Dad's attitudes, I guess."

"Trust me, I was a lot more entertained than embarrassed."

"Okay, good," she said. "Check it out: Mom's face when she heard the word 'sex.'" Stephanie mimicked perfectly my mom's expression of thinly veiled shock.

I cracked up. "So perfect."

"Seriously, though," she said, "I'm glad you know how to relax and enjoy what's in front of you. Believe me, you have more time than you even know."

"I'm sensing that more and more."

"Good," she said. "And as far as this move is concerned, just try to listen to yourself and what you want."

"Okay," I replied. "I can try that."

"I've made some hasty decisions in life just because everything felt so goddamn urgent. You know what I mean?"

"I guess so."

"Well, you can take this for what it is, but in light of recent events, I'm seeing that very little in life is actually urgent. Almost nothing at all."

"That's good to know," I said. I knew Stephanie spoke within the context of her divorce, and for reasons that did not align perfectly with my parents', I was proud of her for the self-affirming attitude she had carried throughout the experience.

We talked for a short while longer, mostly laughing over shared memories of growing up. Soon, she brought up her long drive home and asked if I wanted a ride.

"No thanks," I said, "I'm going to sit here a little longer."

The truth was that I enjoyed the fifteen-minute walk between my childhood home and my apartment, rain or shine, and its ability to clear my head of persistent and unproductive thoughts before going to bed. I started walking only a few minutes after her car's taillights disappeared around the corner.

I'd borrowed one of my mom's scarves from the narrow closet by the front door and now snugged it more closely against my neck to ward off the mist that hung in the cold, lamplit air. I walked through a lonely pedestrian tunnel leading under the highway, kicking at the concrete wall and listened to the juddering reverberations that crashed down the length of the tube.

When I reemerged, I noticed I'd received a text from an unknown number. I had forgotten that Mikey said he would text me. "Hey, didn't want to interrupt your dinner," he wrote. "Just thought you should know that it's calm seas tonight. Not having any doubts about what happened. I had the best day."

I continued walking for a few minutes, mulling over an appropriate response before returning to my phone and texting back, "I'm really glad to hear that. A little relieved, to be honest. Looking forward to our bus ride tomorrow."

Glancing back over the highway, I saw that the moon, a somber puddle of white, hung low with edges softened by the mist into an encircling aura of light. It turned its sorrowful gaze downward, bisected by an instant of ribbon-like cloud that lingered over the farmland to the east.

I looked back at the screen and for a few seconds an ellipsis flickered under my response indicating that Mikey had, willfully or by accident, begun to enter another text. But it soon disappeared and I tucked my phone back into my pocket.

6

My willingness to listen had, a handful of times, placed me into a peculiar conversation with individuals who, although hailing from vastly different walks of life, each described the same phenomenon. There existed at some point in their past an insurmountable inner-struggle (addiction and negative thought processes were examples), which they had suddenly conquered, not because they fought ruthlessly against all odds and lack of self-restraint, but because the requirement of active effort had mysteriously vanished.

My struggle, if I am allowed to invoke the connection, had undoubtedly manifested itself as a daily, interminable anxiety surrounding work and, more recently, the question of whether or not to move. But over the past couple of days, I could not have been paid to care about my career standing, nor to predict the events that would rain down at the end of March. It wasn't that I had somehow acquired all of the weapons necessary to combat such stressors; instead they no longer occurred to me as issues over which to bother oneself in the first place.

It would be tempting to conclude that Mikey had single-handedly towed me up from the depths, but in keeping with the mysticism surrounding others' similar experiences, I felt he was only an accompanying aspect of my new quieted under-standing. The true origin was not something I grasped, but it did not keep me from sleep.

The next morning Mikey looked worse for wear, relative to his regular vigor. I asked him how he was feeling.

"Didn't sleep well last night," he said.

"I'm sorry," I said. "Your text sounded so relaxed."

"I know. I felt pretty relaxed. Just couldn't get to sleep. It happens to me sometimes."

"Maybe it was the nap," I suggested.

He smiled. "I sort of forgot about the nap. Maybe. Naps don't usually do that to me, but who knows?"

We both stood under the eve, scrolling through our phones. I drew a peacefulness from the weight of his presence as we silently conducted our own lives.

After we boarded I slid in against the wall of the bus and Mikey fell into the seat next to me.

"I hope you're able to take it easy today," I said.

"Don't worry about me," he said. "I can nap at lunch if I need to. I also didn't have time for coffee at home this morning, so you're seeing me at my worst. In half an hour I'll be fine."

I smiled. "Okay."

"I have to send a couple emails, but I think I'm going to wait until I get to work. Right now I just want to sit."

"What if you fall asleep and miss your stop?"

"That's why I need you to keep me awake," he said. "You ask me a question and then I'll ask you one."

I thought for a second. "How far is your stop from mine?"

"About three minutes," he said. "Will you ever start writing again?"

"Wow, this is really rapid-fire."

Mikey turned toward me, leaning against the back of the empty seat in front of him and gave me an expectant look.

"I'm sure I will," I said. "Where do you keep all of your

drawings?"

"In my drawing desk. Or on top of the refrigerator. A few other places. Can I read some of your writing?"

"If I can find it, maybe. Why are you so obsessed with my writing?"

He leaned back and looked up at the ceiling of the bus. "We need a rule that says we're only allowed to ask questions that have short answers."

"That seems a little subjective," I said. "Any question can have a short answer. Maybe it won't be a very good answer, but it still counts as an answer."

"Fine," he said. "I'd like to see your creative side. It makes me feel sort of…closer to someone. Is that short enough?"

"Yes," I said. "How long have you been drawing?"

"Since around fourteen years old. I took art my first semester of high school. When did you start writing?"

"Probably around the same time. At least that was when I started to take it seriously." I paused. "What were you like when you were fourteen?"

He thought for a moment. "Honestly, kind of a wild child. A terror to my parents for sure. I didn't have a lot of focus."

"Really? Did you just sort of grow out of it?"

He smirked at me, wordlessly accepting the fact that I had broken the chain. "I guess you could say that. Or maybe I'm just extra buttoned-down around you."

"No, I think I can see it. You've still got a little wild streak to you."

"That's good. I don't want to turn into some boring…I don't know; can't think of anything."

"Accountant," I offered.

"Right." He grinned. "Thank you. Some boring accountant."

I received a text from Jennifer, my coworker. "If you're looking for inspiration," it read, "Calvin is leaving T&D. He doesn't want to move. Fern Hill would be way better with you there. Just thought you should know. See you at work."

"Thanks for the info. See you soon," I replied, then put my phone back in my pocket.

"I don't care if you text," said Mikey.

"It was just a quick work thing. Apparently one of my coworkers is quitting instead of moving to Fern Hill."

"Wow. I didn't realize that was the only alternative."

"They kind of implied it," I said. "It's their expectation that we're willing to move around. I'm surprised he's quitting, actually."

Mikey looked down at his knees. "I doubt that's something anyone takes lightly."

"No," I said. "You're right."

He yawned and warmed his hands on his neck. "Friends rest on friends' shoulders sometimes."

I laughed. "Yes, that is accurate. Do you want to sleep until my stop?"

"Not sleep, just rest," he said. "I'm dying over here."

I patted my shoulder to indicate that he was welcome. He slouched down in his seat a little and tilted his head against my frame. We were both quiet for a few minutes as the bus pounded its way across the bridge and entered downtown.

"You're more comfortable than the window," he said.

"That's good."

He didn't say anything else until we approached my stop and he sat up. "Maybe you should talk to your coworker today. The one who's quitting. See what he has to say about it."

"I was considering that," I told him.

He stood up to allow me access to the aisle. "Cool. See you

after work."

I said goodbye and stepped off the bus.

I arrived at work a little early, and just a handful of staff already milled around. Jennifer nearly plowed through a row of desks to reach me. "Don't let Calvin sway you too much. He doesn't have anything nice to say about T&D right now. They're only giving him the rest of this week."

"Can they do that?"

"Contractually, yes. Not that they should, but they can."

"Alright," I said. "I'm definitely leaning toward moving. I just want to hear his side."

"That's fair," she said.

About an hour into my workday I asked Calvin if he had time to meet at lunch.

"All the time in the world," he said, leaning back with his hands clasped behind his head. During my time at the company, Calvin's initially brusque demeanor had grown on me. Short, moderately overweight, loud and strong-willed, he was an open book and rarely withheld his opinions.

We met for pho across the street and after ordering, he said, "So you're not sure about the move, huh?"

"Right," I said. "Is there any specific reason you're not going?"

"Actually, no," he confessed. "There are a few general reasons, but I mean, it's not like I'm unable to leave the city."

"That's kind of where I'm at," I said. "I just don't want to move. But that reasoning ends up sounding pretty lacking to me whenever I really start to consider it."

"Don't you think if you were really into the job, you wouldn't be hesitating?"

I paused. "I don't know. I haven't really considered that."

"Here's my thing," he said. "My immediate response was

like, 'Fuck no. I'm not doing this shit.' Then later, even though I'd gotten over all the initial stuff, I still had a pretty clear feeling of not wanting to do it. I know if I was obsessed with this job, I never would've had those feelings in the first place."

Our food arrived and he unwrapped his chopsticks. "Actually, it's been good for me because it's helping me realize that I chose the wrong career."

Unexpectedly, his last statement dropped like a lead ball into the bottom of my stomach. It held no nuance or shocking revelatory properties, but nonetheless left me with a distant, icy feeling that faded slowly.

"T&D has been a real bitch about it, to be honest," he was saying. "I really feel like they should have given me more time before cutting me off. It's not like I wouldn't be productive over the next month here. But then again…I'm the one who signed the papers when they hired me."

"What was their reasoning for letting you go so quickly?"

"They said they don't want to continue with someone who isn't headed the same direction as the company."

"Corporate bullshit," I said.

"Exactly."

"So you're thinking you chose the wrong career?"

"I think so. Like I said, if I had no big doubts about it at all, I'd be fine with moving away for a while. Instead I'm jumping ship."

"Okay," I said. "I follow you."

"That's just me, though. Maybe you chose the right career and you just don't want to move to fucking Fern Hill."

I laughed. "Maybe." We ate in silence for a few minutes. After giving it more thought I said, "Your logic is pretty sound, though. I can't be that different from you. I mean, I wouldn't call accounting my passion."

"Well, how not-passionate would you say you are?"

"I don't know. Obviously I'm not feeling much if I'm not totally willing to move for the job."

"Yeah," he said. "Well, you're more undecided about it— that's for sure. It was a lot easier for me to say no. That probably tells you something."

"It does tell me something. It tells me the decision will be harder for me than it was for you."

He grinned. "There you go. Glad I could help."

We finished eating and as we paid at the door he said, "Hey, no matter what you decide, my advice would be to wait to talk to them. I should have just played stupid for a few weeks and stayed on payroll."

I laughed. "I'll definitely keep that in mind."

Mikey texted me after work as I waited for the southbound bus. "Hey, I left work a little early. You weren't at your stop so I'm probably ahead of you. Can I persuade you to come over and hang out today? I forgot to tell you that I'll be out of town for four days starting tomorrow."

"Sure," I replied. "Just boarding now. I'll see you soon." As the bus merged with traffic I reflected back on my conversation with Calvin. The concept of having chosen the wrong career had lost some of its initial bite. Still, I was fascinated by his ability to speak with such pragmatism (and perhaps disregard) about something I considered momentous.

When I arrived at Mikey's he lit up the doorway with re-newed spirit.

"You're looking a lot more rested."

"I know. I did end up napping at lunch. And of course..." He smiled and pointed at the mug in his hand.

I took off my coat and tie after entering and draped them over the arm of the couch.

"Are you hungry?" he asked. "I made some beef and rice last night. There's still a lot left."

"I will need to do something about dinner," I said.

"Let me heat some up," he offered. "I'm hungry, too."

I accepted and Mikey went to the refrigerator.

"Have you done any drawings lately?" I asked.

"Yeah, actually. Last night. It's still there."

I walked over to his desk and studied the sketch that lay on top of a jumbled stack of papers. Two birds (a cardinal and a robin) stood planted in a small circle of grass, the robin pulling taut a worm that was still partially anchored to the soil. Although the lines were not as rough, lending the sketch an augmented sense of finality over what he'd drawn for me, the creatures each possessed the same minimally human expression of unencumbered joy.

"I'm currently obsessing over birds, thanks to you," he said.

"It's amazing, Mikey," I said, to which he did not respond. I considered lifting up the drawing to see what others might lie underneath, but decided against it.

"Alright," said Mikey from the kitchen. "You can come serve yourself if you want. I'll get you a plate."

Once we sat down to eat at the coffee table Mikey said, "I meant to tell you sooner about traveling this week. Sorry about that."

"That's right. I totally forgot about your text. It's alright."

"It's weird," Mikey continued. "I've known about this trip all along, but up until a couple days ago, I never would have thought to let you know about it."

"Before last week you didn't even know me," I said.

"I know. It's so weird," he said.

"Are you flying?"

"I did last time, but this time I'm driving. It's about eleven hours. The Honda's first road trip," he said, smiling.

"That's awesome. Have a good time." I took a few bites and complimented him on his cooking.

"Thanks. My mom and I cooked together a lot when I was growing up. Sorry there are no greens. I ate them all last night. Also the beef got a little overcooked when I reheated it."

"It's a free meal," I said. "It doesn't bother me."

After we finished I insisted on washing the dishes. As I set them to dry, Mikey said, "Do you play video games?"

"Sometimes," I said. "What do you have?"

"Grand Theft Auto might be fun," he said. "We could just take turns and watch each other."

"That's actually one of the few I know."

Over two hours later we remained on the rug together in front of the television, Mikey now at the helm, which I preferred because his lovable, childlike enjoyment of the game buoyed me into my own guileless mood. At times I rolled over into a fetal position, he barely maintaining his composure at my side, debilitated by waves of laughter brought on by our virtual misadventures.

"Sometimes you just have to take the country cruise," he was saying as he guided a 1950s-era sedan down a canyon highway. "Do a little of this and a little of that, and—" The car plummeted off the edge of a curve, scraping its way down a rock face and landing on the shore of a lake. It remained miraculously still operable and we spent over half and hour fruitlessly attempting to sweet-talk it over rocky terrain and back up to the highway.

"I think it's time to admit defeat," said Mikey, who had since offered me a shot at freeing the crumpled-up car. "That was fun, though."

"It was."

"Do you want to do something else?"

"Sure," I said, with no idea what he had in mind.

"It is so fucking hot in here." He went over to his bedroom area and cranked open a long, slim window near the ceiling that ran the top length of another large window by the bed. He also opened a narrow door at the foot of the bed that I had not noticed before, which led out to a small balcony. "If we hang out over here it'll be a lot cooler."

I climbed up onto his double bed with him, which, like mine, had been raised up on stilts so that items could be stored underneath. We lay side by side, looking up at the ceiling for a couple of minutes without saying anything. The cool air that poured over the metal lip of the vent window was as soothing as he had promised. Eventually I tilted my head to the right, watching Mikey's chest rise and fall. He still wore a rather formal white button-down but had untucked it from his pants. The untextured fabric rose up to cloak his pectoral muscles and descended to his slim waist.

He said softly, "I like that we can be quiet like this. It's nice to think that if there's nothing left to say, silence can be comfortable. It's not like that with everybody."

"I know what you mean," I said.

"Not that we need to be quiet. Loud is good, too. We could shout if we wanted—hey, give me something to shout."

"What? I can't think of anything."

Verbatim, Mikey yelled out the words I had just said, jolting me back to full alertness.

I laughed. "Quit it."

He yelled that, too, his voice slamming against the ceiling and every wall in the apartment.

I clapped my hand over his mouth and he tore it away.

"I won't be silenced," he boomed, a gigantic grin spreading

across his face. He held my arm down at my side and wrestled his way on top of me.

I locked my arms around his torso and rolled both of us back to his side of the bed, so that I now lay on top of him.

He struggled for only a few seconds before overpowering me and I found myself on my back once again.

"Okay," I said, "I give up. You're stronger." I relaxed my muscles and let the weight of him sink slowly into me.

"I'm not," said Mikey. He offered a minor thrust, pressing his waist into mine, and I felt that he was becoming hard. I thrust back. He lifted himself up to a sitting position, still straddling me, and unbuttoned his shirt. "It's still so hot and this shirt is way too restrictive."

"Maybe I should join you." I began tearing through my own buttons.

"Yes please," he said. He pulled off his cotton undershirt, tugging it up over his head, and helped me to remove mine. I only had a few seconds to observe his dark, bare chest, which towered above me, appearing more substantial than ever. He lowered himself back down so that our naked skin could meet, and already I felt a cool dampness from the sweat shared between us. Mikey wrapped his arms around me and gave another thrust, firm and definite. I countered and we began to grind up against one another, his pronounced hardness sliding repeatedly over mine through our pants. I was not only aroused, but fully stimulated by the motion. I felt his fingers grip the skin of my back, trapped slightly under my weight as he continued to grate his body into mine.

"Fuck. This is hot," he said. "If we keep going like this, I'm not going to last."

"Keep going," I said.

He pressed on, increasing only slightly in intensity before I could feel the entire nature of his movement adjust slightly. "This is it," he said. "I can't stop it. Oh, fuck."

My consideration for the brutality of his heft pounding into me, the animalistic physicality of him that had advanced into immediate, natural release, and that I had brought this about in him—all of it sent me directly over the edge and I discovered myself climaxing just as he announced his own arrival, so that both of us released at once, coming wildly against one another, into our underwear.

Mikey continued to grind softly against me in small, metered, seizing movements until we had both subsided. He rolled off of me and onto his back. We now panted peacefully, staring up, a pair of heaving chests wet from the heat and activity. Once again we were silent for a few minutes as distant city sounds and scattered voices from the dark street below came gradually back into focus.

"I don't know how else to put this," he said, "but that's really going to help me get through the next four days."

I smiled. "I feel the same way, and I'm not even going anywhere."

A siren wailed by and Mikey got up to close the small door to the balcony. "Do you want a fresh pair of underwear? I'm going to change mine."

"Do you mind?" I asked.

He went to his dresser and tossed me a pair. He then went around the partition to the living room, offering me privacy as both of us changed. Mikey wore a similar, rather tight-fitting style of boxer-briefs.

He offered to wash mine for me and return them later, and I thanked him. "Ooh," he said. "Trading underwear—so sexy."

I laughed as he returned to lie again at my side, both of us still bearing the skin of our torsos. "I didn't even ask you where you were going," I said.

"Boise."

"Where's Boise?" The place sounded only vaguely familiar to me.

"In Idaho. I've spent a little time there already from the last time we helped them on-site."

"Oh. For some reason I assumed all of your clients were local."

"The newer ones are, actually. But when we first started we were casting the net everywhere."

"I see. Well, I hope you have a good trip to Boise. Do you like it there?"

"It's okay," he said. "It's a lot smaller than here. I don't mean Fern Hill-small; it's just not a big city. Some strange in-between size, I guess. But it's clean and the people are nice."

I nodded and we lay listening to the sounds of the night spilling in from outside. I made up my mind to appease my curiosity about something.

"Mikey, I've been wanting to ask. How did your parents die?"

"Car accident," he said. "A truck driver fell asleep and hit them head-on."

"Oh," I said. "Sorry to bring it up. For some reason I wanted to know."

"That's normal. I told you they died but I didn't tell you what happened." He paused. "It was a bad accident so I don't think they suffered."

I folded my arms across my chest. "I'm glad they didn't suffer."

He cleared his throat, pausing for a few seconds before saying, "It's been almost four years. After all that time...I don't feel like I expected I would. It still doesn't always seem like they're gone. It's like they're still around. Somewhere."

I turned his statement over in my mind a few times. "Do you think they really are? Like, somewhere else?"

"If you mean, like, an afterlife type of thing, then I don't know." He turned onto his side, facing me. "I don't have any specific beliefs about that. I guess I don't really think that way."

"I don't, either," I said.

"My aunt always insists they're in heaven. She says that's why I feel the way I do. I've told her that those beliefs aren't...I don't know...a part of me."

I rubbed my eyes. "My mom and I have the same kind of conversations. She's convinced that life must be empty and sad without believing in an afterlife."

Mikey moved once again to his back. He seemed to choose his words carefully before saying, "I would rather be miserable than take something like that on faith."

I turned and looked at him. "That's how I think about it, too."

"I mean, yeah it's sad. It's pretty fucking depressing some-times," he continued. "It's supposed to be that way. You know, not knowing."

I nodded, but didn't say anything.

Mikey got up to close the window. "I'm finally feeling a little cold," he said. "I'm going to put on my shirt again."

I did the same.

We lay together again, wandering through our own minds for a while. Eventually I turned to Mikey, observing his eyes as they darted around the room, lingering in one place for no longer than a few seconds before shifting to the next.

"You look very occupied by something," I said.

He sighed. "Not any one thing. And nothing that I can really put into words."

"What time do you have to head out tomorrow? I don't want to keep you up."

"Around the same as usual. I'll be fine. We'll leave soon and get you to bed, though."

We faced each other, a safe distance between us, and my eyelids began to feel heavy.

"When I focus on you," he said, "I stop thinking about anything serious. It's nice."

I wasn't sure if Mikey referred only to this moment, together on the bed, or if, when we were apart, he also calmed himself with thoughts of me. I just smiled at him.

We both grew increasingly drowsy over the next several minutes, and I said, "I don't want the night to be over, but I'm going to fall asleep if we don't go now."

He lingered for just a second and suddenly I contemplated alternate circumstances, in which I did not report to work early the next morning and Mikey did not embark on a day-long drive to some distant, unimaginable city. We would not be bound by time; we would drift off to sleep in each other's presence and we would come to remove our clothes, crawling under the covers to spend the night together. I wondered if Mikey had considered it, too.

"I don't want it to be over, either," he said. He lifted himself up and crawled off the bed. "I guess four days isn't very long."

"It's not," I said, walking to the living room and gathering my coat and tie. "The work week will go by quickly."

As we traveled home I felt such an unexpected and profound peacefulness that I fell easily back into a state of fatigue, fighting off sleep more than once.

Mikey noticed and insisted that I close my eyes. "I promise I am far from sleep," he said. "Driving does that to me."

I rested my head against the window, abandoning the

waking world for at least a few minutes. At some point I had become aware again but kept my eyes closed, absorbing the hushed vibrations that traveled up from the road through the frame of the car and spread into my side. For a fleeting moment I detected, unmistakably, the back of Mikey's hand meeting with my cheek. It ventured up the edge of my jaw and brushed against my ear before departing. I showed no sign of awareness because I did not want to embarrass him, and because I hoped that it would happen again. It did not, and before long he guided the car off the highway and up the road to my apartment building.

7

Once we were stopped I got out. Mikey pulled the brake and met me in front of the car, where the engine clicked away like a sewing machine and the street was a pool of white. He engulfed me in a tight hug and said into my ear, "Take care of yourself while I'm gone, Chickadee."

"I will," I said. "Drive safely tomorrow."

The next day at work I burrowed underground, clawing through an exceptional amount of back work kicked around by lower-level staff. Though both Jennifer and Calvin voiced their appreciation, I was not inclined to accept credit for behavior derived from boredom and an appetite for distraction.

I wandered into the gym that evening and was approached near the end of my workout by a dark-eyed boy—a man, technically, but certainly younger—with a distinguished face and a solid, compact figure. He was beautiful, I figured, by a kind of objective and widely acceptable token, above which I did not suspend myself.

"You used to show up on my phone as nearby," he said. "You look just like your picture. I never got brave enough to text you, though. I don't see you on there anymore."

"Oh, sorry. I got rid of it," I said, referring to the location-based hookup app Marie had convinced me to download over the summer. "It wasn't really doing me any good."

"Aww, that's too bad," he said. "Well, if you're ever interested it would be fun to hang out sometime."

I spent little time processing a response. "I'm actually taken, but thanks. I'm flattered."

"Oh," he said, "good for you. Well, thanks anyway."

As I walked home, what had felt initially like a straightforward decision unfurled, inevitably, to reveal some problematic aspects. For example, although I had removed the app from my phone, I was customarily unlikely to spurn the brave, in-person advances of appealing men. Actually I was only further attracted by the audacity of a face-to-face proposition.

Another issue lay in the specificity of my response; the only other situations in which I had ever claimed to be taken occurred, in fact, when I was still with my ex-boyfriend (a time when I did not shoulder an air of availability and was rarely ever approached in the first place). I liked to believe I carried no illusions—I was no less single now than I'd been a week ago, or a year ago—and yet my behavior had plainly changed. I still held confidence in my resolve to see Mikey as no more than a friend with whom I had begun to share intimate moments, and now acknowledged the importance in conducting myself accordingly.

Wednesday morning I swayed in my seat at the back of the 40A, flicking idly through my work email, when Marie texted asking if I could meet her for lunch.

About five hours later I hurried down to the street and tore several blocks east to a sandwich shop halfway between our places of work. I was only allotted forty-five minutes and desired as much time as possible to sit and talk.

We collided in energetic embrace by the door. After each of us made our orders we sat down and I said, "Before we get into anything else, I need to tell you that Tandon and Dufresne wants me to move to Fern Hill next month. I'll lose my job if I don't."

"Excuse me?" she said. "You can't move. When did they tell you this?"

"Last week. Marie, I'm sorry I didn't tell you sooner. I was trying to work it out in my mind, and I really just wanted to have fun last time we saw each other."

"It's fine," she said. "Sometimes you've got to process those things." She tore her napkin in two and stored one half in her coat pocket because, as she had once explained to me, she wouldn't need a whole napkin now, and nobody knew what disasters the future held. "How'd you let them down?" she asked.

I could tell she was only partially joking. "I haven't." I said. "I haven't yet."

"Well, those two statements are very different. You're saying this is a situation that can still be saved?"

"I'm not sure what I'm saying," I said. I explained how I was really inclined to go but that I had lingering doubts that were hard to pin down.

"I guess I'd be thinking the same thing if it were my job," she said. "I'll love you no matter what and I promise to visit all the time if you go. But I am too selfish to support the idea of you moving. Make no mistake, Wyatt—I want you here."

"Alright. Acknowledged."

She smiled. "Yeah, you better take that seriously."

"Of course. I'm not going to tell you and then ignore what you have to say about it."

"Thank you."

Our sandwiches were called and Marie jumped up to grab them, commanding me to rest.

"You keep me updated, okay?" she said as she set my food in front of me. "As for our next order of business, Sloan and I are going out tomorrow night and your presence is mandatory. Since it's a weeknight the lines will be shorter and cover will be cheaper. The intention is to get a little crazy."

Sloan served as the third pillar in our European undertaking, and I had not seen him in over a month. "That sounds so tempting," I said. "Aren't we all working on Friday, though?"

"Sloan and I are taking Friday off," she said, tearing gingerly at the red-and-white-checkered paper encasing her sub.

"I'm not sure it's a good idea for me to ditch work," I said. "Not on such short notice, anyway."

"Sloan and I were concerned you might say that. How about you take Friday off and use it as an indicator for whether or not you move to Fern Hill? If they fire you then your decision is made for you. Easy. If not, well, maybe you'll still move. Maybe."

I smirked at her. "That's a solid plan right there."

"Come on, Wyatt. You and I both know that the worst thing you'll face is a slap on the wrist. Besides, if you really are moving then you owe us a night out before you leave. Please let me shame you into doing this."

Her plea was not wasted on me and I felt my mind tilting steadily toward action. "Alright," I said. "But if I'm fired and can't pay my rent I'm moving in with you."

"Oh, let's do that regardless," she said, placing her hand on mine.

That afternoon I approached my supervisor and requested Friday off. She reminded me about the obligatory week's advance notice of nonemergency absence, then granted it, emphasizing the special exception she was making. "By the way," she said, "we're asking all relocation employees to give written confirmation by the end of next week—March 6th. You'll have an email about it soon."

Over the next twenty-four hours I gracefully cast aside any doubts concerning an appropriate reply to such an email. As a tireless Thursday afternoon faded to early-evening, I ditched the elevator for the stairwell and pinballed down six flights to the lobby. I was thankful for the four hours separating me from the planned beginning of our evening adventure, since I had made up my mind to transit home and change out of my work clothes.

I set my phone to wake me before I reached my first stop and slept somewhat well until then, repeating the process after boarding the second bus. I'd stayed up late reading the night before, and throughout the day, fatigue had dangled itself stealthily from my fingertips and eyelids.

I did not spend much time at home, changing and then loading a small backpack full of items for the evening, including workout clothes, overnight items, water and a can of beer that was set to expire soon. I texted my mom to ask if I could stop by after the gym.

About an hour later I treaded across the lawn to the front door, warm, sweating and still in my gym attire.

"You're going to catch a cold," said my mom, who met me as I stepped inside.

"I don't think so. It's so nice today."

"You'll want to shower, right? I got a towel out for you."

We shared a disdain for showering at the gym. "Thanks, Mom," I said.

"When we had that freeze I spent a lot of time there. But I've been running outside since the end of January."

"Good for you."

We continued to make small-talk for a couple of minutes

and then I went to shower. Afterward I found her in the kitchen, where she asked me what I wanted to eat.

"I can help myself, Mom," I said. "You've been at work all day."

"So have you. How about you just let your mother cook you a nice meal?"

I smiled. "If it will make you happy, then by all means."

"It will," she said. "It always does."

I sat on a barstool across the counter and received a photo from Marie depicting two outfits lying on her bed.

"Left," I texted.

"I'm sorry for assuming your friend was gay the other night," said my mom. "You know that's not how I think about it. It's just that I want you to find someone nice."

"It's fine. I don't exactly have a lot of guy friends. You're okay to assume."

"You have Sloan," she said as she chopped vegetables for a stir-fry. "Beef or chicken?"

"Chicken," I said. This was a rather keen observation on her part. Sloan was biologically female and attracted to women, but when I first met him he spelled his name "Sloane" and still identified as a woman. That changed at some point during my third semester at college, and since he was also from Corbin, where we both held down summer jobs and often hung out in the evenings, my parents knew him both prior to and after the gender change. They had handled it with a level of elegant composure that, at the time, surprised me a great deal. It may have helped that Sloan cut his hair short and maintained a decidedly masculine appearance.

"I'll be seeing him tonight, by the way. And Marie."

"Oh. Please say hello for me. I never see either of them anymore."

After the food was done we sat side by side at the bar and ate.

"I've also been thinking a little about your move," she said. "I no longer have an opinion. Your career should not come before your happiness. I can't get your dad on board, though. He thinks you'll be unhappy if you give up your job to stay here."

"Sometimes I feel like I don't have an opinion either." I took a bite of food. "I'm supposed to have one by the end of next week, though."

"Is that when they want you to commit?"

"Yeah."

My mom shifted her weight on the stool, crossed her legs under her pale yellow skirt and continued eating in silence. She always wore a measured amount of floral perfume; its weathered familiarity meant that I did not notice unless, like now, I searched for it.

"Tell Dad not to worry about me," I said after a pause.

"He's not worried. He just thinks he knows what's best for you—both of us do. But we don't know as well as you do."

"Hah," I said. "I wish I knew."

She smiled. "You're not twenty with a child. People decide to wait now and it sets them free. I think Dad and I project our sensibilities onto you from when we were your age. It's not very helpful."

I didn't say anything for a while and neither did she. When we finished, I carried our plates to the sink and rinsed them before loading them into the dishwasher. Out of nowhere I thought of the car ride home, and how Mikey's hand had touched my face when he thought I was sleeping.

I turned to my mom. "If that guy becomes more than a friend, I'll bring him by so you can meet him."

She looked up from a white tablet that lay flat on the countertop. "That would be nice. What's his name?"

"It's Mikey," I said. "If I'm moving, I can't get attached, though. You know that."

"Of course," she said.

I caught the 8:05 northbound and sat at the back. It was mostly empty so I felt unselfconscious about cracking open the beer and downing it quickly. It had been wrapped in a small towel and remained cool, but was not particularly satisfying.

Around nine o'clock I approached our meeting place and noticed Sloan slouched against the scarred brick face of a corner convenience store, buried in his phone. He didn't see me until I was a few feet away.

"Wyatt, where the hell have you been?" he asked, giving me a hug.

"Busy, I guess," I said. "I've missed you. You're still liking work?"

"It's okay," he said. "Not enough of the real meaty stuff. A lot of filing and shit."

"I know how you feel," I said.

"Marie said you might be moving. I hope that's not true."

"I haven't decided anything," I said. "I've still got time."

"How long have you guys been here?" Marie shouted from twenty or thirty feet away. She bustled past a slow-moving group and coaxed all three of us together into concurrent embrace. "There we go," she said. "Bring it in."

"We just got here," said Sloan, half of his face still pressed into my chest.

Marie stepped back, sizing each of us up. "Old glory, reunited. Are we ready?"

We decided to start with beers at a pub in the old part of downtown, which lay only a few blocks away. The interior shrugged with worn and dusty expanses of wood, uninterrupted, as though carved out of a single massive block, joints and floorboards long settled into a final, indelible resting place.

"You guys gearing up for tax season yet?" asked Sloan as we sat down.

"I don't talk shop with friends," said Marie, peering into her drink menu.

I knew this already and so did Sloan. After graduating, Marie began to express her distaste for the topic of work, in spite of (or perhaps because of) the innumerable nights spent wasting at the university library, quizzing one another, sharing homework answers and prepping for exams.

My phone buzzed and I clapped it down on the table, dismissively glancing at the screen. I saw that it was a picture message from Mikey and quickly examined it. He stood in front of a stately looking, large domed structure which I recognized as Idaho's capital building from a three-minute Monday-night Wikipedia research session. Underneath he had texted, "Greetings from Potato Land. Hope all is well with you back home."

I laughed.

"It's him," said Marie.

I looked up and met Marie's eyes, then Sloan's. "How do you know?" I asked her.

"You're never on your phone when we go out. It's one of your things."

"He's been out of town since Tuesday. It's the first time I've heard from him."

A server came by to take our orders.

"Let me see that," Marie said after they left, snatching my phone from across the table. "Oh, wow." Her face glowed opposite the screen as she manipulated the photo to get a closer look at him. "Oh, Wyatt. This man is a fucking find."

Sloan demanded a look.

"I'm not finished yet," Marie scolded.

I reached for it. "What are you doing?"

"I'm texting it to myself." She swatted my hand away.

"Stop," I said.

"Sent." She handed my phone to Sloan.

"Are you dating this guy?" he asked.

"No," I said. "It's complicated."

Our beers arrived.

"To hot people," said Marie as we clinked our glasses gently together. "Has anything else happened with him?"

"We're still hanging out. We've...uh...messed around a few times," I said, grinning.

"Details, please," she said.

"Maybe after I've had a few more drinks."

She rolled her eyes. "You're such a tease, Wyatt."

"And you're so demanding," added Sloan, gesturing toward Marie with his drink.

"You saw the picture. Can I help it that I want to know what the guy looks like with his clothes off?"

"He's not really my type," said Sloan.

"What happened to that girl you brought to bubble tea?"

"She's...I don't know...not that into breasts, as it turns out."

"Did she know?" I asked.

"Yeah, I'm mean...yeah," he said. "Fuck, I don't know. Probably. I thought I made it clear when we first met. Besides, I'm fucking flatter than most guys I know."

I laughed and Marie drank deeply from her beer. "It's her loss," she said. "Anyway, historically you do not have any trouble meeting girls."

Sloan leaned sheepishly against the wall. "I can't argue with that."

"And he's modest, too," she announced, projecting her voice out around the room as if someone eligible was stationed nearby.

Sloan swung an arm out across the table at Marie, who ducked out of his reach. Once she had straightened herself up she said, "I think we should start planning for another trip this summer. Southeast Asia? Maybe India?"

"It will be hard to swing with work," he said.

"Oh, come on. We said we would be like this. And we weren't supposed to listen to ourselves, right?"

"Right," said Sloan. "I remember."

"We said that no matter what was going on in our lives, we'd drop everything. For a month. Just one month this time— remember that?" She turned to me. "You remember, right? We were trying to be realistic about it, so we decided just one month."

I nodded. I also remembered thinking there was no way I'd ever fall so cleanly away from the careening thrill of travel that I could fathom the tragedy of passing up another chance at it. But now the threat to my stability in the coming months, which perched at the edge of cognizance, pecked at a thin membrane of certainty in which I had encased myself. At the time I had told myself that if I ever began to have doubts about venturing out again, I would do everything in my power to fight them. "I think we should set dates right now," I said. "Otherwise we never will."

"That's the kind of energy I was looking for," said Marie, reaching over and petting my hand.

Sloan downed his beer and said, "Alright, let's do this."

Marie bloomed into a fountain of exuberance, shuffling

around the table, squeezing in between us and throwing her arms around our necks. "I love you both so much." She returned to her seat, the server came back and Marie ordered another round, on her.

Each of us was well into our third beer by the time we had concluded our preliminary discussion of this new adventure. The dates of July 15th through August 15th were earmarked, crystallized, inalterable, and I rested a bit more easily on my worn, precarious barstool.

As we finally grew weary of examining possible destinations, looking up hostels and various fares, and the general collective imaginings of sights, smells, sounds and tastes we were destined to behold, Marie turned to me. "Wyatt, tell me about your lover."

Although I had not downed enough beer to achieve any substantive level of insobriety, I felt very relaxed and frankly a little drunk. "Calling him my lover implies that we have made love, which we have not," I said.

"Well," said Sloan, "what exactly have you done?"

"We have ejaculated in each other's presence. Twice."

Marie knocked over her glass, which was thankfully—if not surprisingly—empty. "Shut the fuck up. And this happened when?"

"Over the past week. We've been spending a lot of time together."

"What will happen to you guys if you move away?"

"No idea," I said. "I haven't spent much time thinking about that. Really though, he says he's just into sexual stuff with guys. He doesn't seem to have romantic feelings toward me like he does with girls. So I'm not worried that he'll get attached."

Sloan rotated his glass on its base. "This guy respects you, right? I mean, does he want to hang out for more than just getting into your pants?"

"I really think so," I said. "He's been really genuine. Plus we hang out for a long time after. It can't be just about sex."

"That is incredibly sweet," Marie said.

"I don't know," said Sloan. "Sexual attraction is a big fucking deal. Without it, people have big problems. But if it's a mutual thing..." he paused. "I don't know. It's just this idea of the person who likes getting physical with the same sex, but nothing else. I don't buy it. I don't think it's that simple. If it's there, then so is the potential for real feelings."

"Sloan," said Marie, "not everything has to be read into. If they just want to have fun, then who cares?"

"Of course," said Sloan. "Sorry, I didn't mean it that way. I just don't think some people can recognize how they feel, or they shut it out, or whatever, and they end up sending the wrong message. Then other people get mislead."

"I know what you're saying," I said. "It's okay. I won't be hurt."

"Okay," said Sloan, grinning. "Maybe that was my point. I feel better."

"Did you text him back?" asked Marie.

"Oh, fuck. No I didn't."

"Give me the phone," said Marie, prompting me to cling guardedly to it.

"No. Text your own lover."

"Yeah, shit," she said, "excuse me while I decide which one."

"I am going to die right here if we don't go dancing soon," said Sloan.

I stared off at the far wall of the pub, thumbs at the ready. "Great picture," I texted. "Hope you're having a safe trip.

Looking forward to seeing you when you get back."

A confounding warmth nested in the night air outside. City lights still glowed intensely, filling the space between street surfaces and an omnipresent layer of cloud hanging low in the sky. The weeknight crowd diminished moderately when measured against the clotted veins of a typical Saturday night. Still the route to Sloan's and Marie's preferred nightclub led through near-impregnable segments of sidewalk, where shouting and laughter resounded from glass and brick facades and evaporated into the emptiness above.

Along the way I looked upon Sloan admiringly because of his protective instinct for his friends, as couched as it was vehement. He understood the nature of particular people who behaved recklessly with regard to the feelings of others. He had become seasoned as the unwitting target of this kind of behavior, and he knew tragically well the way it felt to be the focus of another's cruelty. These experiences echoed back from his surface not as anger or projections of his victimhood, but as unadulterated concern for anyone who might be hurt. I felt strong and looked well after myself, but his words concerning Mikey back at the pub had not escaped me.

A couple of hours and no fewer than four shots later my experience had become distorted, although I felt distinctly happy and utterly unburdened. Initially I had worried that the order and sheer quantity of my drinks would make me sick, but the fear eventually left me. Sloan had located an acquaintance at some point, who clung devotedly to him now. They occasionally snuck off to make out in a darker corner of the club. Marie and I would dance mostly together in gradually increasing levels of suggestiveness until we broke out into laughter and started the cycle over again. And all the while the stark presence of strangers in the club, mounting steadily in spite of the five-dollar cover on a Thursday night, devolved for me into a nonspecific entity, the individuals of which becoming all but indistinguishable. I grew tired, but in an isolated, forgettable sense that wasn't truly felt until Marie brought up wanting to leave. By then it was well past one o'clock.

I retrieved my backpack from coat check and paid off my tab. Sloan bade farewell to his companion. We staggered together and giggled our way out to the street, where we began walking to the nearest station.

Marie had a fair amount of trouble walking normally, so she linked arms between us. "You're both my favorite," she mumbled. "Wyatt. I need something to fantasize about. Tell me more about your man, please."

I attempted to gather a few thoughts together, scattered about the floor of my mostly euphoric and unfocused mind. "He's tall," I said. "He has the best body you've ever seen."

"Mhmm," said Marie.

"He's the kindest person. And one time he even touched my face when he thought I was sleeping."

"Don't make me cry," said Marie, limping along. "I will cry forever if you tell me things like that."

"Sorry," I said.

Sloan laughed in a way that was felt more than heard. I glanced over Marie's head at him and he looked back at me with an expression that reminded me to keep my feelings in check, or otherwise accept what may come.

8

I spent the first half of Friday judiciously hungover. Marie, Sloan and I ate sushi for lunch (our first meal of the day) at a place near to her condo in Celadon. The sky had remained solidly overcast throughout the night, trapping in a cradling warmth that now accompanied sunlight as the clouds began to part.

We sat out on the restaurant's terrace along with several other souls clamoring for a brief glimpse at weather that wouldn't find its permanence for another couple of months.

"February," said Marie, "I'm beginning not to hate you so much."

"Too late," Sloan said. "March is two days away."

She bore the expression of someone who had been robbed. "That's ridiculous. It's literally not possible."

"It's literally the end of February," he said.

I, too, took unwarranted offense to this revelation. My six week verdict had shrunk surreptitiously to just over one month, a new span of time that felt vastly curtailed.

Sloan sat propped up on his elbows, purple hood pulled up over his head, the top half of his face mostly hidden behind an enormous pair of sunglasses. "Jesus, guys. At least it means summer is one month closer."

We silently agreed.

I returned to my apartment around three o'clock, peered

into the closet and fished Mikey's note out of a pocket in the lining of my coat. I lay on my bed, opened it once again and studied the drawing. I discovered no palpable details beyond what I'd observed the first time. However I paid special attention to the way the quick pencil lines had fallen to paper, emerging one by one, less through mindfulness than with an effortlessness that saw me feeling, of all things, pacified. I left the paper unfolded and anchored it with a small, smooth stone on top of my dresser.

I estimated the past day to have spit me out sixty dollars poorer—completely unsustainable, although I anticipated no further haphazard spending.

Mikey texted me about an hour later. "Did you know that Yakima is the Palm Springs of Washington?"

"Could you clarify?" I responded.

"It says so on a billboard outside of town. I can't confirm anything. I've never been to the real Palm Springs."

"I haven't either," I texted. "That seems like a strange comparison though. What compelled you to text me about this?"

"Just thought you needed to know. You're welcome."

"Oh, excuse me. Thank you."

He responded with a smiley face.

I did not hear from him again until just after midnight, when he texted to let me know he'd arrived safely at home. "Sorry for texting so late. I stopped in Seattle to see an old friend. I passed your street when I was on the highway. I wish it had been earlier. Maybe we could have hung out. Hope you are well."

"I'm still up," I texted. "Glad to hear you are safe at home. I am free to hang out tomorrow if you're not busy."

A few minutes later he texted, "That would be awesome.

Want to go for a run? I can pick you up if you want."

We relayed a few more messages back and forth, settling on three o'clock because Mikey had work obligations earlier in the day.

As I prepared for bed I recalled a conversation with my dad that had occurred a few years earlier. I'd returned home for Christmas from my first semester at college, where I had morphed into a kind of fortuitous advocate for open communication (something for which my adolescence had hungered in some ways, and by which was completely satisfied in others). I told him how I knew my being gay was not something we had ever truly discussed. I said that if my sexuality made him uncomfortable, we should talk about it. I remembered him foregoing an immediate response to instead stand and tread in his work boots over creaking slats to the fire, where he added a massive piece of chopped pine to the flames, tending it briefly. Once reseated in his worn cloth recliner he turned to me. "If your sexuality made me uncomfortable I would have told you already. That is my responsibility. But it doesn't make me uncomfortable. In fact, I resent the idea that a person's unchangeable qualities would make anyone uncomfortable. That's just not fair, and I hate it."

I lay in bed trying to call up the way Mikey had spoken about his own father. Within the context of who I was, he did not sound like a very accepting man. I sensed that Mikey carried a forceful deference to his parents, which, in their early deaths, I supposed was all but inevitable. I turned inward. If Mikey had held up a mirror for me to regard myself, I would have seen someone frivolous and fortunate—a person whose experience had been unburdened, easy and painless. I felt a bitter pang of ungratefulness seep into my chest. These were not the quelling thoughts I usually focused on before sleep, and

I suspected they were to blame, at least in part, for the unpleasant dreams that followed.

By the time Mikey was due to arrive the next day I felt much better. I had stumbled into a folder on my aging computer which held files containing various poems, snippets and one longer, unfinished project that I'd written over several weeks at school. After inadvertently barring myself for months from accessing this particular interest, my eyes now fell to the words on the screen as if they were not my own. It was a rare and brief opportunity that lent me unencumbered perspective on my writing, to which my reaction was mostly favorable.

Mikey arrived in full running regalia, his hair now cut short on the sides. An easy few inches were also absent from the top.

"My god, your hair," I said. "Take a look at that."

"Got it cut before work this morning. It was time. Kicked myself for not doing it before the trip. I looked like a child before."

"I really like it," I said, surprised at my own audacity as I reached up and ran my hand over the top. He did look categorically older now. "I didn't know you would already be changed," I said. "Let me put some stuff on."

"It's a beautiful day," he said. "Not too cold at all."

"I know. Can you believe it?" I left the door to the bathroom ajar and asked him about his trip.

"It was really great, actually. This time I left myself a little room to explore. It's not a bad place down there."

"I liked your picture. And the Honda did okay?"

"The Honda was a complete sweetheart," he said. "That's the kind of driving I enjoy. Out on the open highway. The city commute just isn't the same."

"I'm the same way," I said, emerging from the bathroom.

The levee seemed a natural destination. It was where our

first impromptu run had occurred, after all. We descended the steps to where he had parked his car and on the landing between the first and second floors Mikey stopped and looked back at me. I halted behind him. His lips spread into a bashful smile. Within his eyes, chaperoned by forthright, inkwell brows that turned slightly downward at the ends, lived a child incapable of driving for hundreds of miles, negotiating with company reps and accepting whatever other liabilities arose from such a situation.

"What?" I asked.

"Nothing," he said. "Sorry. Happy to be back, that's all." He turned away and continued down the stairs.

Once underway I asked Mikey more about his trip.

"They put me up in a good hotel," he said. "They took me around downtown…out to dinner…it was great. Actually, I spent a lot of time walking around on my own. I even took a little time to draw—on a business trip. I mean, fuck. Can't say I've ever done that before."

"That's cool," I said. "What do you think changed?"

He said nothing for a few seconds, then cleared his throat. "I guess I'm just thinking about my experience differently…or something. I'm not exactly sure."

"No need to question what's working," I said.

"Exactly." He signaled out of the passing lane. "So what did you do with the rest of your week?"

I thought a moment. "Nothing big. Actually, I went out late with friends Thursday night. Skipped work yesterday."

"Oh, well that sounds big," he said. "What did you do when you went out?"

"We just got drinks and went dancing. I had a little too much. Well, we all did."

He smiled. "I'm jealous. Haven't done that in a while. Did

102

you meet anyone nice?"

"You mean, like, guys? No. I mean I'm sure they were around, but I wasn't really looking."

Mikey nodded. "Sorry, that's kind of a weird question to ask."

A small, focused arc of light strayed across the dashboard and I followed it with my index finger. "No it's not," I told him. "That's definitely how some people hook up. Can't say it's happened for me very often, though."

"But it's happened?"

"Well, there was this guy in Germany," I said. "His group joined ours at a club one night. He made a really good impression on me. Like, even the next day I was thinking, 'I would bear this man's children.'"

Mikey laughed and I smiled to myself at how much I'd just sounded like Marie.

"I take it you spent the night with him?" he asked.

"Well, yeah. It's funny, though. We only fooled around a little. Mostly we just cuddled and talked and stuff. It was...I don't know. Never mind."

"It was what?"

I paused for a moment as my thoughts spooled up again. "It was, like, kind of sexy in its own way, I guess. I mean, when we weren't messing around." Unexpectedly, telling him this left me feeling awkward.

He moved a hand to the top of the steering wheel. "I think I understand what you mean."

He asked me to tell him more about traveling in Europe. I had mentioned the trip to him before, but only in passing. Presently I attempted to stick to highlights from our travel schedule and list some of the well-known sites we'd visited, but kept lapsing into small, anecdotal pitfalls. I would explain how

Marie's hair once caught fire while we were in Italy, or about a certain night in Prague when we'd become too drunk to locate our hostel. These stories seemed to interest Mikey the most anyway.

"I would really like to travel like that," he said as my rambling waned and we entered a dirt parking lot next to the levee.

I nodded, but didn't say anything in response until we stepped out onto the path, performing absent stretches. "Is there anything stopping you?" The breeze disagreed slightly with my bare arms and calves, but I knew I would warm up quickly once we started running.

"You mean from traveling?"

I nodded, tugging my left foot up to meet with my upper-thigh and butt before switching to the right.

"Just work," he said. "Sophie could take care of things while I was gone. But if she went with me...we'd just have to plan ahead, I guess. It's a worthwhile goal." Suddenly Mikey turned toward the water. "It's a cat," he said, and was gone, stepping down the embankment toward a wall of reeds that grew near the base.

I followed and watched him tempt a siamese house cat out from where it crouched in the tall grass. It approached him with a casual, friendly demeanor, speaking in soft, quick mews. I knelt down next to Mikey and held out my hand. The cat sniffed inquisitively at my fingers, brilliant blue eyes wide and alert. Much of its body was covered in creamy fur, long and light, but the face, spine and tail dissolved into a rich coffee-brown.

"You're such a sweetie," Mikey said, running his hand over its back and up its tail. He looked over at me. "Do you like cats much?"

"I think so," I said. "We had two dogs growing up, but never any cats."

"We didn't have any pets," Mikey said. "Maybe I'll get one someday."

I stood and the creature became cautious, circling back into the limits of its grassy resting place. Before long it had disappeared completely into the taller reeds.

"Goodbye," said Mikey. "Goodbye, my friend."

We climbed back up the rocky slope and started together down the path.

"Did you write anything when I was away?" he asked.

I threw him a playful smirk. "What do you think?"

"You should seriously get back into it."

"Actually, this morning I did find my stuff from when I was in school. If you want I'll send you some of it."

"I would like that very much," he said.

We ran in silence for a while. I was satisfied with the pace, but suspected that Mikey was going easy on me. However, he showed no will to increase his speed. He displayed admirable form, feet dragging minimally across the gravel, arms pumping efficiently at his sides, under apparently little tension.

"Did you ever run cross country?" I asked.

"Yeah," he said, slotting his response between quick, easy breaths. "In high school. Did you?"

"Yeah. I wonder if we were ever at the same meets."

"Probably. I'm sure you guys cleaned house, too. Chickadees had a strong team, right?"

"Yeah, at least when I was there. I wasn't on varsity, though."

Mikey nodded.

After a few seconds I glanced at him. "You were, weren't you? Of course you fucking ran varsity."

He laughed. "Can I help it that I was fast?"

"You're a pretty intimidating guy, you know that?"

"Hah." He gathered together his saliva and spat down toward the water. "That's all just perception."

"What do you mean?"

He looked over at me. "You think I don't find you intimidating?"

"I don't know," I said between breaths. "I hadn't thought about it."

He didn't say anything in response and we were silent again for a while. Mikey carried his phone in his right hand. He eventually checked the time and suggested we turn around. "That'll make it about forty-five minutes. Are you good with that?"

"Sounds great," I said.

As we neared what I estimated to be about halfway back I started to feel significantly winded, though I was confident that I would finish in fine form. I distracted myself by making conversation. "You don't usually work on Saturdays, do you?" I asked.

"No, never. Today was just an exception because Sophie and I didn't want to wait until Monday to regroup. It was just us and our next-in-command guy."

"Sounds pretty exclusive," I said.

"Oh, yeah." He laughed. "Let me tell you, we're very exclusive. Anyway, it sucks but we might have to meet tomorrow, too. Probably just for an hour or two in the afternoon."

"I guess it's different when you've been away."

"Right," he said. "That's true."

We finished the run without incident and cooled down with a short walk around the parking lot. Mikey's calves bulged from activity, large and lean, peppered with short, coarse black hairs. I drank endlessly from my water bottle and surveyed my environment with strange vitality as steady, relaxed breathing flowed incrementally back to me.

Today winter cloaked the swelling promise of spring like worn and dirty fabric, seams aching to split open. The air drifting in from the ocean brought with it smells reminiscent of warmer months; sweet and pleasurable scents swept across the water from blossoming plants in the north part of the city. I welcomed even the occasional quivering odor of industry, diesel exhaust or organic decay that picked its way inland from the harbor.

During the ride home Mikey glanced down at my lap and said, "Those shorts don't leave much to the imagination."

We remained very warm after the run, and now that we'd connected onto the highway, wind trampled through the wide open car windows. So that we were heard, we spoke to one another with intent.

"I wore them just for you," I teased. "Glad you noticed."

Mikey shrunk against the driver door. I looked over and witnessed him adjusting himself through the silky fabric of his basketball shorts.

"You're getting hard," I said. "I can tell."

"No I'm not," he said quickly. "A little. Damn it. I rubbed one out this morning so I could avoid this exact situation."

"So did I. Didn't help much, did it?" I had become completely erect in a span of time I would have previously thought impossible.

"Oh my god. So fucking horny. This is ridiculous." His voice tumbled earnestly forth, deep and hoarse, and his hands fidgeted on the steering wheel.

"Pull over."

"What?"

"Just pull over," I repeated. "Now's our chance. Take the next right. There's a lot down the road that no one uses. My dad used to park his fishing boat on it."

"Okay," he said hastily, slowing the car a bit.

"I want to take care of that for you," I told him, completely clueless as to what mysterious force had apparently just taken me over. "You just tell me if I'm doing anything you don't like, okay?"

"Nope, we're good," he said, tearing off the highway, tires chirping in brief protest. He gunned the engine down the bleak, empty side road.

"Left here," I said.

Mikey parked in the abandoned lot under a sulking oak tree and shut off the car. A meadowlark stated its business from a group of shrubs across the asphalt.

"I've never done this before," he said. "Not in public like this. He handled himself a little through his shorts.

"I haven't either," I said. I'll just jerk you, okay?"

He shimmied his shorts and underwear down around his legs and reseated his naked, dark backside against the cloth seat. "I'm still sweaty," he stated, grinning.

"I don't care," I assured him, marveling at his middle section now as his striking presence swayed a little, directly upright and exposed in plain daylight. He looked over at me and muttered shyly, "You can touch it if you want."

I extended my right hand and leaned over the center console, grasping his sturdiness in a loose fist.

"Fuck," he said. "It feels so fucking strange. You feeling me like that."

"It's okay, though?" I asked.

He immediately nodded, as if to suggest that I would be

crazy to stop. I pulled his foreskin downward, exposing the lighter flesh of the head. I then began to stroke him, starting very slowly, asking him once more if he was okay.

"Keep going," he said.

I increased the speed of motion only minutely, attempting to tug at him in the manner I imagined he would himself. Already he arched his back, his right hand balled into a furious, white-knuckled fist.

Perhaps owing to the run, his voice still emerged with slight rasp, heartbreakingly deep. "You're doing it," he said, gasping. "You fucking know how to do that just right—oh." He lifted his shirt, abdominal muscles delineating themselves as he curled forward. I aimed against his stomach as he began to pulsate and felt rushes of fluid course up through his cock, just under the soft skin of its underside. The thin row of hairs marching down from his navel became drenched in white as he came. His face and chest flushed slightly and he gritted his teeth.

I offered him time to recover, and after about ten seconds he turned to me and leaned his forehead against my shoulder.

"Thank you," came his muffled voice. In another few seconds he sat up and looked around, as if he'd forgotten where he was. "Could you grab the towel from the back seat?" He held the damp gray cotton of his shirt away from the mess.

I handed it to him and let him clean himself up. A small amount of his sperm clung to my hand and I felt, with sudden alarm, the overwhelming urge to taste it. Unsure how he might receive this act of indulgence, I contained myself and wiped it away with the towel once he was done.

Now that the moment was over, Mikey seemed eager to return to the highway. He went to start the car, but then stopped and looked at me with intense concern. "What about you? I need to return the favor."

"Not right now," I said. "When you're ready."

He looked out the windshield, pondering this for a moment. "Okay," he said. "Deal." Between shifts, as his Honda accelerated back toward the highway, he reached out and shook my knee affectionately. "That was incredible, Chickadee. Thank you."

"Of course," I said. I felt grateful for the certainty that he hadn't done anything outside his comfort zone, and reflected that his decision against touching me in the moment stood as further evidence of the cautious nature of his development.

Ten minutes later he dropped me at my apartment. "I'll bring a change of clothes with me next time. Don't be a stranger, okay?"

I promised him that I wouldn't. After he drove off I stood alone on the whitewashed lawn in front of my building for a few minutes. I considered that I could have offered Mikey a change of clothes—we each still had in our possession a pair of the other's underwear, after all—but realized he would probably have asked if he'd truly felt like sticking around. I questioned distantly whether my boldness had overwhelmed him, but decided not to speculate on something I could not know.

I trudged up to my apartment, showered and began hunting for dinner. I scrolled down through my contacts, among which were several numbers for restaurants offering takeout, then cast my phone onto the empty couch cushion beside me. If Mikey cooked for himself, then damn it, so could I. Within minutes I left for the grocery store, where I picked up some staple items and also chicken breast, broccoli and couscous. After another hour I ate contentedly in front of the television, frankly shocked at my tenacious conduct.

It occurred to me sometime after finishing to text Mikey some of my writing. I sent it in the form of three files, one containing a poem in which I took discernible pride, the other two being the first and second chapters of a longer, novel-like project. "Please do not feel obligated," I added once they had transmitted.

I did not hear back from him for nearly two hours, as the minute hand on my wall clock plunged to nearly thirty minutes after eight. "I read everything. Loved it all. Probably need to let it soak in for a while. Maybe I'll go back and read again later."

"I am flattered," I wrote. "Please don't give it too much time or consideration."

After a few minutes he replied, "I was thinking…do you want to come over tonight? I know it's kind of late but I can come get you. We could talk about your writing and/or watch a movie. Let me know if you just want to do your own thing, though."

"I am bored and lonely, to be honest," I texted. "But I insist on taking the bus. There is one leaving in fifteen minutes. See you soon." I donned a black hooded jacket, changed into long pants and was out the door, hurling myself down the hill and into the pedestrian tunnel.

Half an hour later I knocked on his door and he opened it just a few inches, peeking playfully through at me. "Come in, come in," he said, throwing it open. "You never know who could be roaming the halls at this time of night." He made no indication that I should take him seriously.

I trailed him once again into the heart of his home, where we sat together on the couch. "Your writing," began Mikey quietly. "It's like poetry all the time. Even when it's technically not. And I enjoyed the two chapters but I don't have much to say about them. I just really want to know what happens to Charlotte after she leaves for the bridge. I want to believe she doesn't go through with it."

"I don't know if she does," I said. "I don't think I would know unless I actually wrote it." My attempt at finishing a novel had stalled out not long after it had begun; the speaker contemplated suicide and my indecision regarding her fate was probably to blame for the whole story's demise. How should that crucial millisecond of resolution be dispensed? In what capacity would the narrative continue if she went through with it? These questions tumbled around in my head at the time, the answers for which I had not sought with sufficient enthusiasm. The book died with them.

"I can see why it would be hard to pick that back up, without knowing."

"Yeah," I said. "It's weird. Anyway, I'm glad to hear that you liked what I wrote. I've never really had any feedback like that."

"Who else has read your writing?"

"Nobody," I said.

"Oh. Sorry, I don't know why I assumed." He sat back and looked down at the floor. "Wow."

"I mean, no one else really knows about it, so, you know." I guarded my passion for writing with the same uncompromising secrecy that some reserved for a smoking habit or extramarital affair. This mostly unexamined behavior was atypical of me and felt hopelessly peculiar now that I answered for it aloud.

"Thanks for telling me. That's really cool of you."

"I don't know why I've never told anybody else," I said, taking off my jacket and stuffing it down at my side. "It's not like I think anyone would judge me."

"It's okay. I think sometimes it's hard to know why we do the things we do."

I smiled at this.

"Well, I have been appeased," said Mikey, laughing a little.

"Want to watch a movie? All I have is whatever's streaming. I guess I also have some DVDs. Haven't looked through them in a while, though. Who knows what we might find?"

"Let's get them out," I said. "I want to see what kind of movies you like."

Mikey went over to his bed and dragged two small cardboard boxes out from underneath. I joined him and peered down into them after he'd removed the lids. We sifted together through the contents.

"You have a lot of old movies," I said. I recognized many of them as being mid-century films, some even older.

"Yeah. They were my mom's. I watched some of them with her. This was her favorite," he said, handing me a copy of *All the Latest Sunshine*.

I looked it over. "Actually, my mom and I do the same thing. I like this one. Haven't seen it in a long time. We could watch it if you want to." I stopped myself. "Shit. Sorry. Would it make you sad to watch it now?"

He took the movie from me and examined it. "Sure, we can watch it. I've seen it since she died. It didn't make me sad."

Mikey made popcorn for the occasion and after he was finished we settled in on the couch. Throughout the movie we commented periodically on the idiosyncratic elements of the time.

"I love how he just assumes the women are so frail that they should stay in the car while he goes and gets help," Mikey said about halfway through.

"Look at that massive fur coat she's wearing," I said. "They should have sent her."

Mikey laughed.

After it was over we lay on Mikey's bed, once again basking in the cool air that tumbled downward from his vent window.

"Really, though," he was saying. "I can't shake that urge to romanticize everything about the time. The way they spoke, the clothes…the social etiquette for every situation, and it was followed so carefully, too. 'Many happy returns of the day'— how come no one says that anymore?"

I turned to him and grinned. "I don't know."

"Sorry. I tend to go on about this stuff."

"It's fine," I said. "I feel it, too, sometimes. I just don't think it's based in anything real. Those days were just…not so different in the way they seem like they were. And they were very different in some other ways that aren't so good. At least that's what I think."

"I think you're right," said Mikey.

"Don't get me wrong. People dressed better. I'm not arguing with you there."

He looked over at me. "Can you imagine two of the male characters kissing in an old movie like that?"

"No. I can't. It would have been stopped by the censors long before it got anywhere near the audience."

"Yeah, things have definitely changed for the better," he said.

"So you like seeing guys kiss?" I teased.

He grinned. "I'm not sure that I have much of a reaction to it."

I held my tongue for a moment, wondering whether or not to ask. "So I take it you and that guy never kissed."

"Oh. Definitely not. Yeah, it wasn't that kind of thing at all."

"Okay."

"I'm not sure I would ever be into that."

"Alright," I said. "Yeah, it's definitely something more tied with emotions and romance and all that."

He laughed. "And yet I'm fine with a guy touching my dick. It's confusing, I know."

"It's okay. We're all different."

Mikey turned onto his side. "Actually, I'm kind of curious about touching yours. Would that be too weird?"

"You mean, right now?"

He nodded, looking suddenly very self-conscious.

I smiled. "Of course not. Go ahead." I lay on my back, looking down, silently offering him freedom to explore.

At this, he became very excited. "I was feeling so nervous earlier in the car. But now..." With little fuss he undid the button on my pants and tugged the zipper carefully downward.

I had already begun to grow, but was not yet fully hard.

Mikey wondered at this through my underwear and asked, "Can I feel it when you're still soft?"

I moved my pants down around my legs to ease his access. He laid his head back on the pillow next to me and cautiously slipped his hand underneath the elastic band.

As I felt his fingers tremble slightly, brushing over the upper part of my shaft, I exhaled sharply.

"Does that feel good?" He asked.

"Yeah."

He sat up and worked my underwear down toward where my pants still masked my legs. He then remained there, gaping at my cock for a moment before falling once again to rest at my side. Looking down, he placed his hand on my now thoroughly hardened self.

"Fuck," I said. "Sorry, couldn't stay soft for long."

Mikey rested his chin gently on my shoulder so that his fine stubble just barely grazed my skin. "It feels...fuck. It just feels so great in my hand," he said. He tightened his grip, prompting me to let out the smallest whimper and tilt my head toward him. He looked straight into my eyes, concerned. "That's okay?"

"If feels amazing, Mikey."

"I think I want…" he paused. "I want to try to make you come. Do you want to take off your shirt?"

I nodded and did not hesitate to pull it up over my head.

He ran his hand with deliberateness down my chest, fingertips brushing finely over my nipple. He reached my cock and gave it three resounding strokes. "I'm sorry. I'm not sure if I'm doing it right without the foreskin. I want to make sure it feels good for you."

"Don't worry. That is exactly the way to do it."

He grinned and bit his lip. "Okay," he said, providing a few more tentative jerks.

"Oh, shit. This will not take long," I warned.

"It's okay. You're already lasting longer than I did in the car."

I laughed.

He began to tow my rigidness upward, then pull it back down, allowing his hand to slip slightly toward the base. He then continued to tug, faster now, and already I could hardly stand it. I felt his measured breaths land close to my ear; I understood that it brought him new and curious satisfaction to provoke this kind of pleasure in me. And most of all, the thick, solid muscles of Mikey's arm hardened to the task; its dark tones fell starkly against the pale flesh of my chest and stomach.

I exploded, the initial string of myself spanning my upper- and lower-lip, then trailing down my chin. Subsequent bursts fell relentlessly against my neck and then snaked halfway down my chest. Finally my event subsided and I was aware of my right hand, which clenched inside it his other wrist. I let him go and brought it up to wipe the come away from my mouth.

"Thank you," I said. "You are really, really good at that."

Mikey looked extremely pleased. "Fuck. That is a lot of jizz." He hovered, unabashedly gawking for a few seconds before springing into action. "I washed your underwear from the other day," he said. "You can use the ones you were wearing to wipe yourself up and put on the ones you left here."

I removed my underwear and pants completely and did as he suggested. "You're really looking out for me, aren't you?" I said, cleaning up the mess.

I heard him laugh quietly with his back to me as he rooted through his dresser drawer. "You're my guest, Chickadee." He brought the fresh pair over to me and insisted, once again, on washing the dirty ones.

"I'm glad we have a system going here," I told him.

Once I was dressed again and Mikey had returned to my side, we talked softly as the sounds of the night crept through his window. He'd turned off the light in the living room so that now only the streetlamp's glow clambered dimly inside.

Eventually he asked, "Do I have to take you home?"

"Not if you don't want to."

"You could stay if you wanted."

"Sure. I'll stay on the couch," I said.

"You'll take the bed. What if…I don't know. Is it okay if we both take the bed?"

"I have no problem with that."

"Alright," he said.

Mikey offered me a new toothbrush and after a short time we found ourselves undressing to our underwear and slipping between the covers. The double bed did not feel especially spacious now, a fact that did not bother me. We lay shoulder-to-shoulder, propped up somewhat on our pillows. He had pulled a drawing book from his nightstand and flipped through its pages. Sketches of all manner of bird stood in various, illustrative stages of completion.

"I picked this up the day after we met. I've been wanting to practice drawing them for a long time. It was great to finally get to it."

"It's really cool, Mikey."

He closed the book and moved slightly away from me, abandoning his sitting position for something more conducive to sleep. I followed him. He turned his head to look at me. "I've been meaning to tell you this." He paused for a minute to collect his thoughts. "I meet a lot of people because of my job…all these chances to get to know people and maybe connect with someone, you know? Anyway, nobody is like you." He stopped, heaved an immense yawn toward the ceiling and looked back at me. "What I'm saying is that you're a really good friend."

"Thanks," I said. "You are, too. I hope you know that."

Mikey smiled back at me.

It was in this way that we came to sleep soundly, no longer alone, but at each other's side. In my mind, we shared his bed in a capacity unique to us, perfectly different from when I shared with Marie or any other close friend. If I had been asked to articulate this disparity, I would absolutely have failed. But I slept disengaged from worry, and we dreamt tranquilly, inches from one another.

9

I settled back into wakeful existence with the fluttering undulation of a dead leaf, or of a sheet of paper, sidestepping erratically in its journey to the floor. Not one to suffer confusion upon waking, I resumed acknowledgment of my location without pause. Mikey lay still in dormancy next to me, chest exposed, swathed stomach-down by the comforter. With his eyes closed and pink lips slightly parted, his face softened to a faint melancholy that I observed as upsettingly beautiful.

I turned onto my side to face him and realized that part of this action was motivated by the will to assert my presence—as if to say that I am here, another muscled, male human in your bed next to you, the heat from my body uniting with yours, corralled in the tiny space between us, and this is what happens when you invite me to stay. Just in case you hadn't realized what you were up to, then here, behold the outcome of your decision.

My movement caused him to stir and his eyelids blinked open. They slowly closed again and he heaved himself onto his side, now facing me. The inches parting our two faces were in short supply—shorter, I assumed, than he was aware. He said in a small, hazy voice, "So have you...wait, hold on." Eyes still shut, he began again, "So you have very rudely pointed out, and so shall I confirm your allegations: Indeed, there are a few precious aspects of my life over which I retain tragically little control."

He was quoting. I wracked my brain for that single, complementary response and quickly dusted it off. "You're wrong," I said. "Just one aspect."

He smiled and his eyes flicked open for the second time, calibrating lazily on my nearby features. If our proximity just now became known to him, he did not show it. "Good morning, Chickadee," he said.

"Morning. Still thinking about the movie, I see."

He laughed hoarsely and lifted himself to a sitting position, staring blankly out toward his dresser. "Did you sleep okay?"

I moved to my back. "I did. What about you?"

"Like a baby. I don't remember a thing."

"Me, neither."

"That's good," he said. "Be right back." He left for the bathroom and I could not help but appraise his backside as he moved away from the bed, inwardly reeling at the way his bulking upper-thigh more than filled the leg of his underwear.

I checked my phone and set it back on the nightstand. It was after nine.

Mikey returned with his phone in hand and said, "I'm going to meet Sophie around eleven at the office. We still have a few things to sort out before the company meeting tomorrow."

I sat up. "No problem. I'll get going."

"Will you at least stay for breakfast?"

"Sure."

He rattled off some options as we dressed.

"Cereal is just fine," I said. "I don't usually eat much for breakfast."

As we ate Mikey held his spoon in his left hand; with his right he swept across the table, clearing away some invisible detritus from its surface. After repeating this motion several times he looked up at me and said, "If Sophie has a free evening this week, it would be cool if you could meet her. Would you be okay with getting dinner or something?"

"Sure, that sounds fun," I said.

"Awesome." He dropped the spoon into his cereal and seized up his phone. "Let me just look at a few things…" He smiled to himself as he tapped at the screen. "I'm guessing Tuesday will be okay. Six o'clock? Does that work for you?"

"Yeah, that's fine," I told him.

"Okay, awesome. Yeah." He set down his phone. "Fuck, this'll be so cool."

I assured him that I was excited. Privately I was surprised that he'd felt comfortable inviting me in the first place, but I was also more than a little curious to meet a person whom Mikey was so fond of, and who had, I suspected, lent him a great deal of emotional support in the past.

When we were done eating he offered me a ride home but I declined. "I don't want to rely on you in that way," I said. "It's asking too much." I left his apartment contented by the crystallization of this new meeting.

The rest of my day constituted somewhat of a wash, although I was carried on vaguely sore legs to the gym a couple of hours after returning home. Afterward, I proudly consumed leftover fruits of the previous day's incident of rare culinary ambition. Mikey texted later in the evening to inform me that his cousin had confirmed for dinner on Tuesday. I replied to tell him that I looked forward to it.

We did not share a bus the next morning. I fell asleep several minutes into the ride and nearly slept through my stop. Arriving at my desk, a welcome eagerness materialized within me to dive into the pool of documentation lying in wait.

My mom liked to say that a new hollow space in the mouth

feels much larger than the tooth that left it behind, and this sentiment came to mind when Calvin was gone from work that morning. I had forgotten that in skipping Friday, I would be missing his last day.

"It's just as well," said Jennifer. "I think he was a little off the whole day. He didn't want anyone making a big thing out of it."

His legacy (as it were) of throwing caution to the wind remained with me, interminably hovering above one shoulder or the other throughout the rest of the day. I predicted that if this presence persisted through to Friday, my decision would not ascend entirely above its influence.

Upon boarding an unusually full bus after work, I made eye contact with Mikey and he illuminated as I negotiated the aisle back to where he sat.

"Felt like a jerk putting this down here," he said, moving his briefcase from the seat. "Whatever."

"Thanks for saving a spot."

The bus rumbled away from the curb and he said, "I have to drive tomorrow, so come by my apartment in the morning and we'll go together if you want."

"Thanks. That sounds great."

Mikey pulled out his phone and apologized, saying he had a few loose strings to tie up from work.

"You don't have to be sorry for that," I said.

Although I roamed around on my phone as he made a client call, I also secretly listened in, tempted in no small part by his smooth, professional style. He remained involved in his work until our stop arrived, handling another call as we stepped off the bus. We stood together for just a second at the stop. I waved and made to leave for the next, but Mikey reached out and touched my hand. I drew it up to my chest.

"See you in the morning," he said under his breath.

I smiled. "Alright."

Overnight, the outside air covertly disposed of its warmth, which vacated so thoroughly that in the morning I shivered beneath the light coat I'd chosen for the day. Mikey offered to lend me a heavier one as I met him down at the garage, but I refused.

"I'll be fine. The weather just snuck up on me, that's all."

"We'll be eating inside tonight, so don't worry about that."

Once his car had passed beneath the building's low exit and crouched through the dip at the edge of the street, he looked over at me. "Yesterday on the bus—I hate times like that. I really like to keep those calls and stuff inside work hours."

"Well, you weren't home yet. It still kind of counts as being at work, right?"

He relaxed slightly in his seat and his thumb massaged the leather on the steering wheel. "I don't know…" After another minute he said, "I just feel like it's a little too easy for me to lose grip on my schedule." He paused, looked down toward the shifter and then turned up the heat. "After that, work takes over, and then I start to go crazy."

"I see how you feel." I looked away, out my window and said, "I don't want you to have to worry about that."

"Hey," he said, and I turned to him. "It's really good that we started hanging out. You being here is actually helping me out a ton."

"Okay," I said. "I'm glad to hear that."

He turned up the radio just barely and began drumming on his lap, now steering with his knee. "Come on, give me some more travel stories."

I laughed. "If you insist," I said, and we conversed within the warm custody of wanderlust until he dropped me off.

As my Tuesday shift drew in its final breaths, Jennifer slouched at her desk across the barren walking aisle from mine. I looked over and we shared a knowing expression.

"I'm exhausted," she said. "It's so quiet today. Where's Calvin when you need him?"

"I really wish he was still here," I said.

Twenty minutes later we walked down to the lobby together and parted ways. Mikey had texted me the address of the restaurant, and as I started walking north I realized he had likely selected a place close to my office on purpose. The only downside to this was arriving half and hour early; with nothing else to do I sat on a bench by the door. It was an Italian restaurant that I had passed by many times before without ever noticing. An inviting, bread-filled scent flowed from the dining area.

After a short time I looked up from my phone. A woman had come to stand close to me. She wore cobalt blue slacks and a matching blazer with a white blouse underneath. A small, amber leather purse hung from the crook in her arm and her black hair fell directly to her shoulders. When our eyes met she said, "Do you happen to be Wyatt?"

"Yes," I said, standing. "You're Sophie?"

She held out her hand and I shook it. "I thought for sure I would be the first one here," she said, smiling. "Mikey's moving his car, but he should be here on time." She resembled him subtly, and even spoke a little bit like him, in that unequivocal way that only close family can.

"It was just a short walk from my work," I said. "Would you like to get a table?"

She motioned for me to lead the way and a host brought us to a table for four near the back.

"I'm so glad to finally meet you," she said. "Mikey talks

about you nonstop."

I sat down to face her and smiled. "Really? I can't imagine there's a lot to say." Presently I said aloud exactly what I was thinking. If Mikey spoke to his cousin about me at a depth even one foot below the surface, it was certain to invite, at the very least, some level of confusion.

"I don't mean to embarrass him," Sophie said. "He just speaks very highly of you. The company kind of consumed him for a while. It's nice to see him hanging out with people outside of work again."

"Yeah, he talked about that. He said he's been making an effort to cut back."

She nodded. "So, you're an accountant, right?"

"I'm getting there. I've only been in the field about six months. I graduated last May."

"Did Mikey tell you we've been starting to look at hiring an in-house person for our stuff?"

I shook my head. "No, he never mentioned that."

"Well, we've only just started discussing it since he's been back. Actually—" She stopped as a server came by to take our drink orders. Sophie ordered a glass of wine and I followed her example. "Actually, I'm the one who really thinks we need it," she continued. "Plus, I'm sure he didn't want to suggest that you come work for us—especially with you guys being close outside of work. It's not always a good idea."

"Right, I see what you mean," I said. "It's awesome that you two work together so well, though. Mikey said he couldn't do it without you."

"He's incredibly driven, so I'm sure he would have done well on his own. But I did study computer science. You could say I'm classically trained. He picked a lot of it up on his own and was missing some of the foundational knowledge. That's probably been my biggest contribution. Anyway, we've been messing around with coding stuff since junior high." She smiled at this. "We were probably destined to do this together."

"That's so cool," I said. "Actually, Mikey never talked about what he went to school for."

"Well, he also started in CS, but he never had a chance to finish. When my aunt and uncle passed away...you know...it really derailed him. In the end, he didn't need to go to school, though. He's a strong self-starter."

"Oh," I said. "I see, okay. He's told me a little about his parents. We haven't really talked much about the accident, though."

"He doesn't mind talking about it," she said. "I really believe he's dealt with it in a healthy way. Obviously he still carries it with him. I do, too. But it's been almost four years, and we've processed a lot of it together."

Our wine arrived. Sophie sipped at hers and I did the same.

"I'm so glad you were there for each other," I said.

"Yeah. And of course he had Alice, too. I don't know if he's talked about her at all." She laughed. "I should probably just shut up and let him tell you this stuff."

"Alice was his girlfriend, right?"

"Right. She gave him a lot of support. Alice wasn't..." Sophie paused. "I don't believe they would have lasted. No matter what had happened."

"I see. This whole thing is a little weird, to be honest. I haven't known him that long. But we are getting pretty close."

"Yes." She nodded earnestly and set down her glass. "I know. I understand."

"It's just really interesting talking to someone who knows him. Someone who's not him. I feel like I have a million questions...or none. I don't know. It's just good to meet you."

"Definitely," she said. "I'm glad this was something he wanted."

"Me too." I realized we had talked almost exclusively about Mikey. "So your mom lives in town, right?"

"Yes," she said. "I live with her. Well, her house has a private suite on the ground floor. That's where I live. It's just south of Brickhouse."

"My sister lives in Brickhouse. That's a pretty long commute, isn't it?"

"It's not that bad. There's a park-and-ride at Northend Station, so I leave my car there. The train ride is about twenty minutes. Or sometimes I drive and take Mikey's spot in the garage."

"That's the Emerald line, right?"

"Yes."

Just as Sophie looked toward the front door, Mikey showed up. He approached the table and said, "I see you guys have already met."

"Yes," said Sophie. "We've just been talking about you."

"I'm going to pretend you're not serious." He sat down next to Sophie and smiled at me. "Sorry, they're doing construction work on the garage so I had to move the car. This is what I get for driving."

"You said you had something going on at lunch?" I asked.

"Yeah, we took a couple of clients out to eat," said Sophie. "It was just easier to coordinate with a car."

"They're not clients yet," Mikey said.

"We have a verbal agreement," she clarified to me.

I nodded. "You guys sound so busy. I just kind of clock in, put in my time and leave at five."

"Mikey's getting good at leaving by five," she said. "I'm trying."

"You're not trying," Mikey said, grinning and turning to look around the room. He turned back to face her. "But you don't stress, either."

She silently accepted this. "Where did you move your car?"

"Southgate," he said. "It's free on weeknights. Did you know that?"

"That's Westgate. You have to have a city pass for Southgate."

"Fuck," he said. "Or else what?"

"Or else they tow you, I'm guessing."

Mikey pulled out his phone and looked it up. "Fuck," he repeated. "You're right."

"I know I'm right."

"Damn it. What a fucking pain." He looked at me. "Are you okay here if I go and move it again? Sorry about this."

"I'm sure I will survive," I said. "Don't worry about it."

"Okay. You guys just order. Actually, get me the Alfredo if they come by before I'm back. With chicken, please."

Once he was gone, Sophie dug through her purse for her phone. "I'm going to ask him if he wants wine or beer to drink. He's so ridiculous. Seriously."

"He cracks me up," I said.

After she finished texting she set down her phone. "Actually, I'm glad we have a little more time to talk. He told me a few things..." She paused. "Sorry, I don't want to make this weird, it's just that he told me you were gay, and the way he talks about you makes me wonder what he's up to. I don't know. I don't mean to be brash."

"It's alright," I said. "You can say whatever you want."

"Okay. Well, the thing is, I've known Mikey my whole life. He's like my brother. Sometimes it's like...there are these things that I've come to understand about him, maybe even better than he does."

"Yeah," I said. "I can see how that would happen."

"So let me ask you this. Are you interested in him at all? And I don't mean to assume something like that. I'm honestly just curious."

I searched for a helpful answer, since I was not sure of my own feelings. Suddenly I said, "I'm trying not to be." I surprised myself with this statement, and immediately knew it to be true.

"Right," she said. "Well, he's an attractive person." She glanced down at her napkin and folded it in half lengthwise, seemingly without intent, then looked back up at me. "I guess what I'm saying is, I wouldn't give up waiting on him, if you're interested. He's truly a good guy. I promise you that. He's the best one I know. He's also very confused about himself. But the way he described you..." She looked past me for a moment, collecting her thoughts. "Well, most of all, he talked about you like you were golden, and I feel like he's a good judge of that sort of thing. If he finds someone, I guess I just want it to be a person who shares some of his good qualities. Am I making any sense at all?"

I offered a small nod. "I think so."

"I honestly believe he'll figure himself out, even though it might still take some time. But I'm also taking your feelings into consideration. If I didn't think he was worth your time and emotions, I would be telling you something very different right now." She stopped herself. "If this is confusing at all, I'm sorry. I just felt like I should say something. I don't even know if I'm reading the situation correctly."

"I think you are. And what you're saying is honestly very helpful. I'm grateful that you told me all of this."

She pressed her hand against her chest. "Okay. That's a

relief."

"Yeah," I said. "It's really considerate of you."

"Good. I was debating all of this earlier today—you know, whether or not to say anything, if I had the chance."

The server came by again. Mikey hadn't responded so we ordered another glass of wine for him along with our three pasta dishes.

"It's a carb explosion," I said.

"All the best meals are."

I laughed.

"So," she said, "Mikey's always telling me that I have trouble getting to the point. The truth is that I've been waiting for the day when he would start talking about a boy. It's always been this imminent thing in my mind. A not-if-but-when kind of thing. It's kind of selfish, but now that it's here, I'll do whatever I can to help the situation along. Even at the risk of you thinking I'm a crazy person."

I laughed. "I really don't think you're crazy."

"You're very understanding. Anyway, I'll try to talk to him about it soon. It's just that I don't want to push him away. It's really the only thing he won't open up about."

"Actually...well...I don't know. He told me he was going to try to get over some mental blocks, or something like that."

She sat back. "Really? He told you that? Wow, he's never said anything like that to me. He must really like you."

"I don't know."

"Just give him some time. When he tells you he'll do something, he's good about following through."

"Okay," I said. "I will."

I wished I had more time to give. I suspected now that one of the few things Sophie did not know about me was my impending departure. As Mikey returned once again to the table and took his seat, I considered that his lack of awareness concerning an elusive aspect of his being did not isolate his experience from anyone else's. As grateful as I was that Sophie had disclosed these things to me, especially given the short time I'd known Mikey, I wondered if similar conversations ever transpired about me, between two people who shared my acquaintance, when my back was turned. Although well-intentioned and untarnished by betrayal, the details she had relayed to me still felt like they were not yet mine to know.

Mikey beamed at me from across the table. "Don't believe a word she says."

I laughed and took a drink from my wine.

The conversation meandered throughout the rest of dinner. I appreciated Sophie's discretion as she backed away and entertained with stories from their childhood days together. At first Mikey seemed to study my reactions in a covert way as Sophie spoke, but later he softened and threw me an occasional affectionate glance.

Toward the end of the meal, when Sophie left for the bathroom, he said, "Thanks for coming out tonight. It was important to me that you got to meet her."

"Of course, Mikey. I'm really glad you wanted me to."

I looked down, but after a few seconds, sensed that he had not finished regarding me. When I raised my gaze back to him, he looked away.

"If no one else," he said, "let the sunshine pour over you. You can bathe in all the love the sunshine gives."

10

By Thursday the city had descended into a strange, bitter cold, which I believed optimistically to be winter's final death rattle before yielding to spring. The radiated heat inside Mikey's apartment was befitting now, and not at all uncomfortable as I stretched out opposite him on the couch. At his suggestion I had thrown together a change of clothes and ventured over after dinner. We would leave for work together in the morning.

Tuesday night's dinner had wormed into discussion and Mikey lifted the bulk of his arms, interlocking his fingers on top of his head. "Sophie likes to talk," he said. "I don't know if you noticed when you were alone with her. She'll sort of lead the conversation sometimes."

I shrugged. "It didn't bother me. I thought she was really nice."

"Yeah, and I don't mean to say it's a bad thing. She's great at jumping in whenever there's a lull in meetings with clients." He lowered his arms and cuddled up against the couch cushion. "What did you guys talk about when I was away?" he asked, only casually disguising a furtive curiosity.

"You, mostly," I said, hiding part of my face with a throw-pillow.

He closed his eyes, head resting against the cushion. "Part of me knew that she would talk about me if I wasn't there. I don't mind, really. As long as she didn't make me look like an ass."

"She didn't," I said. "I promise." It was the first time since dinner that he'd shown anything other than a passing, joking interest in what Sophie and I had discussed when we were alone. I found this heightened fascination problematic, owing to the disparity between my will to hide nothing from Mikey, and a sense that full disclosure would be, apart from everything else, unhelpful. It might also be disastrous in terms of Mikey's confidence and amassing effort to understand himself. I tried to imagine how it would go—explaining how things had gotten quite overt, and that the conversation had been almost entirely about him, about how Sophie had come to accept, beyond question, this relegating truth about him that he could not yet see. And above all, that this man who, for example, had professed explicit lack of interest in ever kissing another man, was of such crushing substance that it made him into someone for whom biding my time wasn't a complete misadventure. In spite of compliments diverted toward his character, the reductive, don't-worry-he'll-come-around tone of the conversation rubbed shoulders with offensiveness. I wanted to protect him from that.

I had spent Wednesday wondering intermittently about Mikey's motivation to have Sophie meet me.

He could not have anticipated that we would have such extensive opportunity to speak in his absence; on the other hand, I trusted he knew his cousin's nature. Maybe he sensed something about her intuition with respect to him. Perhaps, during the plausible instant that she and I were alone, he sought to have me know things about him that he himself could not explain. Ultimately, though, my predilection to overthink things exhausted me; these thoughts were outlandish and at the moment impossible to confirm.

"I got the idea that she's happy we're hanging out," I said.

"She thinks really highly of you. She said you're a good guy."

"Naturally," said Mikey with a grin. "Yeah, I remember when I was telling her about you she got all excited. I haven't held on to a lot of friends from my past, and she gets worried when I'm not being very social. Really, there's nothing to worry about, but I can't convince her of that."

"She cares a lot about you."

"Fuck yeah she does," he said, pulling his knees to his chest. "She's three years older. When we were younger, that gave her a lot of authority over me. Sometimes it still kind of seems like it's there. It's not really on her terms, though; if anything I'm imagining it."

"She may always be that kind of figure for you. My sister is for me."

He nodded. "I don't mind that." After a pause he said, "It sucks that it's so cold tonight. I wanted to walk on the seawall near downtown. Should have done it when I had the chance."

"You'll be able to again soon."

He smiled and rose up. "I want to play video games. Will you join me?"

"You don't even have to ask," I said. "I've been craving a little GTA."

"Who hasn't?" he said, kneeling in front of the TV stand.

We played for over an hour before Mikey rolled over on the floor. His on-screen persona stood still, swaying a bit unnaturally and performing the occasional subtle gesture at random.

"I've had enough," he said, laying on his side and facing away from me. He tossed the controller over his shoulder and it thumped across the rug, landing near my knee.

I had set a large pillow against the coffee table and leaned my back against it. "You're so reckless," I said.

"I'm reckless? Who shamelessly mowed down fifty people

with a Lamborghini half an hour ago?"

"You don't know the difference between a game and real life."

He shrugged. "Blow me."

I laughed. "You realize you need to be careful what you say around me," I told him. "I just might take you seriously."

He was silent for a couple seconds, his back still turned to me. "What makes you think I'm not serious?"

I sat forward and tugged hard on his shoulder, rolling him onto his back. He looked up at me, his upside-down expression all but vacant, awaiting my response.

"If you're serious," I told him, "then I don't want to waste any time. I would hate for you to change your mind."

Mikey looked down at his lap and then back at me, a detectable blip of wonder surfacing in his eyes. He unbuttoned his pants without breaking eye contact. "I want you to do this to me," he muttered.

"Stay where you are," I said. "I'll do it." I moved to where I could access him, spreading his legs and positioning myself between them. "Are you comfortable enough here?"

He nodded.

I knelt before him now on the rug, pulling down his pants zipper, fingers brushing past the rapidly growing presence that waited beneath. "You're kind of big, you know."

He stared up at the ceiling. "I think I'm about the same as you."

"Yeah, well, I'm kind of big."

"I'm aware," he said.

I pulled his pants down around his legs, just as he aided me by lifting his backside briefly from the floor. As I relieved him of his underwear he managed a small laugh. "I'm going to feel, like, indebted to you if you actually suck my cock."

I paused, inches from him. "We can figure that out later," I said. "Just relax, okay?"

"Okay, Chickadee," he said.

"Actually, there's just one thing—if it happens." I paused, and he glanced down to meet my gaze, dark eyes shifting to focus on one eye, then the other. "If you come," I continued, "I want to swallow you. I don't want you to be caught off guard when I do it. Is that okay with you?"

He looked back at the ceiling and smiled. "It's okay. I want you to have that, if that's what you want."

Then I held him in my hands, noting that he was just shy of fully erect and angled easily toward me. I pulled down his foreskin and took him artlessly, halfway into my mouth. He did not taste like anything but smelled minimally stale, just as I would expect by this time of day. I leaned far over him now and glanced down to see the toes of his left foot curl and tighten. I advanced downward, letting him slip cleanly back into the hollows of my throat. Against my lips I felt the mild coarseness of his trimmed black hairs, hemming in the base of his cock. He was wholly engorged now, filling my mouth at least as much as I'd ever experienced. However, because it was Mikey, and as I presently realized just how badly I had wanted this, his bulk—swelling against my tongue, the roof of my mouth, the back of my throat—felt all its own, unique and unprecedented.

"How the fuck do you do that?" he asked quietly.

I did not answer him but drew myself upward, detaching completely, then descended again upon him. I pressed on, no longer parting from him, attempting to incite in him the greatest amount of pleasure my abilities could sustain.

During these moments he moaned softly, eyes shut. His head rolled to one side and he lifted his hand, feeling my hair and neck. He warned that he was close and went so far as to push against my shoulder, attempting to usher me up and away. I stood my ground and he flattened his hand against the floor. His body turned rigid and his arms lifted him slightly. To my contentment he began to thrust, concurrent with the first blast of his semen, into my mouth. I buckled down on him, holding him there as he continued to transfer himself into me. I swallowed rapidly so that none of it was lost.

Once he finally broke from me he breathed deeply. The scene was tidy, the light-brown skin of him just slightly dampened by my saliva. He looked down, and then at me. "It's all gone," he said. "You swallowed all of it."

"That was the plan," I said, sitting back and smiling.

"Oh my god, that's so hot," he said. "Like, it's all in your stomach now."

"It is," I said. Remnants of him, tasting slightly bitter now, lingered in my mouth and caused a tingling feeling in my throat. It had been a long time since I had done this, and I felt privileged to have done it for Mikey.

He coaxed his underwear and pants up around his waist, raising his head and squirming up against the broad leg of the coffee table. He remained like that, neck canted in a fashion that looked uncomfortable to me. "That sort of exhausted me…in the greatest way possible. I am officially indebted."

I shook my head. "No, you're not. I wanted to do it to you, probably even more than you wanted it."

"I guess I can understand that. Lately, I've kind of been curious what it's like. You look so big—I can't imagine it in my mouth. I'm scared to try."

"You don't have to if you don't want to."

"I never thought I would. Never, ever." He steepled his fingers above his stomach, inspecting them silently for a moment. "With you, though…I'm starting to feel kind of different about it." He laughed a little. "It's not that I'm wanting a dick in my mouth all of a sudden. It hasn't happened to me in that way." He paused again, carefully gathering his thoughts. "But…I mean…if the person it belongs to is really incredible, then I guess that's why I'm starting to want it. And not just a little. Because it's a part of them that they're giving me."

I looked away, toward the kitchen and grinned. "You're not deliberately trying to get me all emotional, are you?"

He laughed, sat up and hugged his knees. "Of course not. But it's how I feel, and I wanted you to know."

I smiled at him. "Thank you, Mikey. Really."

He stood and asked what I wanted to do.

"Can we watch another movie? Maybe another old one?"

"Whatever pleases you," he said with a grin. "You're the guest."

"You need to stop saying that."

"Maybe. Once you've been over here a lot more, maybe then I'll stop. But that time has not come yet."

"Alright, alright," I said, dragging myself across the floor to the foot of the bed.

Together we sat and once again sorted through his ragged stacks of DVDs.

"*African Queen*," I blurted out. "Nailed it."

"But we haven't even looked at half of them."

"Hey," I protested. "I thought I was the guest."

"Piece of shit," he muttered, clasping a hand to my shoulder and rocking me back and forth.

"I'm kidding," I assured him. "Let's see what else is here."

"Actually, I'm good with *African Queen*, seriously."

"Alright, then. If you're sure."

Once again we watched casually, and about ten minutes in, Mikey asked, "Have you ever seen interviews with Katharine Hepburn?"

I told him I hadn't.

"She's unlike anyone else. Well, I mean, the only other people even kind of like her came out of the same world. Females in movies from that time."

"Why do they have to be female to be like her?"

"Because that's all part of it. To have all these ahead-of-the-time opinions, and shout them out in interviews—if you were a man, big fucking deal..." he trailed off, reaching out and performing a masturbatory gesture over the coffee table before continuing. "It was a time when, if you were female, half the people out there—no, more—assumed, before you even opened your mouth, that a man had already said something of greater value. So fucked up. You know what Bette Davis said was her biggest mistake in her marriage? She said it was picking someone who wasn't as smart as she was. Well, I mean, she said it a lot more eloquently than that, but still, can you imagine the courage that took on her part, to put it that way? And at that time?"

I shook my head.

"Sorry," he said. "Just some private interest of mine, I guess."

"It's fine," I said. "I mean, I don't disagree on any particular point."

He just smiled, his eyes unfocused and wandering a bit.

We watched about half the movie before Mikey confirmed that he was too tired to go on. "You can still finish if you want. I'll just fall asleep here."

"Let's go to bed," I suggested. "It's late enough for me."

A blue ceramic mug sat near the edge of his small bathroom

vanity, in which he kept his toothbrush. After he'd finished preparing for bed I took his place to find that the one I had opened on my previous stay remained in the mug, next to his.

I washed up, removed my shirt and came to his bedside to find him lying with his eyes open, pillow propped up somewhat against the headboard. His stout, bare shoulders cropped up just above the comforter. I removed my pants unreservedly and climbed into bed next to him. He remained completely still as I did so. I turned to him and asked, "Is everything okay?"

"Sorry, just woke up a little as I got ready for bed, I guess. Start thinking about things and then I can't stop."

"I know how that feels," I told him. "Is anything bothering you?"

"Not really. It's sort of a sad night for me. It happens sometimes. I didn't think it would tonight, though. With you here and all."

"You can feel however you want with me here. It doesn't matter."

He nodded and started to speak, but the words hung in his throat. For a time all I could hear was the low whine of a streetlamp at the corner through his vent window. He shifted and said, "When my parents died, I began to feel so many unexpected emotions that eventually nothing surprised me. But there's this one thing that has stuck around, and it still catches me off guard, even now. It's their voices—and I have to say, I never would have expected it to be like this."

"Their voices?"

"Yeah. It's like, I can imagine so clearly either one of them saying all this shit they used to say. The sound of it...it comes to me as if they were alive yesterday. My dad hounding me to keep applying for scholarships. Or my mom telling me to stop paying for my own bus fare. I swear to god, for the rest of my life, I'll always remember exactly what they sounded like."

In these final few words, Mikey's own voice took on an unfamiliar quality, and I glanced over at his face to see that there was now a single, small dewdrop tear, whose thin trail glossed the skin of his cheek.

"Sometimes," he continued, "it's like I start to conjure them up a little, and then I can't stop. It's hard to deal with. Then I wonder, like, if it will always be like this. Like if this one small part of it will always feel so fresh. It'll suck if that's true."

"Mikey," I said. "Can I do anything?"

"It's fine," he said. "I'm glad you're here."

"I'm glad I'm here, too." I paused and then asked, "Would it help to talk about it some more? Can you tell me more about that day? What it was like? But I guess...don't tell me, if you don't want to."

"I can tell you all about it," he said. "That part isn't so hard for me." He turned onto his side to face me, flattening his pillow a little. "It was in the morning," he said. "I was at school. City campus. I got called from class. Did you know they don't make you identify the bodies unless they absolutely have to? I didn't know this until then, but it's really just this trope type of thing that always makes it into movies and shows for dramatic effect. I didn't even see them until the funeral. Actually—" He paused. "Actually, I never really saw them again. It was strange, for sure, seeing what used to be them, but it's not like I was looking at who they were anymore, all made up in a box."

I nodded, facing him so that our gazes aligned from our separate pillows, and he itched his nose before continuing. "Anyway," he mumbled before his voice descended to a sort of heavy tone, "they were headed east on the freeway. There isn't much of a center divider for a stretch once you get past

Celadon. A truck driver crossed over and hit them. I mean, there's not much else to say about that part of it—something so definite. How can you even try to pick it apart? You won't find any answers doing that."

"Right," I said. "I understand."

"Man," he said softly. "This is weird—telling you all this. Good, I guess. What else do you want to know?"

"What was it like for you after that? Like, what was life like?"

His eyes fell to the pillow and remained there for some time. "My life changed. It was kind of this bizarre, violent change that I could never have fathomed before it happened. It's even hard to put it into words now…but I can say that I remember being convinced that part of me had died. I think that's a cliché for a reason. My existence became pretty terrible. Most of me was just…gone." He stopped to ruminate on this for a moment. "And I had this sensation of being absolutely certain I would never get that part of me back. I was thinking, this is my life now. In general it will be very unpleasant, every day, forever." He stopped himself again, folding his hands up under his chin. "Anything else?"

"Wow," I said quietly. "I don't know. I guess I want to know where you're at with that now."

"Oh, well, obviously I don't feel that way anymore. But the way it all started coming back to me, so incredibly gradually…it's like the most unsatisfying progression I could have imagined. I went through my own grieving process, but for quite a while, even after the nastiest parts of that, life was still shit. Sleeping, eating, working—everything kept going, more or less, but it all came to me through this hazy, awful filter. And then it was like…one day…I would realize that, for weeks, things had been slightly less shitty. And I was at total fucking loss for what in particular had gotten better. When had it changed? And then, weeks later, it would happen again. I would think, shit, this week actually feels a little like the old days." He paused and looked me squarely in the eyes. "I can't tell you what had changed, or when. I wish I could. That sensation of having lost most of how it felt to live day-to-day — I don't get that anymore. I am once again the complete person I was before it happened. But I don't know when I began to feel like myself again." At this, he stopped talking and looked away. He seemed only just now aware of how much he'd said. His expression lay hijacked by apprehension, soliciting some kind of verbal response.

"Mikey," I said. "I'm just really glad you found that part of yourself again."

He smiled. "Thanks for listening, Chickadee. The funny thing is, for a long time, I couldn't get emotional about them — at least not in any recognizable way. But now, with everything I've gotten back…this sense of normalcy…in that context, I cry when I think of them. I don't think it's bad at all. I try to welcome it. Memories come up lately, and I cry. That's really the extent of it, you know?"

"Yeah," I said. "I know." I thought for a moment and said, "I wish I could have known them."

"Me too," he said. "I think you would have liked them. I know they would have liked you."

"I can't even imagine them. Can you give me something? What's something you like to remember?"

I watched him reflect. Then his face changed all at once, flooding with warmth, as if some prevailing shot of consolation had finally arrived through a vacuum tube extending back into his past. "There was this trip we took to the interior," he said. "I think I was already eighteen. It was just me and them — we hadn't done anything like that in a long time. I sat in the middle seat just behind them in the van. My mom was handing me some kind of snack—I don't remember what it was—and we were playing this endless license plate game. I remember feeling like I was just a kid. Normally, by that age, I hated feeling that way. I hated anything that made me feel like a child. But in that moment...I don't know. It was just different in that moment. I felt really safe with them. I felt like it would be okay if it stayed like that forever. I wish—" He stopped himself. Gone from his expression was any perceivable degree of solace. He sighed and his words crept out precariously onto some imagined threshold, "I just wish I had known it was the last time I would get to feel that way."

Mikey stopped talking altogether now. He reached under the edge of his pillow with both hands and lifted it, curving it up against his face. In this way he couched his countenance from me, as he held very still. He was silent. For a period of several seconds, I don't believe he breathed at all. Then he drew in a mammoth breath, so enduring as to be inhuman, like a ship keeling to one side. He held it for an instant and then released, shuddering slightly, the air slipping unevenly forth.

I waited for what felt like a long time before saying, "Mikey, what can I do?" I wanted desperately to put my arms around him now.

His voice cracked slightly, muted and deep through the pillow. "You've already done so much for me."

I did not ask his permission as I moved closer to him. I sent my left arm up over his side, just below his shoulder, and pulled him tightly against me. His pillow-barrier remained and separated his face from my chest. He wordlessly lifted his head and dragged the pillow out from under him entirely, casting it down near his feet. He burrowed into my chest and stayed put, breathing softly in and out. I felt him relax incrementally with each whisper of hot air against my skin. A period of time passed, after which I felt all but certain he was asleep. I tucked my mouth and nose slightly into his hair and smelled him. My comfort asked for no change in position. Accepting now that he had been put completely at ease, I, too, relaxed.

In the morning I woke up, once again before Mikey, as well as before the alarm we'd set. I lay on my stomach, halfway on top of him, arm slung around him, the side of my head pressed cleanly into the center of his chest. My other arm was stuffed underneath me and alongside his; we held hands here, I realized, against the cotton of my underwear—a meaningless barrier between us and my bulging flesh.

Caught off guard by this surprise advancement, I jumped enough to wake him. I went to lift myself off of him.

"Stop," he grumbled. "Where are you going?"

My own voice far from prepared for the day, I rested again on him and mumbled, "This seemed a little intimate."

He said nothing for a moment and then laughed. His chest rumbled beneath my ear. "Don't worry," he said. "We're doing a terrible job at being fuck-buddies, that's all."

There was nothing else to say, so I just laughed along with him.

11

Mikey broke away from me with apparent reluctance, canceled his alarm and then stood haphazardly on the bed in order to crank closed the window near the ceiling. "Damn, it's cold," he said. "This should not have been open all night."

The sight generated above me was magnificent; I looked away out of a strange new estimation, perhaps tied with our recent revision in intimate dealings.

He sat, throwing himself quickly back under the covers. A small separation between our bodies now made its return; I did not resent it, nor did I expressly welcome it back.

He kicked his left foot out once, toes skimming the side of my calf, adjusted his pillow and tilted his head toward me. "What's going on at work today?"

I closed my eyes briefly and said, "I have to confirm that I'm moving today. For my job."

"What? So soon?"

"Well, the move is only about three weeks away. They need to know so they can make all the arrangements. They're the ones paying for it, after all."

"I meant to ask—are they paying for your housing, too?"

"There's a stipend for that, but it's pretty small. They said they'd cover the moving costs, though."

"Okay," he said. He picked up his phone, fiddled back and forth between home screens and set it back down on his nightstand. "What happens if you change your mind after today?"

"I'm not sure," I said. "I know it would be very frowned upon. And then obviously I'm out of a job."

"Right. Gotta take care of yourself. Three weeks. Okay." He shifted his weight restlessly and seemed to puzzle through something, but said nothing else on the subject.

We chatted back and forth for the next few minutes about nothing in particular. Mikey offered for me to shower before him. The bathtub, which I supposed to be original, sat proudly on stubby legs and was adorned with a green curtain that hung from an elongated chrome hoop, completing one full lap around its rim.

As I waited for him to finish showering, I flipped through the handful of drawings sitting atop his desk, an act which by now felt entirely permissible. He had sketched at least two more birds (sparrows, or something) and a mid-rise building, about a century old in appearance, which I did not recognize.

Once Mikey had rejoined me I asked him about it. "Where is that building? The one you drew, I mean."

He stood in front of his dresser, buttoning a white shirt over a tight cotton undershirt. "It's in downtown Seattle, right along the I-5," he said. "It kind of stood out to me on the drive, so I looked it up later."

"Oh. I see. It's a great drawing."

He smiled. "Breakfast?"

There wasn't much time left over, so we quickly downed some cereal and left the dishes in the sink. I grabbed my coat off the rack as he fastened the gleaming black buttons of his peacoat. Around his neck he cinched a checkered tie.

"You look handsome in that," I said.

"No compliments," he said. "You're fueling my ego."

Mikey seemed content to be by my side as we stepped down to the street, although we said little to each other during this time, a reticence that persisted as we waited together for the bus. I grappled with the raw facts this morning—to be clear: fact. Calculations based on my current trajectory would land me in Fern Hill at the beginning of next month. At some point I had come to understand that I would, with certainty, confirm my willingness to move. No longer did this register as a decision, nor, for that matter, any other sort of enigma with more than one possible outcome. Maybe I had always known that I would go. It was just that this day in March held, trivially, the moment in which it all became official.

To assert that I had thought it through would suggest that I knew what it was to do so. More accurately, I had thought about it until I did not recognize how to think anymore, and now no longer thought of it at all.

On the bus, Mikey said, "I don't know if moving was a hard decision for you to make, but either way, making it official is a pretty big moment. You can take this or leave it, but just know that what I said hasn't changed. I'm rooting for you."

I looked over at him and he looked back at me, adding, "You know that, right?"

"Honestly, that means more coming from you than from anyone else I know."

This statement seemed to satisfy him a great deal. He smiled broadly and looked all around him, surveying (with fondness, I imagined) the faces of other riders, and simply taking in the day, still in its youthful hour.

"What's going on at work for you?" I asked.

"For me? Fuck, who knows. I've got a video conference with the Boise people. I'm sure there will be a shit ton to do other than that. There always is. But I can't even think about what that entails right now."

"That's fair," I said. His voice had come stormlessly forth, convincing me that the small details truly did escape the outer limits of his headspace. After a time I said, "Thanks for talking to me about all of that last night. It really helps me to understand."

"It helps me, too," he said. "To understand, and to have someone else who understands."

I nodded. As we crossed over the water I motioned out the bus window and asked, "What do you think about ships?"

He looked at me quizzically. "I'm all for them," he said with a small laugh.

"Like, when you think about them—if you've ever really thought about them—what do they make you think about?"

He did not answer immediately. "That something so large can move around freely relative to the space around it—I am impressed by that. It seems impossible to me because movement in my daily life doesn't occur on that scale. Cars, pencils, thinks like that. Those I can imagine."

"And you can imagine those things and their movement being influenced by humans, too. I have trouble thinking about humans being in charge of how the ship moves. It's like it's its own creature, or something."

"Okay, I see where you're going with that. I honestly hadn't thought about it." He paused for a few seconds, looking ahead. "Tectonic plates," he said, turning back to me. "There's some truly massive movement. And in that case it's true. A human has no influence over it."

I smiled. "That's right."

Jennifer and I arrived at the office at the same time. As we rode the elevator to the sixth floor I asked, "Do you know how you're going to phrase your commitment email? Is it like a formal thing or just a basic line or two?"

"Wyatt," she said with a grin, "you're slacking. That's not like you."

"It's due today, right?"

"Well, yeah. But I mean, you could have done it any time. I sent mine last Friday. I just assumed you had already, too."

"I guess I didn't think about it that way."

She patted my shoulder. "Took you a while to make up your mind, huh?"

I was quiet for a few seconds. "Well, not completely. I guess somehow I thought I might still decide not to. I mean, that wasn't actually going to happen, but still."

She laughed. "I'm glad you decided to go. I don't know what I'd do without you up there." As we walked out toward our desks she said, "To answer your question, it's not a big deal. Literally just say you'll do it. Make sure your signature gets attached. Send. Think you can handle that?"

I rolled my eyes at her and sat down at my desk. In five minutes it was done.

At lunch I crossed over to the pho place where I instead ordered banh mi and walked with it to a nearby park, which occupied about two-thirds of a city block. I liked the park because of its proximity to work and because old-growth trees grew densely around most of its limits and throughout, affording it an impressive degree of seclusion for its location.

I found a bench near a decommissioned fountain at the park's center and sat. Few other people hung around, as the weather had fallen once again out of favor.

Here I experienced an effective silence in the sense that noise from the street, while still audible, was indistinct and hard to attach to any particular source. Under these qualifications I was able to block it out completely. The trees surrounding the small open square—mostly oaks and a few pines—took on an air of having been entombed, a status of which they seemed nearly aware, as they sagged dustily and did not rustle whenever a breeze picked up. To my mind, these were qualities not unlike sadness. The air nagged at my hands as I ate my sandwich, and when I had finished I gladly tightened up my scarf and stuffed them into my front coat pockets. A cluster of dry leaves kicked around in the basin of the empty fountain, overlooked by a timeworn statue of an angel with a blank spot where her face would otherwise have been. In the next moment, as I sat, nothing moved at all.

After work I stood on the bus out of downtown, clinging to one of many vinyl stitched handles suspended from the ceiling, designed for the very purpose of steadying oneself. I had mostly expected Mikey to be present because he was often on the 5:10, but instead I was alone and did not hear from him for the rest of the evening. That night at the gym I found myself overwhelmingly excited by the raw specter of men in various stages of toil and, because I opted not to change at home, undress. If tonight had instead been the night when that unnamed boy-of-a-man approached, I felt with some positivity that I would have gone to bed with him. I was thankful it didn't happen that way, and once back at home, took care of myself in solitude.

The next morning I slept in until ten, when my phone rattled across my nightstand and fell to the floor. Doubting I would actually need it, I had set an alarm just to be certain I wouldn't waste the day away in bed. I must have underestimated my exhaustion; it shook me from deep sleep, and I saw that Mikey had texted about ten minutes earlier.

"Was wondering if you wanted to walk the seawall with me today. It's still pretty cold but it looks like there will be plenty of sun. Let me know and I will come pick you up."

I told him not to go out of his way, that I would catch the northbound bus.

"Ok," he replied.

I showered and ate a small breakfast. The 40A dropped me off just before eleven and I soon climbed the stairs to his apartment.

"Do you want me to wear my peacoat again?" He asked after greeting me at the door.

"If you feel like wearing it," I said, "I am unopposed."

We did not linger at his apartment. Once we had been driving for about ten minutes, Mikey asked, "How long have your parents known you were gay?"

"I came out to them when I was sixteen," I said. "I mean, I'm sure they knew before then, but if not then yeah, I guess they've known for about six years."

With some hesitation he said, "But you don't seem like someone who would've been very obvious about it, or whatever...based on how you act, I mean." He winced after saying this, which suggested to me that he hadn't liked the way the words materialized.

"I know what you mean. Honestly, their first clue was probably my internet search history."

"Oh," he said, laughing a little. "That would make sense."

"But actually, I know there were other things. My mom and I have talked about it. It's hard for her to explain, but she's said she could always just sort of...sense it."

"Okay."

"Like, it was just supposed to happen that way, I guess. Apparently she's always had a sense of that."

"And your dad? How did he handle it?"

"Pretty well, I think. It was weird with him, because after I told him, he didn't say or do much about it. We almost never talked about it. I always thought it was because it made him uncomfortable, but I found out later that he just cared so little about it that he didn't feel like there was much to discuss."

"Wow," Mikey said.

"Yeah, I always try to remember that I lucked out in that way. I never had to deal with any adversity at home."

"It's so incredibly cool that your parents are like that. So they just sort of switched over to asking about boyfriends instead of girlfriends, and all that?"

"Well, there never really was a switch. They always said things like 'the person you end up with' and other stuff like that. I don't think they ever had any big expectations either way."

After a pause he said, "That's really fucking cool of them."

We didn't say much else about it until we had reached the seawall, parked, and begun walking east toward downtown. In the distance, shimmering, silvery greens and blues of countless glass condominium towers rose up suddenly, like a single cliff, over narrow beaches lining the water. A photograph of the day would have belied the cold, and I noticed Mikey's words were accompanied by tiny puffs of rapidly condensing air.

"Another thing that amazes me is how you knew yourself so well at sixteen."

"The more I've thought about that," I said, "the more I've decided that people must know themselves in very different ways. It just wasn't hard for me to recognize it about myself. It got to a point where it just wasn't a question anymore. I was never going to be with a girl. Beyond that, I do think I have my parents to thank for their welcoming attitude. It's not like that was ever a barrier for me."

"Yeah," said Mikey. "I wish I knew myself better in that way. In the way you know yourself, I mean."

I looked over at him.

"That thing you said about your mom sensing it in you," he continued. "It makes me wonder if a lot of parents have that kind of sense. Like, what if my parents..." he trailed off for a moment and looked briefly out at the water. "I was pretty young when my dad first talked to me about it. I remember it being after he had picked me up at Davie School, so I couldn't have been older than eleven. He, like, pulled the car over to be all dramatic—he was like that sometimes—and made me look him right in the eyes. 'Ke' and 'tut'—those are some of the Thai words for it...and I knew what they meant already when he used them that day. To be like that was the most horrible thing. It was dishonorable and disgusting and everything else like that."

His expression had turned sour and he seemed to hold himself back momentarily from continuing, so I said, "It's not fair that you were treated like that."

"What fucking eleven-year-old even knows who he is? My dad had some good qualities, but sometimes it's hard for me to remember him in a positive way."

"I think that's okay," I said. "You don't have to forget about the bad side of him."

"Maybe it would be better if I did. Just so I could pretend that he never even felt that way."

I smiled a little. "Maybe."

"As I think about it, my life just starts to sound like a big cliché. Still seeking my dead father's approval and all that. Is that really all this is?"

I hesitated and then said, "I don't think anything is that simple, but it sounds like that could be a part of it."

Mikey scowled and kicked his shoe into the surface of the dirt path. "Anyway, I think it's something I can get over if I really try."

"I bet you can."

"That whole internet history thing. Can you believe I've never even thought of that? I'm sure they found stuff once I got a little older. Porn, teen health forums, stuff like that. Fuck, I'm sure they knew. We never talked about it."

I paused. "Did you watch gay porn back then?"

"Well...yeah."

"Do you watch it now?"

He laughed. "Slow the fuck down, Sherlock. Yeah, I do. But I've only recently been able to acknowledge that I do. I'm a mess, I know."

"You're not a mess, Mikey."

"I know what it says about me. What it means—I know that now." He took another few steps and then gave my shoulder a tiny shove. "It's just, having you around...you're giving me a lot of reasons to want to acknowledge it. And to be okay with it."

"I'm really happy to hear that," I told him.

"I've heard that for some people it's like, others call you gay before you even realize it about yourself. Well, no one has ever called me that. Not in a serious way."

"I know what you're saying. It makes it easier to...I don't know..."

"You can say it. It makes it easier to hide. Totally. I played a lot of sports in high school. Most of my friends were guys. People judge others based on the stuff they like to do, who they hang around, all that. I never gave anyone a reason to think I wasn't, you know, completely straight."

I nodded. "I don't know how much you've heard about it, but a lot of people do think of sexuality as a spectrum."

"I guess so. That stuff makes sense to me. It's funny though, because I wouldn't have the first idea about where to put myself."

I thought for a moment and then said, "Maybe you're, like, definitely on the heterosexual side, but not all the way at the end."

"I don't know. I guess."

"Sorry," I said. "I don't mean to make any assumptions about you."

"It's fine." He stopped, walked to the edge of the wall and leaned up against the green metal railing.

I stood next to him and pointed out at a squat, wide boat lumbering across the water toward a distant cluster of tall buildings. "You ever take the Seabus?"

"Not in a long time," he said. "I don't do a lot of business north of the water."

"Oh."

"I was just thinking about how it was with Alice," he said. "Honestly, it's kind of hard for me to remember."

"I've wondered about her sometimes," I confessed. "I mean, that's how you would know you're attracted to women. It was good with her for a while, right?"

He shuffled his hands around in his coat pockets. "For quite a while, yeah, I would say that it was good with her. Part of how we got together in the first place was our conversations. We had the most amazing conversations." He interrupted himself to say, "Okay, just so we're both clear on this, I'll be candid with you. For me, the sexual stuff was not exactly...well, undesirable. We even had intercourse sometimes, and I enjoyed it."

"If you're attracted to women then that would make sense," I said, grinning.

"Right. I guess it would. Damn. I feel like there's something here I'm having some trouble getting at."

"Is it different with me?" I offered after a pause.

"Yes," he said. "Transcendently."

"Oh, fuck. There's a ten-dollar word."

"Yes," he said. "There it is."

I cleared my throat. "That seems...well...notable."

"Yeah. It is notable. And I keep thinking back to that first night, at your apartment, when I said I preferred girls. You asked me, and I gave you that answer, but now I'm feeling some kind of accountability—to you, I mean—to make sure I'm being honest about that."

We stepped along the now-brick pathway in silence as I thought about how to respond. "Mikey, you can take your time and figure that out for yourself if you want, but don't think you have to answer to me. I don't really give a fuck about the preference thing. You're a person and I'm a person, and something's working here, between us—whatever it might be. If you can agree with that, I think we're good."

"Okay," he said. "Yes, I can agree with that."

We had lunch together at a seafood restaurant on the water, an indulgence for which Mikey insisted on paying; such an arrangement had never come up before, and he was adamant.

"We both work hard," he said as we walked back toward his car. It was after a period of vague distraction on his part, during which I could tell he had thought it over. "Our compensation is different in a way that feels arbitrary to me, and also unfair."

"Okay, I understand. I guess it's good that most of the things we like to do together are free."

When we arrived back at his apartment, Mikey fell onto the couch in a way that would indicate exhaustion. However, he seemed anything but, drumming his palms on his chest and singing something from Belle & Sebastian.

I sat on the floor below him, back against the couch and said, "'Write About Love'," as the track title came to me.

"Right," he said. "Title track. Man, you know your music. I bet you've got it on vinyl, too, huh?"

"In fact, I do. Is that alright with you?"

"Of course. I would expect nothing less from a good hipster like you."

"Fuck yeah," I said, flicking through my phone, ignoring his bait.

He tapped me on the shoulder and I twisted myself around to face him. "I kind of want to suck you off now," he said.

"Kind of?"

"I've been wanting to all day."

"Okay," I said. "That is certainly something we can do— right here, you mean?"

He sat up on the couch, square in the middle and motioned me over. "If it works here, then yeah."

I listened for any measure of hesitation in his voice, but there was none. I rose up and felt myself through my pants with one hand, outlining for him the growing, partially defined shape of me. I laughed quietly at the absurdity of putting on this kind of show for him.

"I really think I'm ready for this," he said.

"I know. I trust you when you say you are. Do you want to take your shirt off? I don't think I'll have any trouble finishing and I'm not sure where you want it to go."

He began to undress his upper-body. "On my chest, I guess."

"Okay," I said, unclasping my belt.

Now with his broad chest exposed, he looked up at me with the surrendering expression of a person who places the whole of their security into the hands of another. I removed my pants and stood before him in my t-shirt and underwear.

"I'm glad to see you're ready for this, too," he said, looking down at my middle section.

I peered down and then back at him. I tore my underwear to the floor and stepped out of them. I then took two steps forward and straddled him on the couch, half-kneeling in order to level myself with him. His mouth was no great distance from me now; he placed his hands at my hips and pulled me just slightly toward him. Because my cock stood straight out when erect and did not tend toward either the right or left, there was almost no space left between me and him. I looked up so that he could feel more fully an unattended freedom to explore. I no longer saw him, but felt the warm, wet inside of his mouth suddenly envelop me.

He pulled back after a very short time and laughed. "Man, this is crazy. I don't know…it feels so much bigger in my mouth."

I looked back down at him. "Don't do anything you don't want to."

"Are you kidding?" He took me between his lips once again, evidently caring little about whether or not I watched.

I could see now how he tested this new and peculiar circumstance with evenhanded, glimmering curiosity and an absolving lack of shame. With Mikey, more than with anyone else, I had noticed that a staggering majority of my pleasure during intimacy had so far been derived from a conceptual premise. As a habit I thought a lot—too much, to be sure. During sex, I thought about Mikey, about the man he was in an ideal sense (indeed, how ludicrously hot) and related it to his present actions. I had grown so attracted to him that, although he had absolutely no clue yet how to handle me inside his mouth, the sheer concept of being within his warmth, in this way, saw me profoundly stimulated.

He pulled back from me and laughed again. "Fuck, Chickadee. How the fuck do you do this? It's hot as hell for me, but I can tell I'm not doing shit for you."

"Yes you are. You don't have to take it very far in. Just keep sliding it in and out. That's all I need, I promise."

With renewed confidence he did as I had described. Already I felt an inevitable storm mounting inside me and knew that I would not last much longer. All at once he slowed, gripped me more firmly at my hips and beckoned me into him. I felt my length move with a soft pop, cleanly back into his throat; he had all of me now, his lips arriving with finality at my base. He gagged plainly but not distressingly and released me.

Something about him seemed fulfilled now as he returned to his earlier motions, and this sent me precisely over the edge. I warned him and tore myself away. I did not stroke but aimed downward, let out a short vocal gasp and shot myself over an extensive portion of his chest. At first we had made brief, fierce eye contact, but then he laid his head back and closed his eyes as I emptied onto him.

When it was all over I stood and stepped back. He looked down, immediately worked downward his own pants and began to jerk himself with great fury. I stood in silence and watched him perform this act, unashamed. I don't believe I would have had the ability to do anything else; I was transfixed during this very brief period, at the end of which his seed exploded forth, mixing in over and over with my own and canvassing the shadowy expanse of his chest. He let out a tiny whimper as the event occurred and then lay back, still fraught with small spasms.

The next moment basked in a faint afterglow. Mikey did not

say a word and I didn't feel the need to speak to him. Many seconds passed in this way before I moved toward him and offered to help him clean up.

12

Mikey and I sprawled together on his bed later that evening. It was dark outside, but not late. No longer apprehensive about arranging myself attentively toward him, I lay on my side while he rested on his back; my arm was slung loosely over his stomach.

"We don't last very long," he was saying. "You know, when we do stuff."

"Does that bother you?"

"No, not at all. It's normal, then?"

"I definitely wouldn't be concerned about it. We're still extremely excitable around each other, I think."

"So, what, we'll probably last longer later on?"

"Seems that way to me," I said. "Once we get used to it."

He smiled faintly. "Good thing we have all this time."

"Oh," I said. "I guess…yeah, well I'm sure we'll still hang out, even after I move."

"Right, yeah, I was thinking that, too. Okay."

I felt an immediate desire to continue with the thought, but Mikey changed the subject and it did not come up again.

Because I would be living out of town soon, Sunday-night dinners had taken on a new urgency among my mom's various machinations. The next evening I walked over in the rain and was fairly soaked by the time I arrived.

"Wyatt, where is your umbrella?" she demanded.

"I don't know," I said. "I'm not sure if I have one." I crossed the living room and sat with my back to the wood stove. "I'll dry off here. It won't take long." I grinned at her. "Feels nice."

"Help your dad out and tend to that if it gets cold," she said, stepping back toward the kitchen. "Stephanie should be here soon. She probably hit traffic on the bridge. It's so unpredictable during the weekend."

I sat alone for a few minutes, glancing through news stories and texts before initiating a system update on my phone. As I left it on the floor next to me to conduct its business, my dad came down the hallway from the bedroom. He had likely been napping, his common practice in preparation for a merciless workweek. He managed a team of freight shipment laborers at the main harbor and, in his mounting age, had finally escaped most of the backbreaking manual loading and unloading. Meanwhile my mom worked an early shift in midtown as a PA, at a hospital a couple miles north of Mikey's neighborhood.

"Wyatt," he said, sinking into his chair, "put your old man's mind at ease. You're sure about your move?"

"I'm sure," I said. "It's official, anyway."

"You're feeling good about it?"

"Yeah, I am," I said. "I know it's the right thing for me."

"Well, that's what's important. You do what's right for you."

I nodded. My mom had clearly done a number on him. "What's going on at work?"

"Same as ever. We've caught up on everything since the labor strike. Upper-management is still breathing down my neck. They've been doing that for the last twenty years, though. They'll do it until the day I'm done. It's not so hard to ignore, these days."

I smiled. "I wish I could ignore that kind of thing."

"With time, you'll learn," he said, and then heaved a booming laugh of a duration too long to match the humor in his statement, a characteristic that I had grown to love about him, if only since leaving home.

I stood up and looked out the front window in time to see Stephanie's Camry pull up along the curb. She sprinted across the front yard in the rain and stamped her feet on the porch before opening the door.

"Hello, hello," she chanted upon entering. "I'm getting over a cold so don't touch me."

"Stay away," came my mom's disembodied voice.

Stephanie kicked off her boots and unwound her scarf. "Oh," she said, noting my position near the stove. "That fire, my savior." She hurried over to stand next to me, bending a little to massage the backs of her thighs.

I bumped my shoulder affectionately into hers.

"Knock me over, why don't you," she said.

"Mom, do you need help?" I asked, projecting my voice toward the kitchen.

"Yes, Mom, we can help you."

"No. Almost done."

"Want to watch something, Dad?" Stephanie asked. "You look like a zombie."

My dad sat with his feet flat on the floor, hands cupped over the ends of the chair arms, staring blankly out toward the television, which was not turned on. He snapped back to alertness and looked up. "No thanks, Steph. Thinking about work. How was the drive?"

"Not that bad," she said. "Seems to go by faster when you're not in a hurry."

He smiled, taking his time to acknowledge the sentiment.

"Did you get that serpentine belt on yet?"

"No. I need someone to hold the tensioner loose while I take off the old one. I can't do both at once."

"I'll take a look after dinner," he said.

"I don't have the new belt with me, though. I left it at home."

"Alright, but it's got to get done soon. That old one isn't looking good and you don't want it to snap in traffic."

"I know, Dad. It's okay. I've got someone who can help me. I'll do it tomorrow."

Her voice took on an odd quality as she said this, prompting me to ask, "Who, exactly?"

She grinned. "None of your business."

"Oh my god, who?"

"I work with him," she reasoned, as if that would dispel my curiosity.

"Don't let him screw anything up," my dad warned. "Some guys just want to prove to you that they know their way around an engine. I promise you, they don't. Wyatt, are you listening?"

"Yes. Be suspicious of helpful men. Got it."

Stephanie laughed.

"You little weasel," he said. Again came his booming laughter.

"Come eat," yelled my mom.

I added a piece of wood to the fire and then trailed them to the dinner table.

"Curry," she said as we took our seats. "There are bell peppers in it, and beef, and some other stuff. I left the meat in big pieces so that it can easily be left out if desired." She had directed this statement at no one in particular, but would not have said it were Stephanie not at the table.

"Thank you, Mother."

"Stephanie's seeing someone new," I announced while I slipped some rice into my bowl.

"Oh my god, Wyatt," she whined. "I am not. Give it up already." She did not look especially annoyed.

"Who is he?" asked my mom.

"She's not saying," I explained. "But they work together. I was able to fish that out of her."

"He took me out to dinner the other night. I think we both enjoyed it. That's it. That's what's happened outside of work."

"Whoa, hold on," I said. "What's happened inside of work?"

"Stop, Wyatt," she insisted.

"Wyatt," said my mom, "You're so silly tonight. It makes me wonder what you're thinking about—or maybe whom. Yes, whom."

My mom did not often put her cleverness on display. Because of this, she sometimes caught me off guard, which was probably all part of her plan. Apparently blind to such outcomes, I had not anticipated how this situation could turn on me. And more to the point, did Mikey actually have an observable effect on my behavior?

"Nothing," I said. "I mean, no one."

Stephanie nearly choked on her water. "Oh, wow. What a master of deceit. Since you've decided to make a spectacle out of my personal life, maybe I should point out how obvious it is that you're still hanging around that guy."

My mom clasped her hands together and drew in a long, elated breath. "Oh, is it true? You promised you'd bring him by, Wyatt."

"I didn't promise," I said. "I'll have to see. Anyway, it's not like it's going to last. There's nowhere for things to go. I'm moving. Or did everyone forget?"

"No one forgot, sweetie."

I turned to my dad, who looked content but a little bored. "That reminds me," I said. "They'll pay for a moving van, so there's no need to get the old truck out again."

"Oh, I see. I was honestly looking forward to it," he said. "See if they can just get you the cash for it. We'll use the truck and you can pocket the money."

I nodded. "Sounds good. I'll check with them."

As we continued to eat, Stephanie cast a deliberate smile in my direction; I knew it had all been in fun, but it felt oddly exonerating to see that such playfulness had brought her a similar satisfaction.

"Mom," I said eventually, "how is work?"

"It's tiring. I feel like I'm not enjoying it quite like I used to."

"Wow," I said, swallowing another bite. "I didn't know you were feeling that way."

"It's nothing major. Some people have retired. There are a lot of new hires now. As for me, I'm stuck somewhere in the middle. There are so many young people on staff...it just doesn't have the same feel that it used to have." She smiled vaguely to herself. "I used to be one of those young people. I guess I'm the only thing that's really changing. But that's how it goes, right?"

"Mom," said Stephanie. "If you're not enjoying it, you could always change careers. So many people are doing that now."

"That's what I told her," my dad muttered.

"I just want to wait until we're a little more secure," said my mom. "We've still got a few years and then the mortgage is paid. Maybe then."

My dad looked down at his plate and shook his head, but did not say anything.

I remained generally mindful that my parents had bank-rolled my entire college experience, but moments like this brought the overwhelming significance of it all back to the forefront. I considered now that remaining steadfast in my career advancement had certainly been the more dutiful choice. I felt at once very good about this.

After finishing our food we began to clean up. Stephanie coaxed my mom from the kitchen as I packed away leftovers.

"I find it hard to relax when I'm perfectly capable of pitching in," she lamented.

"No one's expecting you to relax," Stephanie said, guiding her to the couch. "I'm just asking you to sit still for once in your life."

When it was just the two of us alone in the kitchen, Stephanie said under her breath, "Dad has told me recently that they're set to retire early. They have plenty of savings. I think Mom is being too cautious."

I thought this over for a moment before muttering in reply, "Maybe she's just afraid to look for something different."

"I think that's exactly what it is." She scrubbed at a pot for a few more seconds and then set it in the sink. The edge of the counter was finished in white ceramic bullnose tiles, cracked and chipped in places, stained slightly in the battering deluge of time. Stephanie leaned against them now, peering out the small box-window which overlooked the backyard, bathing in the day's failing light. "She thinks she still has to answer to people other than herself."

"Hmmm." I began loading plates into the dishwasher. "People like who?"

"Well, us, I guess. Dad. You and me. She can do literally anything she wants. I just want her to know how true that is. I want her to believe it."

"Have you told her?"

"Not as plainly as that, but yeah, I think I've made my thoughts known."

"And what does she have to say about it?"

"Not so much." Stephanie returned to her responsibilities in the sink. "I think I need to approach it with her in a different way—and maybe with a little more delicacy. The way Mom and I are with each other…I really don't know. She's just so…I don't know." She hauled the ancient green-enameled dutch oven over to the stovetop, where it was perched on a burner to dry. "I just need to work on being more delicate."

My mom's life—a saga to my eyes, a true legend—was elusive, Delphian, something I felt I would never fully assemble in my mind so that it could be understood from its dawning until now. A cluster of concealed horrors she'd faced in her childhood (countable on one hand, according to her, but no less than unspeakable) made her experience into one with which my own could never be compared. I had concluded at some point in college that, although I could never know her completely, I would seek further understanding whenever a conversation lent itself. It was all I could do not to take her presence in my life for granted, a passivity of which I realized I had been recently quite guilty.

"Overall, though, do you think she's happy?" I asked.

Stephanie's reply was short and not loud enough for me to hear, but her expression sufficiently conveyed her uncertainly. We had been speaking like stowaways, which in itself could be enough to elevate my mom's suspicion.

"Won't you need a car in Fern Hill?" Stephanie asked in a plain voice. "How will you come home to visit?"

"I've thought about that a little. It's cheaper to live up there, but not enough for me to get anything nice." I laughed. "It'll be something as old as I am, probably."

"You know Dad'll want you to get something Japanese. My neighbor is selling his Civic. It looks at least ten or fifteen years old. He's probably not asking too much."

"I can do without for a while. I need to save a little first."

"Mom and Dad helped out with mine," she said. "Don't be afraid to ask."

"Yeah," I said. "I know."

Once the kitchen had been restored to a general state of order, we joined my parents in the living room. Together they looked comprehensively tired, which prompted Stephanie to suggest skipping a movie.

"That's okay with me," said my dad. "Wyatt, let's talk a little about your move. I assume you'll want everything from your apartment. Is there anything you'll need from storage?"

"I don't think so."

"That Saturday—it's the 28th, right? I assume that's when you want to leave? Or maybe we can pack all day Saturday and leave Sunday morning."

"Sunday morning sounds more realistic."

"Do you know where you'll be living up there?" asked my mom.

"Not yet."

"I don't think that's something you should put off, Wyatt."

"I'll start looking at places online. Otherwise the company has made arrangements with some agencies for fast-track leases. But I heard there are better deals if you look for them independently."

"Well, don't kill yourself over it," she said.

We discussed minor details for a while and then channel-surfed somewhat collectively, landing on an early episode of *Friends*. Before long my parents made their way toward their bedroom. Stephanie and I said goodnight to them and were soon left alone.

"Do you need to get going?" she asked.

"Soon, I guess. Not yet."

She stood and went to the front door. "It's really not that bad out here," she said, hanging onto the doorframe and leaning out into the night.

We situated ourselves on the porch swing, overlooking the front lawn. Stephanie had carried with her one of my mom's massive old quilts and we bundled ourselves tightly within it.

"I'm not going to catch your cold, am I?"

"I really don't think you need to worry," she said. "I just like scaring Mom."

For a minute or two we didn't talk. I listened to the faint roar of cars on the highway, sequestered, as if it were not the sound itself, but just the memory. The cold, damp air nuzzled against my cheeks. I turned to her. "You're doing okay with everything?"

"I feel happy," she said. "I am happy. But I'm a little ambivalent about my situation with the new guy."

"So it is actually a situation?"

"Yes," she said. "It is. A new one, but a promising one. The problem is that I'm not ready for another situation. Or I don't want to be."

"You don't want to be?"

She took her time responding. "It's good to be alone for a while. Part of me wants it to last forever, but another part of me is scrambling every second to get back into something with someone. It's infuriating."

"It sounds like it."

She said little else about it, but I accepted that because she had shared this much with me, I owed her the same. Before I spoke, however, my phone buzzed in my pocket. Mikey had texted.

"I need to see you tonight, if possible," he wrote. "I messed things up with Sophie. I don't know what to do."

"Sure," I replied. "I'm at my parents' now. Can you pick me up? Do you remember how to get here?"

There was a brief delay before his next text, during which I apologized to Stephanie. "It's him. I think he's coming to pick me up. He's got a family thing he needs to talk about, I guess."

"Don't worry," she said. "Do what you need to do."

Mikey's reply arrived. "Not quite. Text me the address if that's okay. I couldn't stay in the house so I was out driving around Corbin. I'm not far. Sorry about the short notice."

I replied, telling him not to be sorry, and ended with the address. I then turned to Stephanie. "It's funny that he just texted me—Mikey, I mean. I was about to update you on all that."

"And?" she beckoned.

"Well, I guess it's kind of a similar situation. Even if my reasons for staying single are more external. You said things with this new guy are promising. I'm definitely feeling the same way."

She nodded. "Do you know what you're going to do about that?"

"No. No idea. But I can't change my plans for him. Not big plans like this. He's not out—in fact he's only barely out to himself. There's just...so much going on with that situation. But in another way it's like, nothing is happening."

She nodded.

"I'm sorry, I'm just tired. It's making me lazy about how I describe it."

"It's fine," she said. "I think I mostly get the situation."

"On a more tangible note, I think he'll be here very soon. Would you like to meet him?"

"Yes," she said quickly, as if she might miss her chance. "He's comfortable with that?"

"I believe he is."

His car rounded the corner in the next moment, as we began extricating ourselves from the confines of the blanket. I had imagined leading Stephanie out to the street so that they could meet, but he pulled speedily along the curb and his engine shut off. He had strode, quickly but without urgency, halfway across the lawn by the time we stood up. I stepped down off the porch and said, "Mikey, this is my sister, Stephanie."

He reached out and shook her hand as they exchanged personal introductions. "It's so good to meet you," he said. He stood back a little and said to me, "I'm sorry to come by so late. And to interrupt."

"Don't worry, Mikey."

"You're not interrupting anything. I need to go home soon, anyway," she explained. "You two enjoy your night." At this, she flashed a sort of sideways, clandestine smile, which communicated much more to me, I was certain, than it did to Mikey.

I hugged her goodbye, and Mikey and I stepped across the yard to his car. We rode down to the next corner and he said, "I really don't take it for granted that you're here for me tonight."

"I'm glad you texted me," I said. "Please tell me what happened with Sophie, if you feel up to it."

He pulled out onto the uncrowded highway and accelerated to the limit more slowly than usual. "She started asking about you. Just a few pointed questions, I guess. She asked if I felt attracted to you. It was so out of nowhere. She wasn't even trying to accuse me of anything, it's just..." He trailed off.

I remained quiet, lending him time to gather his thoughts.

"Anyway, I blew up at her," he said. "I really fucked it up, Chickadee. I just denied everything. A big fucking wave of denial."

I thought about suggesting that we find a place to park before continuing to talk, but the fingers of his right hand hooked casually, confidently over the stitched bottom rim of the wheel, as if his manner of conducting the vehicle did not answer at any level to his agitation.

"It just felt so...shitty." His chest heaved a little and a small breath fell from his lips.

"I'm so sorry," I said. "Mikey, if she was rushing you in any way—"

"She wasn't, though," he insisted. "It was time to talk about it. Overdue, actually. I should have already brought it up. But hearing her say she'd always wondered about me...I just felt so hurt, somehow. It's as if she feels like I've been hiding this for so long. Does she think I'm someone who wants to hide who I am from the world?"

"Hiding. That's what you said before. It isn't the right word."

"Then what is the right word?"

"I don't know," I said quietly. "But it's like, you didn't even know what the fuck you were hiding. You didn't understand it. Until recently, I don't think you really even believed it was true."

Mikey did not respond to this.

"It's so obvious how much respect she has for you," I said. "She told me you're the best guy she knows. You might think she's passing some kind of judgment on you, but that's just not true."

"I know it doesn't make sense. It's just, if she's felt this way about me for so long, I wish she had brought it up a long time ago."

"Maybe she didn't feel like it was the right time. Maybe she thought it would be too soon."

Mikey sighed. "Fuck. I guess it would have been. I don't know."

We didn't talk for a couple of minutes. Eventually I said, "What do you think you'll do?"

"I have to tell her what's going on with you and me. I owe it to her. And I am so disappointed with how I reacted. I need to apologize for that."

"The way you reacted," I said. "Mikey, don't beat yourself up too much over that. She must know how difficult this is for you. Just cut yourself some slack, okay?"

After a pause he said, "I pride myself on having my shit together. At this point, I don't feel like I do."

"It's okay. I promise you'll feel better soon. You're dealing with this. You've worked so hard to understand it." I took a breath and was met with that yet untouched, synthetic scent of his car's interior. "My god, Mikey, you've come so far in the last few weeks, and your support group isn't exactly—well, it's just not what I had. You have your shit together more than I ever could hope to."

"Yeah," he said, mustering a laugh. "You're not going to convince me of that."

I shrugged. "Fine, don't believe me, then."

"Fuck all of this," he said. A soft peak of mitigation had arisen in this voice. He turned up the stereo and then wiggled the shifter back and forth before selecting a lower gear. The car accelerated firmly and we roared west through the night, toward water.

"This song," I said. "Have you listened to it much?"

"All the time, Chickadee. I never skip this one."

In the next moment we belted out the lyrics together. His mouth moved exactly as mine did, through precisely the same motions—his voice, also, reaching for that same isolated, lofty note, before we broke back down together.

I glanced at the speedometer to see that Mikey drove just over one hundred miles per hour. "You maniac," I said.

"Sorry." The car slowed. "It just happened."

"Where are you taking us, anyway?"

"I'm not sure," he said. "The levee, I guess, if we don't change direction now. This is Paradise Highway, right? Doesn't it dead-end there?"

"It does."

"Is there any parking?"

"There is." Still occupied by what we'd discussed, I thought a moment, touched his arm and said, "Just so you know, she and I talked about it. About you maybe being attracted to me and all that. It felt weird not to tell you. I'm sorry I didn't say anything sooner."

He glanced at me and smiled a little crookedly. "It's okay." He cleared his throat. "I could have guessed. I did guess, I mean."

"She was so respectful of you. I promise she was."

"I know that."

Minutes later we landed by default along the western levee, farther south than we'd previously journeyed, left the car behind and climbed a flight of concrete steps to the top. We still wore our coats, but the air flowing gradually in from sea lacked the biting chill that persisted inland. The ocean, past a ribbon of tall foliage and marshland, slept still tonight beneath cargo handlers and fishing workers, whose vessels emitted faint, scattered dots of light far across the water. Somehow they seemed more distant now than the stars, which shone overhead through a vacant atmosphere.

"There's a beach out there, at the water," I said. "I remember, from when I was a kid. It's just a small patch of sand, after you walk between the bushes."

He followed me down an unofficial trail. The plants grew taller until soon we were deep among them. A pulsating breeze murmured between the branches and vines.

"Are you sure this is okay?" came his low, hushed voice.

"Why wouldn't it be?"

"No reason. Just a little creepy here. If you think it's okay, though…"

Without thinking I reached back for his hand. He offered it to me without pause. As I led him down the rest of the trail I considered that he had never divulged to me this hint of fear or apprehension toward something so concrete, and that it made me want to pull him close, to squeeze him tight at his waist and to protect him from everything by which he had ever felt threatened.

The trail opened up suddenly onto the sand and Mikey appeared immediately back at ease. "Fuck. This is beautiful." His shoes and socks leapt from his feet. "The sand's still wet from the rain earlier. But it feels so nice."

So that I could feel what he felt, I joined him, and we stepped barefoot together over to where silty saltwater lapped at the tiny beach's edge.

"It's been forever since I've been in a place as peaceful as this," he told me.

"Me too."

"I said something awhile ago, about kissing. Do you remember that?"

"Yes," I said. "You won't kiss a guy. I know."

"I can't stand for you to think that somehow—" He caught himself for a moment, then continued. "I never want you to think you're not worth it to me. To try something new, I mean, even though it's somewhere I never thought I'd go."

I guessed what he was indicating by this remark, but did not act. I waited instead for him to make the next move in case he had (unthinkably) meant something different. I didn't wait long.

He stepped toward me in the sand. Never before had he looked so tall. "If I'm reading this wrong," he said, "I mean, reading us wrong, what this is—you should tell me now."

Somewhere far away, my feet froze in the wet grit, but I could not feel that now. With great effort I cobbled together a response. "There's nothing to say, Mikey."

"Then I'm going to kiss you, Chickadee."

I stepped into him and felt his arms surround me. His lips fell with immediacy against mine, and were much softer than I had expected. As the fine stubble of our upper-lips interlocked I shuddered slightly, releasing some small knot of doubt, discovering only in its parting that it had ever been there at all. Mikey cared for me in the same way I cared for him; whatever fixation was shared between us fell cleanly outside the realm of casual play.

I ran my fingers down his cheek, feeling at first the coarse black whiskers below his sideburns, then a smoothness in the center where they did not grow, and then their return near his chin. Neither of us found cause to shave during the weekend and I did not resent the rawness it lent now to our embrace.

Mikey moved his hand against my cheek as well, felt, evidently, at my similar roughness and broke just barely away from me. Tender and feverishly warm, his lips still brushed agonizingly against mine as he said softly, "The facial hair thing. For some reason I wasn't expecting that."

"Haven't ever kissed someone like me, huh?"

"Not that I can recall."

"Are you okay with it?" I asked.

The earthen dark of his eyes, never before so close to mine—as if our lashes would soon intermingle—reflected perfectly the half-pearl of a moon. I felt a tiny rush of his breath against my lips. "You don't need to wonder about that."

He kissed me again, openhandedly feeling my neck and cheek with redoubled ardor and after a few seconds, our tongues met. I let his slip cautiously over mine and then, for a moment longer, we moved our hands over one another with passion, opening our mouths slightly, moaning softly in turn.

He broke away and held my hands. The moonlight lit a gap between us. He cleared his throat and said, "I want to save something for another time."

I did not know exactly what he meant by this, but didn't dwell on it.

During the car ride back to my apartment I mentioned that my feet were still ice-cold inside of my shoes.

He sent the heat to the floor and said, "Just so you know, I didn't plan to kiss you tonight. I only meant to tell you about Sophie."

"I didn't think you did."

"Okay," he said. "Cool."

I smiled to myself, listening to his music as it trickled through the speakers, and to a dull roar of wind blasting over the slick metal shell of the car as we hurried through the black.

13

While lurching through my routine the next morning, I tossed around the memory of the kiss with a kind of detached amusement, as if it had been a dream, even laughing it off as I took stock of my sleepy appearance in the mirror. It really did feel like a dream, and that tiny beach was now a world apart from here. I had been exhausted at the time, without fully realizing it, and remembered very little of preparing for bed once Mikey dropped me off at home.

I thought about work while in the shower, then of my mom, imagining what kind of new occupation she'd be willing to take on, after having toiled for decades in the same place, much longer than I had been alive. She sewed like mad in her free time, read on it and watched videos about it. She had crafted many of her own dresses. I made my way down off the hill to catch the bus (it was a clear, sunny day, and also cold), considering that she must have deliberately avoided paid work as a seamstress for one reason or another.

It took Mikey's absence on the second bus to force me into acceptance. It wasn't that I didn't want to remember. I think it was the smell of him, his quick, hot breaths and the light sweetness in the taste of his mouth, most of all, that pulled acutely at me. Thinking of these things made me ache with compulsion to feel it all over again, the roughness of his face, his tongue testing mine, his dark features closer to me than they had ever been. There was also the way he stood barely over me, so that I had to angle my head back just slightly to meet him.

But I was easily aware that in remembering so much, in wanting it to happen again, my actions and desires did not line up correctly with the path I had chosen. The circumstances were not convoluted. The factor of risk, to my mind, lay in the potential for one or both of us to be hurt when I left. It struck me as vital at this time to affix my longing to the kiss itself, to his physical body, and not to the boy—in general, to an intimacy that was only sexually charged.

It helped that Mikey wasn't on the bus. I thought back to the nature of his appearances before we had ever spoken; he had always been either present or not, without explanation other than having simply left at a different time than I had and catching a separate bus, or driving. Maybe I could now seek relief in the fact that this aspect seemed not to have changed at all. Even after sharing our first embrace only several hours earlier, he'd made no effort to be here now, to discuss himself or his actions. And he didn't need to be. It worked to preserve whatever small but important dissociation we still shared. I felt that holding on to that would facilitate our parting considerably.

Work that day was consuming and ordinary. I had packed lunch in an effort to save money and stood from my desk only a couple of times as the hours droned on.

"Chickadee," Mikey texted as I departed from the first bus home, "I am so sick. I think it's the flu or something. I hope I didn't give anything to you last night. I'm sorry. We should hang out when I'm better."

"Maybe I was carrying it from my sister," I replied. "She

said she had been sick. I'll never forgive myself. Do you need anything? I'm nearby."

After walking a half-block my phone buzzed again. "Don't worry. I just need to sleep right now. We'll catch up soon."

As I passed his street I peered down a crowded wall of ancient buildings, making out the white metal railing of his tiny balcony and also the window next to his bed. If he looked out now it would be possible for him to spot me. I hurried on to catch the 40B.

It occurred to me that I would have gladly visited him, completely unconcerned about catching whatever he had. Absurdly, being sick alongside him seemed entirely pleasant; how fortunate would it be for us to quarantine ourselves from the world as we recovered? How much closer would we become? With my selfishness in check, I quickly acknowledged that Mikey should never have been sick in the first place, and I should be happy to give him the solitude he desired to ride it out.

I contacted Marie at lunch the next day, asking if she had plans after work. "I am on a budget," I added.

Her reply floated in sometime around two. "Darling, do you need a sugar daddy? Come live with me. I can be that for you."

"I don't need that," I texted. "Mostly I just need to talk. Is it rude to invite myself over?"

"Perish the thought. I'll be on the train home around five. Please come."

A few hours later I found her standing underground at the city-center station, blue shoes pressed together, near the edge of the platform.

She reached up and hugged me. "Just got here. I was hoping we would catch the same train."

Soon we were swept up in a tepid and stale wind as three

cars came moaning and squealing through the tunnel. When the doors opened Marie hustled through to the gangway, freely pushing her way between passengers. I followed her lead.

"I need to stand, if you don't mind," she said, grabbing ahold of a metal bar at the edge of the rubber corridor.

"I don't mind at all," I said. "I've been sitting all day."

"It's horrible," she said. "The fucking man...making you and me sit all day." She regarded me with terrible concern. "And he's making you move away."

I nodded.

"Oh, Wyatt. Tell me you decided not to go."

"I confirmed with them, on Friday. It's already set in stone. I'm sorry."

She flitted her free hand dismissively. "Please stay with me when you visit home, okay? Don't stay out with your parents. What person ever really needed parents, anyway? Parents are complete bullshit, Wyatt."

I stared at her blankly across the narrow passage, then settled into a quiet, prolonged laugh.

"What?" A broad smile took over. "They are. I'm telling you."

"What's Sloan up to?"

"Same as us, I'm sure. We texted a little yesterday. Working hard for the money. Chasing love."

I cleared my throat a little. "That does sound familiar. And are you having any luck in your pursuit?"

"Pursuit? Of love, you mean? Not at all. There's nothing. No sex, either, which might be the bigger tragedy of my life at the moment."

"You and Anthony are finished forever?"

"Forever. We haven't said a word to each other. Not even a text."

"And that's the way you want it, right?"

She looked at me intensely for a second and then said, "Almost all of the time, yes."

I nodded to indicate that I understood.

"It's not him that I miss," she said. "It's just…you know. I'm not totally built to be alone. I wish I was. I'm sure you understand."

"I think I said something very similar to you when we were still in school."

"You did," she said. "It stuck with me. That's not to say I am unhappy right now. I'm really feeling quite fulfilled, for the most part. Food is my intimate companion. That and looking forward to travel."

I smiled. "If I had to, I could be alone for the rest of my life, as long as I travelled the world and ate good food."

"Now you're getting it," she said.

Such was the topic of discussion for the remainder of the train ride, and even until after we had entered her condo. Together we laid down an intricate, imaginary brickwork of plans pertaining to our activities when visiting certain countries. There were, for example, particular Vietnamese dishes we would be seeking out. Eventually we acknowledged that the discussion was all but invalid without Sloan's input.

"It's not fair to him," said Marie. "We have to stop. Put your coat in here." She pointed through her bedroom doorway, toward her bed. "I hate it when you wear it around like you aren't staying long. Here, give it to me." She reached up and lifted it off of my shoulders. "I should be checking to see if there's any black hair stuck to this," she muttered, laying it on her bed. "What the hell is happening with Thai Guy?"

"With Mikey."

"Right. What the hell is happening with Mikey?"

As she went over to make us drinks I let her in on a few basic developments, mostly to do with his own self-discovery.

"It's a good sign that he's willing to take such an honest look at himself," she said. "That kind of thing is never as common as you hope."

She set my glass in front of me and I thanked her. "Seriously," I said, "he's got to be one of the most genuine and interesting people I've ever met."

"And hot."

"Yes," I agreed. "Most importantly, that." I took a sip of the clear drink as she joined me at her narrow kitchen table. Outside, the sky threatened to rain down on the streets far below.

"Actually..." I began, planning to launch right into a brief but careful retelling of Sunday night's event. Instead I came right out with it. "He kissed me. On Sunday night, in a very romantic way. I'm not sure what to think about that."

Marie covered her mouth with part of her hand but I could see a gigantic smile forming behind it. With some effort she composed herself enough to take a long drink, then set down her glass. "Are you glad that it happened?"

"I can't help but be," I said. "I'm starting to really, really like him, Marie."

"A kiss," she said, sort of to herself. "A romantic kind of kiss. Wow. That was really unexpected coming from him, right?"

"Well, yeah. He told me not long ago that he could never kiss a guy. I didn't think he would ever want any kind of romantic involvement." After a pause I said, "We were supposed to be friends with benefits. That's all."

She shrugged. "How long do you think those kinds of relationships really last? It's only so long before they die, either because they turn into something more, or one person involved finds someone else."

"I guess I thought it might just continue that way, especially since I'm moving. As in, we'd mess around with each other when I visited home and that's it."

"Yeah, I see how that might have worked for a while with you moving away. And I don't mean that those relationships represent a bad decision, like, inherently, as long as both parties recognize that they're unsustainable. But all of that aside, as far as fuck-buddy status is concerned, the two of you were doomed from the beginning."

"What makes you say that?"

She paused. "I mean, look at you. You're obviously too good together for something like that. I swear, you're meant for each other."

For an instant I shook internally with alarm. "You haven't even met him, Marie."

"No, but I know you pretty well, Wyatt. You don't act this way for just anybody. You've slept with a few guys since your last relationship and none of them had you waiting by your phone—or seeing their face in a crowd when they aren't actually there. You're acting like a crazy person, and I like it."

I couldn't help but laugh. "I hate you," I said. "I fucking hate all of this."

She laughed along with me. "Why? I want to be you right now. I want someone to make me feel that way."

"Really?" I asked. "You want to start falling for someone just as you're moving away? That sounds appealing to you?"

She quieted down, still smiling and poking at a submerged ice cube with her finger. "Maybe. It could be. Anyway, it's better than what I have going on right now, which is nothing."

"Alright, if you're sure about that."

"I am."

"So," I announced. "I come to you seeking your advice. I will hear it, no matter what it is. How do you think I should proceed, given that I am leaving town at the end of the month?"

"I think you should forget that you're leaving, as far as he is concerned."

"What? Seriously?"

"Yes," she said. "Just do it all. Live it all. If you're dying to fall for him, then let yourself."

"Honestly, that sounds reckless to me."

She nodded, smiling.

"If either of us—or maybe both of us—is really going to get hurt at the end, I'm worried I couldn't handle it. I'm worried it might keep me from leaving."

"Isn't that the point?" she asked. "Your job has all the control over where your life is going. Your employer, I should say. I don't think that's healthy. Let this boy situation have some of that control. Let it have all of its weapons. Then they can do battle with one another properly. At the end you'll find out which one prevails, and you can know in your mind that each had a fair shot."

I stared at her for a moment and then took another drink. "It just sounds so reckless," I repeated.

She continued to smile at me.

"There's no mindfulness involved. It's like setting up all the conditions for a science experiment, and then letting it run its course. That's how you're making it sound. Is that all life is? Just a set of experiments?"

"Yes, Wyatt, it is."

I rolled my eyes. "That sounds like something from a movie."

"Obviously I don't live like that all the time, but sometimes I do, with some aspects of my life. I'm saying to you that you should, right now, based on everything that's going on with you."

I paused. "I don't know if I can."

"Just try. That's my advice, okay?"

I nodded. "I asked. And I said I would hear you."

"You did."

We didn't say anything for a moment, just sipped silently on our drinks until hers was gone and mine dwindled.

"Are we alcoholics?" she finally asked.

"Yes," I assured her. "Damn it, Marie, one problem at a time."

Our discussion eagerly shed its grave colors as it marched on into dinner. Marie shared with me leftovers from her refrigerator. I left just as the sky grew completely dark, thanking her for everything and promising that we would meet again soon.

The next day I stood up at my desk not long after noon, stretched and left for the break room. Jennifer joined me after a few minutes.

"I'm following your lead," she said. "You're not the only one who knows how to pack a lunch."

I smiled at her. The company culture tended toward eating out every day, leaving the lounge area and kitchen surprisingly unburdened, considering the significant number of employees among whom they were shared.

"I have a question for you," she said, smacking a container of yogurt down on the table's rubbery surface and returning to the fridge. "Do you have a strong preference for living alone once we're in Fern Hill?"

"I don't think so," I said. "Now that you mention it, not at all."

"There are a lot of two-bedrooms available up there. Who

knows why. The rent is only slightly higher than the one-bedrooms. I think it only makes sense to share one."

"You're talking about you and me, right? Because I don't think I'd share with anyone else in the office."

"I'm touched," she said.

"Sure. Let's do it. Shit, maybe this will motivate me to finally look for a place."

"We can look this afternoon," she said. "We'll sneak it in."

That it might seem desperate did not cross my mind until after I texted Mikey on my way to the first bus home. This concern was fleeting, as it felt strange and unfitting when filtered through our friendship.

"You feeling well enough for me to come by on my way home?" I had written.

"Sure," he replied. "I would like to see you. I'll leave the door unlocked. If I'm in the shower when you get here then let yourself in."

Mikey answered the door, not long after I knocked, wearing only a towel. His hair was still damp. The broad, soft tract of his chest glowed in the yellow light from the hallway.

"You haven't been sick," I said. "You've been working out."

He summoned a weak smile and welcomed me in. "I can promise you that's not true."

"Has it been really bad? How are you feeling now?"

He shrugged. "I'm getting some energy back. I haven't thrown up since yesterday."

"Mikey," I said. "That sounds bad. I could have brought something. Do you have everything you need?"

"That's really thoughtful, but please don't worry about me. Are you sure you're okay here? What if I'm still contagious?"

"It doesn't matter," I said. "I think you should get more rest. I won't stay long."

He shrugged again. "You can sit down if you want. Tell me what's going on with the outside world."

"Not too much, really," I said. I took a seat on the couch and he went over by his dresser to put on clothes. I did not watch him. "My coworker and I picked out an apartment in Fern Hill today."

"Really? Were you up there?"

"No, just online, I mean. Sight-unseen, except for pictures."

"I thought you'd be living alone when you got there, for some reason." He came to slump down opposite me.

"I was," I said, "but it's much cheaper to share rent on a two-bedroom."

"Oh, okay."

He did not look completely recovered. Our eyes met for a few seconds.

"I talked to Sophie," he said. "I had to, I mean, to tell her that I wouldn't be at work. Maybe it was better that I was feeling so shitty. I didn't have the energy to even think it over. Everything came out. I just said it all."

"Really?"

"Well, first I said I was sorry for how I had reacted when she confronted me. But yeah, you and me fooling around, my attraction to guys, all of it. How I'm starting to...um..." He paused. "Well, whatever made me kiss you the other night. I told her about that, too."

"How did she react to all of it?"

"I could tell she was ridiculously happy about it," he said. "But I think she tried not to show that too much."

"Okay."

"She's been doing a lot of stuff for me," Mikey said slowly, "especially over the last few days. I'm not sure how I can pay her back."

"Is your business doing okay with you gone?"

"Yeah, it'll be fine. She told me it's not too much to handle." He smiled. "She said it's better with me out of the way."

"She's probably just happy you opened up to her."

"Yeah," he said. "I think that's true."

We didn't talk for a moment. Mikey lifted his feet up onto the couch and faced me.

"I'm fine with talking about Sunday night, by the way," he said. "How are you feeling about it?"

"The kiss, you mean? It's fine. I'm okay with it."

"Alright," he said. "So you're saying…that kind of thing… it's alright with you if we just let it happen?"

I thought back to Marie's advice from the day before. "If we both want it, and I think we do, then yes, I want to just go with it."

Mikey's eyes let go of some of the dull grayness which had so far weighed them down. "Okay. That sounds good to me, too."

At the risk of annoying him, I asked again if I could do anything.

He raised an eyebrow. "Nothing that doesn't require a lot of contact. And I don't want you to get sick, too."

I laughed. "That's not what I mean."

"I'm kidding. Honestly, if you would play Playstation with me, that would make me happy. Just a few races."

Despite his ailment, Mikey won one after another, until finally after five or six, I edged past him in the final lap.

"Get the fuck out," he said. "I won't be insulted in my own home."

"I should leave on a positive note anyway. It's better for my self-esteem."

"No," he protested, realizing I did actually intend to leave.

"You can't go."

"You need sleep," I said. "You'll never get better."

"I will," he said. "I have a strong immune response."

"Prove it," I said, standing. "Anyway, I'm meeting with my parents this evening. Tax season is upon us."

"You're helping them with taxes," he said, remaining slouched down in the cushions. "That's really sweet."

"It's not that big a favor," I said. "Theirs are pretty basic." I put on my coat. "Get some rest, okay? Don't go back to work until you're ready."

"How about we do something Friday night, if I'm feeling better?"

"Of course," I said.

He did not get up to walk me out as I went to leave, but threw me a half-smile and said, "Thanks for coming by. I really appreciate it."

"I wanted to," I said. I told him to feel better soon and left for my parents' house.

On the second bus I reflected, expecting to feel something negative in response to our latest agreement—some pang of worry or regret chewing at the edge of my thoughts—but it couldn't be conjured. I felt no adversity at all, and any anxiety (if it could even be so labeled) took the form of an occasional lightness, like a tiny balloon humming around in the upper reaches of my chest. Each time I felt it, I smiled.

14

"You know, I've never really thought about it," my mom was saying.

"Come on. That can't be true."

We sat on metal folding chairs, crammed side-by-side under the keyboard tray of her small desk.

"Well..." she said, staring blankly at the cluttered bulletin board above the monitor, "I suppose it's not. Anyway, I've never given a lot of thought to it. Just a little every once in a while."

"So, what do you think?"

"I think you're very talented. Your dad won't believe we got through all of it so quickly. He'll want to check it over, of course—"

"I'm talking about the career thing, Mom."

"I know, sweetie. It means a lot to me that you've thought so much about it. But I'm really just not ready for a change like that. Plus, it's a big sacrifice in income just to be doing something different. What makes you think I'm good enough to find stable work? And even if it were stable, the money wouldn't be very good."

"It's not a question of whether you're good enough," I insisted. "I'm telling you right now that you are. These days people want hand-made everything. Everyone's scrambling to be the world's most ethical consumer. If you can prove your fabric comes from anywhere besides a sweatshop, you're practically golden."

She leaned away from me in offense. "I wouldn't dream of buying supplies made in a sweatshop."

"That's exactly what I'm talking about, Mom. Jesus, make that your slogan."

She scowled. "You have the strangest ideas." She laid her fingers briefly across the keys, then returned them to her lap, softening. "I'm listening. I understand what your saying. If anything, it sounds like wonderful retirement income."

"I guess," I said. I laid my head on her shoulder. "Do you really think Dad needs to check my work? We can submit these any time."

"We'd better let him. He likes to have his hand in this stuff."

I nodded, rocking her slightly. The house was silent except for the distant rattling of change in the dryer.

"I should get it in writing that we're allowed to visit you as often as we want."

"Don't say that. It really won't bother me." I sat up, scooted my chair away from hers and faced her, slouched over with my elbows resting on my knees. "I think it's going to be a little lonely up there."

"You have a friend from work who's also moving, right?"

"Yeah, she's great. We're actually going to split a place. But we're not that close."

She opened another tab and scrolled through one of her sewing blogs. "I'm happy to hear you'll have a roommate. That should help somewhat with the loneliness, I would think."

"Maybe you're right."

"I forget how long you said they'll keep you up there."

"Now it's looking like it will be at least two years," I said.

She turned away from her desk, staring somewhere just over

my left shoulder. "That's a long time."

"I know."

"But I really think it's going to be fine."

"I know. I think so, too."

She pushed the issue of dinner rather aggressively but I refused, reasoning that I would get sick doing crunches at the gym and throw it all up.

"That's disgusting, Wyatt. Make sure you eat plenty after you're done."

"Alright," I said. "If Dad has any questions, he can text me."

"Okay, I'll tell him."

I stood and she followed me to the front door.

"Did you hear about the murder in Sand Hollow the other night?" she asked.

"Nope, I didn't."

"Someone just out walking. Completely unprovoked. No connection with the killer at all."

"I'll be careful, Mom."

"Please do," she said.

Thursday passed so quickly that I found myself dashing through work, periodically stumbling in an effort to keep up. I did not hear from Mikey. I had not expected to. Marie texted as I settled into bed late in the evening to read, the heavy and enduring novel splayed open for the thousandth time across my lap.

"How about another late night in the city tomorrow? I insist on buying your drinks this time. Sloan wants to discuss the trip. I'm sure you do, too."

"Awesome," I replied. "Don't worry, I'll buy my own. I just won't drink very much."

"We'll see about that."

I knew her skepticism was meant for my declaration of restraint, not because I lacked any in particular, but because she so clearly planned to treat us to multiple rounds and was certain that I would not refuse within that context. I made up my mind not to reply, giving my phone a perfunctory smile and turning my eyes to the page.

My gaze fell on Mikey's building the next morning in time to see him step down onto the crumbling sidewalk. He wore a light gray suit jacket with a slim pair of matching slacks and held a briefcase in his gloveless hand at his side. He shouted something I did not understand and then advanced toward me. I met him partway down the street under the faded red awning of a small bakery.

"Look at you," I said, aware of the wide, stupid grin beaconing from my face. "Back from the clutches of death. How are you feeling?"

He pulled me into a quick, tight hug before we set out for the bus stop. "More like beyond the grave," he corrected. "I'm pretty sure I just died at some point before you visited last. I've made up my mind that I'm some kind of spirit now."

I shrugged. "Well, either way, as long as you're sticking around."

"That's the plan."

"How long has it been since you were in the office?"

"Since Friday. Fuck, it's been a week."

"Got a lot of catching up to do?"

He jammed his free hand into his pocket. "Nothing too overwhelming. Sophie's been working her ass off. She's completely showing me up, actually."

"Sounds like nobody needs you."

He laughed. "They really don't. And I'm not just saying that."

"I wasn't being serious," I said. "They'll be glad to have you back."

"Yeah?" he said. "I'm not so sure."

We didn't talk as we stood beside the bus shelter, falling in with the silence among several other regulars who waited around and within it. After a short time we boarded and took our seats together near the back. He pressed his shoulder just slightly against mine and left it there.

Turned mostly toward the window he said, "You're... Well...you're looking really handsome today."

I managed to keep calm. "Thanks, Mikey. That's really nice of you to say."

He looked ahead and smiled. "I think today is going to be very good, actually."

"Really?"

"Yeah, I mean, I'm just going to attack everything head-on at work. It feels like it's all going to be great." He thought for a moment. "I hate to say it, but I'm really feeling like I should stay late, though. We can still hang out, but not right after work."

Suddenly I remembered I'd agreed to meet Marie and Sloan. "Shit, I totally forgot we made plans to hang out tonight. I told some friends I could go out with them. I'm sorry. Let me see if I can cancel." I pulled out my phone.

"Don't," he said. "We didn't actually make plans. I only said if I was feeling better. I don't expect you to put your life on hold for me. That's ridiculous."

After some thought I said, "Could you meet up with us? Would that be something you'd be comfortable with?"

"I think so," he said. "It would be cool to meet your friends. I don't want to impose, though."

"I can guarantee that they won't mind."

"Oh," he said. "Okay then."

The bus juddered through its gears as the driver remerged with traffic after another stop. Along the roofline about halfway to the front was an advertisement that read, "Kick the commute. Live in the city. It's no longer something only your boss can afford." Underneath, a website was listed.

I turned back to Mikey. "You definitely seem like you're feeling better."

He nodded. "Like I said: strong immune response." He beat his chest twice with his fist. "Young, virile."

"Mhmm," I said. "You're sure going out tonight won't be overdoing it?"

"Not a chance," he said. "I am excited about tonight."

Awhile later I left Mikey alone in the seat, clutching his briefcase to his chest, and departed into the daily throng. My wool coat felt hot and burdensome for the first time in several days, so I shed it as I shuffled west among the crowd to the front steps of my building.

Toward the end of the day I checked my phone to find texts from both Marie and Mikey.

"We can meet in the same place as last time," wrote Marie. "Is eight okay? Early start."

"Yes, that's fine," I replied. "Can I bring Mikey along?"

"You don't even have to ask. I can't wait to meet him."

Mikey wrote, "If you're not going home before heading out tonight, feel free to come by my office." He included the address, then later added, "Let me know if you decide to come. 9th floor."

Once I was finished for the day I told him I'd stop by around six.

I ate pho for dinner, lodged against the back wall in a small establishment closer to Mikey's office and cheaper than the one next to mine. I'd never tried it before and found it to be at least as good.

"Coming up," I wrote a short time after, to which he responded, "Awesome. Suite 900, by the way. I'm at the back by the windows."

I caught glimpses of his company's interior before entering, through open blinds in the hallway windows. There were no cubicles and workspaces were homogenous, back-to-back and rested on two rows of wide wooden tables with legs pushed all the way out to the corners.

I entered quietly to see that two of these tables sat alone at the far end with some space between them, arranged perpendicularly to the rows. Mikey stood up at the left one, emerging from behind a large silver computer and silhouetting his form against the light of the evening sun.

"You made it," he said with a smile as I stepped toward him. "What do you think?"

The space gushed with light, seeping from the bright gray walls in spite of unlit overhead bulbs and a declining natural source. A bank of gunmetal ceiling fans resided high above, each swinging its three long blades in diplomatic relations with the surrounding air. The amount of open floor space astounded me and struck me as diametrical to my own place of work, where even one additional desk would prove to be an obstacle.

"I love it," I said, draping my coat over the back of a nearby chair. "Very open and modern. A little startup-ish."

He nodded. "We're a little startup-ish."

"Right."

"Let me show you around," he said, leaving his desk and leading me toward a conspicuous red door near the center of the western wall. "Through here is our break room. Our conference room is up one floor. We share it with a few other businesses."

A large blue exercise ball rolled peacefully away from us, across the polished wood toward a lounge-like sectional, low and gray. A full kitchen of gleaming metal appliances lined the north wall of the room.

"It's really nice," I said. "Better than where I work."

"We moved here in the middle of summer. We barely made any changes. All of this was here." He led me back out into the cavernous main room. "Half of these tables were moved from our old place. We ordered more of the same when we came here. Sophie likes to keep things minimal, and so do I."

"Do you think you'll stay here for a while?" I asked.

"Looks like it. I really like it here, and we have plenty of room to grow." He paused and then added, "If we must."

"Still not so into that, huh?"

"Not so much," he said, wandering back toward his desk and the wall of massive windows. "It's looking inevitable at this point, though. I'm at peace with it as long as I can delegate tasks and, you know, keep personal stress levels low."

I stood facing him next to the glass. "I understand."

"This side of the room is mostly our coders. There are eight of them," he said, indicating to the right. "Five women, three men. Try finding that anywhere else in the industry."

"Impressive," I said. "Six if you count Sophie, right?"

"Exactly. And the spaces on the left are usually our consultants. There are three. We also have two people who mostly do marketing. And we have in-house design. That's Morgan. He usually sits next to Riley, because they have this thing going between them. I don't think they know that I know. Sophie told me. Riley has to sit at that computer by the door because he's our receptionist. All the rest can sit where they want but most people kind of have their spot chosen." He brought his hands to his hips. "Anyway, that's about it I guess."

"Sounds like a fun group," I said.

"We're an interesting mix, for sure." He surveyed the vacated room, then turned back to me, wearing an irrepressible smile.

"You're happy to be back, aren't you?"

"I really am," he said.

"How did today go? So far, I mean."

"It's been awesome. But it's true, I'm not finished yet. Sophie's out getting dinner. Shit, do you want me to text her and see if she'll pick up something for you?"

"It's fine, I just ate."

"Alright. And when are you meeting your friends?"

"Eight, supposedly. It's sort of early, I know."

"I don't think I'll be done by then. But I can certainly be out of here by nine."

"Really, Mikey, take your time with whatever you need to do. Just text me when you're free. I don't want to hold you up anymore, so I'll get out of your way." I went to grab my coat but he stopped me.

"Chickadee," he said, "you know when you've been sick, and you start feeling well again, and then it's like, you feel really, really good? Since, you know, you've been feeling like shit for so long?"

"I think so."

"Well, I think that's part of why being back at work today feels so good." He paused for a moment before continuing. "But even more, I think it applies to you and me. I'm not going to take it for granted that I'm a healthy person. I want to make the most of it, and this time we have while you're still living here."

"Okay," I said. "Me too, Mikey."

Together we looked out at the sweeping expanse of surrounding steel, brick and glass, the shock of the sun hanging low over the water, and to the clogged web of streets below.

"I never get tired of looking at this place," he said.

"Me, neither."

He took ahold of my hand and pulled me closer to him. I turned away from the window so that I faced him again; we hugged each other and did not let go.

"It's so weird," I said into the soft tissue of his neck.

"What's weird?"

I paused to collect my thoughts. "It's just this feeling, like I've missed you, somehow. I've missed you so much."

He squeezed me more tightly to him. "I want to kiss you again so bad. I've wanted to since the first time."

My chin rested in the basin just above his collarbone. "I don't know if you're waiting for my permission, but you have it already."

"It's just…having been sick…I don't know."

I broke slightly away from him and went in. I pressed my lips neatly to his and ran my hand lightly over the clipped black hair at the back of his head. Through his white button-down, the muscles of his chest asserted themselves firmly into mine. Both of us were shaven now, but the new smoothness of his face against mine only fed my eagerness to feel him and know him in each embodiment.

My tongue did not meet with his. He seemed almost to melt against me for a period of several seconds, exhaling fully, a tiny shiver creeping through his back. He placed his hand on my shoulder, stepped slowly away from me and said, "I'm sorry. Sophie could be back any time."

"It's fine. I understand."

"I wouldn't be embarrassed," he said. "Not really. She

knows now. I think I should be okay with her seeing. It's just that it would be a little awkward."

"You don't have to explain. It's okay, Mikey."

He smiled. "Man, this is still all so new to me."

"I know."

He paused. "Will there be drinking tonight? Maybe dancing?"

"Both are very likely," I said. "Does that work for you?"

"I think it will be good for me." He sat on the edge of his desk and looked down at his shoes. "I'm a little nervous to meet your friends," he said quietly.

"You don't have to worry. They're really nice. It's just two of them—Marie and Sloan. They'll be glad to meet you."

"You're sure? I feel like I'm barging in on your personal life a little."

"You're not, I promise. That's not how it feels to me, okay?"

"Okay," he said. "And you and me—when you introduce me, I mean…we're just…"

"We're friends. You're my friend, Mikey."

He looked relieved. "Alright. Sorry. I know, I'm overthinking things. I always do that."

"Yes," I said. "Me too. I'm trying not to."

"It's hard, isn't it?"

"Fucking impossible."

He laughed a little, then reached out and grabbed my arm. "What's going on under this suit?" he asked, grabbing my bicep firmly in his hand.

"I would really like to show you," I said.

"Oh, man," he said. "Fuck, it's been so long. You'll have free time this weekend, right?"

"I've got plenty of time. You just focus on work right now. I'll be around. We can spend the weekend together if that's what you want."

"That's pretty much what I want."

"Then I'm yours," I said, and told him I should get going. "Text me when you can meet us, okay?"

"Alright, I will."

We said our goodbyes and I left him alone to work. The elevator door opened up to the lobby, where Sophie stood waiting.

"Wyatt," she said in near-alarm, "how nice to see you again."

"You too," I said, moving in a half-circle around her as we traded spaces.

She held the door open with her elbow, juggling her purse, cup of coffee and a sack of takeout that smelled like Thai food, although I couldn't tell for sure. "You must not have stayed for very long. I didn't think I'd miss you."

"No I didn't. But I'm sure I'll see you again soon."

"Yes," she stammered as the door attempted again to close. "See you soon."

I descended the building's steps to the street, noting that I had over ninety minutes to burn. Somewhat absentmindedly I headed east, bound for Chinatown, which lay just south of Old Town, where we had agreed to meet. During the first part of my journey the rays of the setting sun permeated the street and reflected in magnificent golds and oranges off the mirroring immensities facing back toward sea. Twenty minutes later, and most of the way to my hazy destination, this soothing glow was all but gone, and the accompanying warmth went away with it. I lifted my coat up onto my back, buttoned it slowly as I walked and then folded my arms. The vibrant, imposing Chinatown gate passed steadily over me not long after.

Beneath the veneer of unfurling, pagoda-like architectural

embellishments and strings of zigzagging paper lanterns, the street level teemed with stores and small shops selling practical items and excellent food. Off the main street, wedged in one of the narrow connecting vessels rested my preferred haven, a small bao shop which sold, among other things, handmade dessert buns filled with lai wong (or nai wong, Sloan contended), a sweet, eggy condensed-milk paste. I ducked between produce stands, which remained open past regular hours at the end of the week, and into the passage. The shop owner greeted me warmly and I indulged, exchanging a small stray bill and some change for three of the buns.

Jumbled against the edge of the alley was a tiny scrap-wood table with a cluster of threadbare chairs chained to it. Taking my seat, I noticed two vertically-oriented signs flickering separately above, one yellow and one green, so that the cold dark was scared off by a kind of inconsistent lime-flavored glow. Even this small open space between buildings bustled in the heat of the day; I'd seen it before with my own eyes, but now it was mostly abandoned. A hunched-over elderly woman wearing dirty clothes and a small ragged blanket moved incrementally over the clattering bricks, pulling a creaking, rusty cart behind her, moderately burdened with what might have been all of her possessions. As she passed close to me I held out one of the buns. She took it silently, her face lit by the green, and one side of her mouth curled up.

I sat for what felt like a long time. The shop owner stepped outside to smoke and asked where I was from. He looked surprised upon hearing that I lived in Corbin.

"You'll get your clothes dirty from sitting out here," he said.

I told him it was okay and watched him take a long, final drag, the ember screaming less than an inch from his lips. He quickly stamped it out as thick silver smoke streamed from his face, then went back inside without another word.

I watched the smoke rise up one floor, then perhaps two, until I imagined more than I saw. It crept past shuttered windows, hung momentarily under the eaves four floors up, then leaked into the night sky, dissipating by way of a slow breeze.

Otherwise I languished inside my phone, tumbling through travel blogs and social media. Not long before eight I headed north, passing through a block or two of displaced people. I was solicited twice by drug users, both searching for information. One asked how late the train ran; I told him it ran all night. The other, a rail-thin, frantic woman, sought a nearby bookstore; I said I was sorry but I didn't know of any in the area.

Even—or perhaps especially—the parts of the city that many viewed as unfavorable held an unwavering goodness, of which I was made distinctly aware tonight. As I entered the much busier Old Town I was struck with the feeling that I couldn't stand to move away from such a city. Like a fresh wound, raw and exposed, my emotional state suddenly surged with pain. I cried silently but openly as I walked. Then my mind began making frantic reparations; everything hardened quickly over and I straightened up. My face cold and damp, I blinked a few times, feeling extremely out of place in the wake of this brief but bizarre upheaval. I wiped at my eyes with the backs of my hands, glancing around suspiciously, looking for anyone who might have seen, and believing, for some reason, that it mattered.

I gradually looked past knots of people as I edged closer to the harbor, admiring instead the relative permanence of brick and stone, sustaining itself not because of anything I did or did not choose, but exactly in spite of it. Stephanie had relayed, some time ago now, that I should take care not to approach each challenge I faced with indiscriminate urgency. It was that specific tendency which I suspected had presently taken me over. I wasn't leaving now. Even next week I would still be here. And tonight my experience would be a shared one; serendipity towed me closer yet to three people whose impacts lifted me considerably—in particular, Mikey's. I ached for every single encounter. I took in the prosperous energy of awaiting events as a symbol of my good fortune. I knew immediately that no matter my angle of observation, life was brimming, and I had so much to look forward to.

15

Any lost composure had been regained by the time I arrived outside the pub—a good thing, because although I was a few minutes early, Sloan crept up beside me almost immediately.

"Wyatt, buddy, how's things?" he asked, grasping my hand firmly and pulling me close.

"Pretty good, and you?" We framed ourselves against the brick exterior so as not to block the narrow sidewalk.

"Not too bad. Same as last time we saw each other, I guess."

I indicated toward the pub's entrance and said, "Same place."

"Same fucking place, dude. We're an exciting bunch, let me tell you."

We both laughed at this. I had always been a bit taken with Sloan's presence. All told, he wasn't much taller than Marie, and surefooted in every meaning of the word. He possessed a stockiness not only self-described, but from which he derived a sense of personal pride. It felt good to be with him again.

"Marie tells me that we're meeting your man tonight."

"Is there some message thread I'm not a part of or something? Word sure gets around."

He laughed and smacked the wall with an open hand. "Well, hers and mine, I guess."

"Oh, right. Anyway, he's just a friend, and I think you'll like him, Sloan. He's a really good guy."

"If it's the Mikey I'm thinking of, then I already know him."

"Wait…oh, fuck. High school, right?"

He nodded.

"Sorry, I totally forgot you went to Brighton."

"It's okay. I don't talk about it much," he said. "Not too many fond memories from that age."

I smiled. "He even said he was a Bengal. I'm just surprised you never came to mind."

Sloan shrugged. "Yeah, when I saw his picture on your phone he looked familiar to me. But I didn't think much of it until Marie said his name."

"Crazy," I said. The temptation became too great and I asked, "Do you remember anything about him?"

He grinned. "Well, the fact that I remember him at all should tell you he was popular. I didn't give a shit about people in high school. But he was a pretty prominent guy." He paused, eyeing me a little.

"What?"

"You're loving this, aren't you?"

"You got me," I said. "Obviously I'm obsessed with him. Stop teasing me."

"Okay, okay. Honestly, it's not like I ever talked to him. Not to mention he was a grade up. He was a jock. He was rowdy and annoying in the halls just like the rest of the jocks. Let me think…he was a lot skinnier. Like…tall but—I don't know—scrawny. If that picture is actually him then the guy's really bulked up. Good for him. Man, I'm putting myself to sleep with this shit."

I laughed. "Don't hurt yourself. I just wanted to know if he was a nice guy."

"I don't remember. But I don't think it matters. People

change a lot after high school."

"They really do," I said.

"You could have gotten a table," said Marie after nearly blasting past both of us. She grabbed our wrists and pulled us toward the door, letting go only as her purse slipped down from her shoulder and into the crook of her arm. "Whoops. Got to keep my moneybag secure, seeing as tonight is on me."

"Only it's not on you," I protested as we stepped inside.

"That's what you think," she said. "Is this table okay with everyone?"

Marie ordered us a pitcher and we took it in gradually; she claimed two full glasses for herself, which was only fair. "I think," she declared as she poured the second, "that we should consider a direct flight to Bangkok, or maybe Saigon. Then we can hop around as we please."

I nodded. "Flights to Bangkok aren't bad. But Seoul is cheaper. We're still doing Seoul, right?"

"Well, if price is the biggest factor, then we should go straight to Taipei," she said. "I'm just stuck on Thailand and Vietnam. I could literally spend the whole month in only those two countries. And yes, we can do Korea. I'm just being selfish because I've already been. Several times."

"If we go to Seoul, it would help a lot that you speak Korean," said Sloan.

"Are we going to Hong Kong, too, Sloan?" she asked, poking a finger at him. "When exactly do we get to take advantage of your Cantonese?"

"I hope we're going to Hong Kong," I said.

"Everyone speaks English in Hong Kong," said Sloan.

She shook her head. "Nope. That's not true."

"Fine. But a lot more than in Korea."

I placed my hands flat on the table. "Let's just assume we're going to have issues communicating in most places. I mean, none of us speaks Thai or Vietnamese, right?"

"True," said Marie. "So it sounds to me like we're talking about more countries and shorter stays. That's okay with me. It'll also be more expensive, but I really do think it's the way to go."

"No matter how you slice it, it's cheaper than Europe," said Sloan.

"Very true," I said, taking comfort in the fact.

We launched into a discussion concerning the solidification of flights. It was settled that we would first fly nonstop to Taipei, explore for a few days and then depart for Bangkok.

Marie snatched up her phone and began taking notes. "Cheap is good for the long flight," she declared. "I'm on board with that now."

"I've always wanted to visit Taiwan," said Sloan, wearing a dreamy expression.

For another half-hour we continued chipping away at a vague order of events.

"I would feel better saving some more money before booking flights," Sloan confessed.

"Thank you," I said.

"Totally fine," said Marie. "It's too early to book anyway. And we need more time to let the plan sink in. We'll reconvene—oh," she said, turning to me with an injured expression, "we'll have to meet up online, if you're away."

"That's fine," I said. "Yes, I'll be gone by the time we book flights. It's okay."

She continued looking at me, her eyes narrowing in casual suspicion. "It's not okay, but we'll deal."

"That's right," said Sloan. "We'll deal. The good thing is that we're guaranteed a month with you this summer."

"Exactly," I said.

Sloan's words seemed to have chased off any of Marie's immediate concerns. She smiled and began waving vigorously until she had obtained the attention of a server. "Can we do shots?" she asked, once he arrived at the table.

I was unsure whether the question was meant for us or for the tired-eyed employee who stood patiently at my left. "If you're buying," I said.

"Tequila?" she pleaded.

"No," said Sloan.

"Fine. Whiskey it is." She turned to the server. "Just the house stuff, if you please. I am a working girl."

He nodded and left for the bar.

My phone rang in my pocket and Marie gasped. "Is he coming? Should I order another?"

"I don't know," I said, fishing it out. "Hold on."

Mikey's voice greeted me through the earpiece. "Just wanted to make sure you guys are still there. I'm like ten minutes away."

"Yes, we're still here—hey, have we ever spoken on the phone before? This feels weird."

His laugh crackled through. "I felt like being old-fashioned. Also I tried texting but almost walked into a pole."

"Whoa. Be careful out there."

We said goodbye and I resurfaced to find that Marie had ordered another shot for Mikey.

"I don't know if he does shots," I told her.

"If he doesn't, I am confident I can change that." She began to stare me down, eyes wide. I started laughing but still she did not break.

"Okay," I said. "I'm confident you can, too. Please, just stop that right now."

"You're kind of terrifying," added Sloan.

In the coming minutes I realized how fortunate I was to be facing the door. My positioning made stolen glances toward it less detectable, which permitted a successful masking of my general disquiet as I awaited Mikey's emergence. When it finally did occur, he scanned the interior briefly before his eyes fell squarely on me. The building's supporting beams hung low; his height was apparent as ever and he carried an unlikely air of nervousness—although this seemed to be fading presently by the second. His tie was gone, the top two buttons of his pale blue shirt undone. The shirt itself was untucked. He carried his coat as he approached and hung it on the chair next to me.

I stood as he arrived and introduced him to Marie and Sloan, who also stood and shook his hand across the table.

Marie said nothing except for her name. She spent the next moment in what was, to me, a shocking state of repose.

"I think I know you," said Sloan, once we had reclaimed our seats. "I graduated from Brighton in 2011."

"Right, okay," said Mikey. "I was 2010. Hey, were you by any chance a year ahead in math?"

Sloan grinned. "Mr. Huang. Yes. You were definitely in that class. I remember because he would post grades—"

"And we kept swapping spots, right?"

Sloan all but lunged forward. "Yes. That was you? Shit, man, you're kidding."

Marie broke her curious silence. "What, like a ranking?"

Sloan nodded. "Yeah, and he would use our student IDs, but I mean, fuck, everyone knew who the top ones were."

"And that was you guys," she said.

Mikey grinned shyly. "Right."

"And who ended up getting first?" I asked.

Mikey pointed silently across the table.

"Come on, Sloan. You never told me you were a year ahead in high school math," said Marie. "And the top student, no less."

He shrugged.

Mikey cleared his throat and said, "Your hair used to be longer, right?"

Sloan laughed. "Yes, my hair was longer."

"Sloan identifies as a man now," Marie clarified.

"Cool," said Mikey. He paused, glanced toward me, then added, "I know I've learned a lot about myself since high school."

"Wyatt and I were just saying that earlier," said Sloan. "I think it's true for everyone. There are a lot of discoveries to be made."

Mikey gestured toward the four shots, squared up at the center of the table. "What are these doing here?"

"They're for you," said Marie. "It's sort of an initiation thing. We all had to do it."

Mikey smiled cautiously at Marie. "Are you sure we're not sharing them?"

I reached for mine. "She's just giving you a hard time."

Marie stuck out her tongue at me and raised up the tiny glass. "To self-discovery."

Each of us tossed one back, and a short time later, Marie appeared to have warmed to Mikey considerably. She smacked her phone down on the table and said, "You, my friend, have a little catching up to do."

Mikey indicated toward our empty pitcher. "I'll order another if you want."

"Let me," she insisted.

"No way," he said, quickly flagging down the server and pulling out his wallet.

As we waited for our next round, Marie leaned in toward Mikey. "Wyatt here says you are fluent in Thai."

"I grew up speaking it at home."

She nodded. "And would you care to join us on a trip to Bangkok and beyond?"

Mikey shot me a quick glance, then asked, "How do you know I'd be a good travel companion? We just met, after all."

"I'll take Wyatt's word for it."

I cleared my throat. "I never said anything about whether he'd be a good travel companion."

She heaved her purse up onto her lap and began to rummage through it. "You just take some time to think about it, Mikey."

"Okay," he said, laughing quietly.

"Behold," she said. "I've got to keep these lips soft. You never know what the night has in store." As she applied the balm she cast an ominous look around the table.

Sloan's hand beckoned for it and she passed it to him.

Much of the newest supply of beer was deflected toward Mikey, who gave in only because he had paid for it and because, I suspected, he saw that there was indeed catching up to do. He fielded several meat-and-potatoes questions from Marie, and one or two more once Sloan could get a word in. He handled both the inquisition and the alcohol handsomely, the former possibly aided by the latter.

The entire time I felt the subject of his parents swim just below the pine surface of the table, and just as I thought it had sunk out of reach, Sloan said, "Your folks are still in Corbin, then?"

"They're gone," said Mikey. A speck of hesitation followed. "But it's okay."

Neither Marie nor Sloan asked for any clarification. Sloan

sat back slightly and said, "Sorry about that."

Mikey offered a subtle raising of his glass and drank. Each of us did the same. The moment was somber but short-lived, and five minutes later we had forgotten about it entirely.

"Give it back," Sloan was wailing to Marie, who had stolen his phone as punishment after he suggested she would be a terrible driver. "Please, give it back." He reached aggressively for it and she held it tightly against her chest. They both laughed wildly, but neither was ready to back down.

"No. Say you're sorry."

"Fine, I'm sorry."

Slowly she released her grip and he snatched it away, lifting the device above his head and waving it like a prize. After pocketing it he said, "All I meant was that I couldn't picture you behind the wheel."

"That's not how you put it."

"Alright. Fair enough. That's how I should have put it."

"It still sounds mean. You'd better dance with me at length tonight, and not disappear with another lady-friend like you did last time."

"I'll stay with you. Or better yet, I'll find you someone to disappear with instead. How's that sound?"

Marie appeared genuinely hopeful. "That sounds nice. Look," she said, gesturing over at Mikey, "we're boring the new guy to death."

Mikey laughed. "Fuck, I'm just enjoying the show."

She smiled warmly at him. "You're a very good sport. Come on, everyone, time to get out of here."

Marie and Sloan walked ten feet ahead, leaving Mikey and me momentarily on our own.

I turned to him after we had pressed through a crowd outside an adjacent bar. "So, can Mikey dance? That's what I want to know right now."

He stumbled playfully a few steps ahead of me, covering his face with his hands. "No, Mikey cannot dance. I'm terrified."

"That was a trick question. Everybody can."

"Shut up. That's not even technically true."

"Oh, I agree that it's not technically true. But through one's own personal definition of dancing—"

"Stop." He held up his hand. "I know what you're going to say, and I hate it already. There must be some kind of public consensus over what is good dancing and what isn't. I've hardly danced since high school. I know my limitations."

"You know what? Fuck public consensus. Fuck all of that. I'm going to think you're fucking great, no matter what." I hung back for a moment, concerned that this concoction of words had solidified, for all the world to see, my state of insobriety.

Mikey just regarded me in silence for a second before throwing his arms around my torso, clasping his hands just below my shoulder. We continued precariously forward as he planted an instantaneous kiss on my cheek. There was the slightest wetness to it, for which he apologized, wiping at the spot with his thumb.

"Leave it there," I insisted.

He backed away and we returned together to our stride, hands in pockets, as if nothing had happened.

"I missed you, too," he said.

"What?"

"Earlier, at the office, you said you'd missed me. I'm saying that I missed you, too."

I offered him a smile and noticed a thick wave of black hair had slipped down almost to his eyes. I reached over and brushed it up out of the way. "I'm glad you left it long on top,"

I said.

"Really? I was thinking maybe it should have been shorter, like yours."

"You're wrong," I said. "Short is good for hair like mine, but black hair is just so...spectacular. It deserves some presence. The more the better."

"You know, some people don't like black hair."

"They're completely fucking crazy."

He laughed. "Hey, before I got mine cut it was getting long enough to put into a bun. I could have been like the guy from Mulan."

I shook my head. "You racist," I joked. "You're not even Chinese."

Mikey shrugged. "People tell me I look Chinese. Even Chinese people say that. Maybe I have some in my blood. A lot of Thais do."

"Yeah? Well the guy from Mulan is pretty attractive, now that I think about it."

"Oh, the dude's a total babe."

We hurried along to rejoin Marie and Sloan, who had just entered the line for the nightclub.

A courtesy storm raged between Mikey and Marie over paying for cover. I insisted on paying for myself, which would be the ultimate outcome for everyone. Ten minutes later our presence fell under a barrage of colorful, strobing lights and rhythmic pulsations, which dove immediately and unapologetically beneath my skin. I concluded that I must have been flat-out drunk by the beginning of our previous visit and this time retained my wits in greater number. That, or Mikey's presence boosted my awareness; he presently beamed at me and handed me a shot.

"This is for you," he said.

"Thank you." I took it from him and leaned in close so that he could hear. "What are you trying to do to me?"

He just raised his eyebrows. We drank them at once and joined Marie and Sloan on the dance floor. It became clear to me after only a few minutes that Mikey held his own in this unfamiliar setting. As he danced he was not rigid, nor was he self-conscious; he relaxed and allowed the music to pound through him. He lacked the skill and control of Sloan, the only person among us who had any formal training, but was easily on par with Marie and me. And more than anything else, he seemed to enjoy all of the activity immensely.

"Why the fuck don't I do this more often?" he yelled to me at one point.

I, in turn, fought to suppress moments of urgent attraction. This particular club was no stranger to the occasional shirt cast aside. Mikey made do with releasing another button on his own, totaling three from the top. He wore nothing underneath.

As the night carried on, Sloan and Marie stuck close, dancing on increasingly provocative grounds. So did many others in the club. We had since split two more rounds of shots, and as our gazes met again, I saw that Mikey's eyes now harbored a more persistent desire. When I looked con-spicuously down toward the exposed portion of his chest, he took my hand and brought it up against his skin. He was warm, damp with sweat. We danced against one another now, packed in among the crowd. This was new territory for Mikey—it was public, but our identities were scrapped among the club's wild mass of patrons. He ground himself hard against me at the waist. Cautiously, I rotated myself so that my back was to him. His lips landed repeatedly against my neck. He brought his arms around me, up, felt my chest, and again thrust his waist quietly, firmly into me. I felt his pressure against my backside recede.

He said into my ear that he needed to step outside and cool down, asking if I would come with him.

"Of course," I said.

The cold night air was an instant blast of relief. We had not bothered to retrieve our coats from the check, but I had worked up enough body heat to sustain me for some time. My ears felt like they had been jammed with cotton.

"Thanks," Mikey said to me. "It was getting a little too hot in there."

I was all but certain he spoke figuratively, or else had intended both meanings. I told him that I agreed.

"Fuck," he said. "Twelve-thirty. How late do you guys like to stay out?" He laid his words down deliberately, but they stepped slightly over one another.

I shrugged. "Until whenever. I'm ready to go any time." I noticed my own voice slurring as I spoke. "Let's get our coats."

"What about your friends?"

"Don't worry about them. They don't give a fuck, really."

"We should at least tell them we're going," he said.

"Right, we'll find them and then go to coat check."

This plan agreed with him and we stepped somewhat resentfully back into the hot and humid mess, pressing indelicately through until we had reached them. I told them we were ready to go and apologized for bailing.

"Go," yelled Marie, pointing drunkenly and with a slightly bent finger toward the door. "My god, look at you two. Young, healthy and both fit as fuck. How are you not fucking each other's brains out right this second? My mind is literally blown. Go," she repeated.

Sloan stood by with his arm around her shoulder, looking rather drunk himself, but he gave me a single small nod and a smile to indicate that the situation was under control.

Mikey tipped the person at coat check handsomely and once we were back outside, called for a taxi. "Let's indulge tonight. No messing with the bus. I think we'll miss the last one anyway."

At first, for whatever reason, we kept our distance in the back of the car. After a minute or two, Mikey turned to me and said, "Do you want to stay at my place tonight?"

"Yes."

"I just don't want you to feel trapped. I can give you money for the fare back to Corbin—"

"Mikey," I said, looking him up and down, "if it's okay, I just want to stay with you."

"Of course it's okay," he said.

So far the driver paid absolutely no attention to us at all, just listened to his radio and dug his foot deeply into the throttle each time a light turned green.

Mikey unbuckled his seatbelt and slid over to the middle seat, next to me. He laid his chin on my shoulder and spoke directly into my ear. His voice rose barely above a whisper. "What happened when we were dancing? At the end, I mean."

I felt myself grin. "You were sort of...taking me from behind."

He paused for a second. "I want to do that. If you're ready, I want to actually do it tonight."

Encased within myself, a warmth crept steadily over me and I had the sensation of sinking deeper and deeper into the cushion of the seat. I ran my hand along the ridge of his tight, weighty bicep. "When we get home," I whispered into his ear, "I want you inside me."

"Seatbelt, please," said the driver.

Mikey kept his eyes on me as he shrank back to his side of the car. Soon he became visibly resigned, obviously aware that he could not have what he wanted right at this moment. He eventually fell asleep, for about five minutes, waking as I directed the driver down his street. I wondered briefly if he had changed his mind, but as we climbed the stairs he said, "You're gonna have to guide me through this."

"Don't worry, I will," I said, very much still into the idea.

He had achieved some kind of second wind, pummeling the stairwell with his feet and stepping quite literally in circles around me. "I'm nervous, but like, I'm also not."

I laughed. "Actually, me too."

"I'm also kind of drunk," he said.

"Me too," I said. We entered his apartment and I told him I needed to step into the bathroom.

"Okay," he said.

I returned to him after less than a minute. "This is a good time for it," I told him. "I can tell."

He nodded silently.

I suspected that it was still an area of complete mystery for him. I detected a hint of concern in his expression, but it was easily outgunned by his expanding lust. He began to strip off his clothes and I hurried to keep up with him. We stood naked in front of one another, exposed and unrepentant. I had not seen him in this way for too long; his appearance, down to and past his rigid flesh, was jarring and beautiful. We immediately embraced. Our mouths were open and wet; we ran our hands over every reachable part of one another. Mikey sidestepped to his bed; I held tightly to his arm and let him tow me onto the covers.

"I have this lube," he said, tearing open the drawer of the nightstand. He turned over the bottle in his hand and looked at me a bit shyly. "I've been trying some things out."

I grinned. "Explain later," I said, throwing myself onto my

back.

We prepared ourselves quickly, during which Mikey leaned in twice to kiss me. "You're so beautiful," he said. "Stay on your back," he told me, "unless you really want me behind you. I want to be able to see your face."

"I'll stay where I am."

"Do you want me to use a condom? I know I'm clean, but I have some."

Before Mikey, and after my last relationship, condom use had been assumed in every one of my sexual encounters. But now I shook my head. "I know you're clean, too. Besides, I swallowed you already."

At a level somewhere below the surface, we seemed to mutually acknowledge the nature of our circumstance, and the subject was abandoned.

I spread my legs apart and made myself ready for him. I felt the solid mass of Mikey's cock against me.

"I can help guide it in if you want," I said.

"It's okay," he said slowly. "I think I can do it."

Sure enough, just as he finished speaking, he found the brink of me. He sunk at least half of his length into me. My body rang out in the wake of this shocking, abrupt intrusion. Beforehand, I had briefly considered asking him to be gentle and start slowly. After all, he was bigger than some, maybe most. But I longed for his playful energy and enthusiasm to extend, unencumbered, into this new terrain. I didn't chase after agony, but I also did not want him to restrain himself— not even a little. The pain now flooded me, but this was Mikey, and after another few seconds, it was all of him.

"Oh my god," he said. "It's really tight. Does it hurt you?"

"It feels incredible," I said.

He flashed a broad smile, teeth visible in the blue light from the window. "Fuck. I can't believe this is happening." He pulled out to around half his length, then thrust himself all the way back in. "Fuck," he repeated. "This is the most amazing feeling."

"Keep going," I said to him. Tears surfaced at the outer corners of my eyes and descended in two tidy trails toward my ears. Thankfully, there wasn't enough light for him to see. It would not last.

As he began to thrust more aggressively, the pain fell to parity with a quickly rising tide of pleasure. Soon after, it left completely, and I swam only in elation.

Maybe the alcohol had numbed Mikey's senses to his benefit; this time he was in better control of his release. His arms straddled my torso and suspended him with little effort above me. He slowed up and looked down into my eyes. "Everything's okay?"

I nodded.

"I was about to finish," he said. "I had to slow down. I don't think I can put it off much longer."

"Don't," I said. "Let me know when you're about to. I'll finish when you finish."

"Think you'll be able to?"

Without hesitation, I nodded. "Just let it go inside me, okay?"

"Okay," he said. He started in again, slowly at first, gradually increasing his intensity. His expression moved from vague uncertainty to outright excitement. "Fuck, you're really liking this, aren't you?" he said.

My own mounting pleasure was clearly visible. "Don't stop," I said. The thickness of him spread me completely apart. I felt with odd precision the textures of his solidity moving along the outside edges of me. But each time his length reached the end of its inward travel, I felt him the most. I lost my senses completely in the depth at which he placed himself.

"It's about to happen," Mikey said. "It's happening."

I reach down to touch myself, but knew suddenly that such stimulation was not needed. I began to climax at once.

He bucked against me in pronounced release, no longer pulling back at all, just reaffirming his entire length again and again until he finally subsided. His face beat down at me, flushed and damp. Very slowly, he left me. He moved back and knelt before me as if waiting for further instruction.

"Mikey," I said. "That was really good."

"Did I hurt you?"

"No," I assured him. "You didn't hurt me at all."

"Do you need to use the bathroom now?"

"Yes," I said. I left him alone on the bed, where he lay back on a pillow, naked and still hard, hands behind his head.

I invited him to shower off with me. We grabbed at each other playfully as we soaped up, then stood close under the hot downpour. Mikey swayed with exhaustion. I don't think a word was shared between us after we brushed our teeth and slid together beneath the covers. He faced me and I faced him. Our hands landed upon one another's between us, amassing into a small pile. Mikey fell asleep immediately, and soon after, I followed.

16

Mikey's hands covered his face after he propped himself up against the headboard the next morning. Out the window, his building cast a commanding shadow across the street and halfway up the next row of structures. Otherwise, the sun shone new and bright, completely unimpeded.

"Oh, god," he said into his palms. "Last night. I can't believe we did that." He removed his hands, confirming what I had suspected to be his familiar coy smile—which I was relieved to see.

I lifted the comforter over my face, feigning embarrassment. "I know. You really laid into me."

"Oh, god," he repeated. "Okay. So it's happened. You're feeling okay about it?"

Mentally, I surveyed myself. "A little sore already," I conceded. "But that's nothing to be upset about."

"Jesus. So…one gets sore, then, after that."

I nodded, still undercover. "Yes, Mikey, one gets sore."

He tore the comforter down off my face and I grinned up at him. "Okay," he said. "Just making sure you were into it."

"Into it? I was at least halfway responsible for it. Probably more than half."

"Okay," he said again. "I don't mean to dwell on it. I just didn't want to spend the whole day wondering."

"I understand. And I'm happy to dwell on it. I mean, fuck, you completely plowed me."

"Stop," he said.

"I'm serious. I could think about it all day."

His face flushed slightly with embarrassment. He rolled halfway on top of me and placed his hand over my mouth. "Another subject, please."

I pulled it off, down to my chest. The thought came to me suddenly. "Say something to me in Thai."

"No," he said. "Thai is an ugly language."

I pushed him off of me. "No it's not. How could you say that?"

"What? It's all nasal and whiny. I don't like using it except with family."

"It only sounds that way to people who don't understand it."

"Oh, and you understand it?"

I paused. "No, but I understand that it's an entire language that can communicate everything about how someone feels in life. Love, sadness—I don't know—regret, fear, joy, just… everything."

Mikey fell silent. The corners of his mouth turned up, as if he was determined not to smile. It all amounted to something akin to admiration. He sighed. "Maybe sometime, Chickadee." His words sank with finality.

"Okay," I said.

Mikey cooked eggs for breakfast and I poured us both some cereal.

"It's warm out," he said, staring wide-eyed down at his phone as we began to eat. "That changed fast. We should walk by the water."

"The levee or the seawall?"

"I want to go to the levee. Maybe farther south again, where we were before. We could stop by your place first, if you want."

"Sure," I said. "I can grab my running shoes. It would be nice to change clothes, too."

"Alright, yeah, let's run. I'm going to be slow, though."

"Yeah right," I said.

Each of us also chugged down a fair amount of water. He told me he felt a slight headache, which he attributed to last night's nontrivial degree of consumption. I remarked that I felt good as new, which surprised me.

Mikey hustled his Honda down the street, around a few corners and out to the highway.

"Shit, I forgot what a sunny day looked like," he said to me.

"I hope it's here to stay," I said. "Where I'm headed, it doesn't get warm until May or June."

"That's terrible. That's, like, a sin or something."

I just nodded.

As we climbed the rickety stairwell to my unit, Mikey said, "I haven't been here in a while. We should really spend more time here."

"Anytime you want," I said. We entered and he waited by the door as I went over to my dresser.

"You can sit down if you want. I don't mind shoes on the rug."

He shook his head. "My mom will haunt me if I do that. She was always very strict about it."

"Mine, too, actually. She shamed little-Wyatt many times over it. But I guess it had its intended effect," I said, indicating down at my shoeless feet.

"Aww." He laughed. "Poor little-Wyatt."

I went into the bathroom and changed into fresh underwear, a t-shirt and running shorts. I mulled over the fact that he had just spoken my given name. Actually, I had turned my name into a phrase, which he had then repeated. This reduced the significance a great deal. But I had felt slightly odd—disarmed, truthfully—in the seconds after he said it.

"Does your mom haunt you often?" I asked once we were back in the car and continued to the levee.

He laughed dismissively. "No. She's gone. They're both gone. I don't actually believe in that kind of thing."

"Alright," I said.

"Should we drive down Paradise again?"

I shook my head. "You can just stay on this road. It'll hit the levee, too. Then we can run south to where Paradise ends. We can even go back to that little beach, if you want."

He said the idea sounded good to him and continued straight on. Soon, he tore up onto the small gravel lot. We grabbed our water bottles and left the car behind. We ran in t-shirts, but had each brought along zippered, hooded jackets. His was similar to my own, although instead of black, it sang out in a deep royal blue. He slung it over his neck; I folded mine over my arm.

About a quarter of a mile down the trail, Mikey said, "I really liked meeting your friends last night."

"Yeah? I didn't really know what you would think of them."

"I thought they were great. I guess I did sort of know Sloan already. He seemed really put-together. And Marie…she had a lot of energy."

"She's a big personality," I told him.

"But I like that," he said. "She's a little like Sophie, I guess. Says what's on her mind."

"That's true. They are a little bit similar."

He laughed. "So, about that trip to Asia…"

"Mikey, I think she was joking. I have no clue. Anyway,

she's not expecting an answer."

"I figured," he said. "It sounds like a lot of fun, though. I'm so happy you'll get to travel again."

I told him that I was, too. "Honestly, everything is seeming a little...I don't know. A little up in the air right now. Everything about my life. It's not the greatest feeling."

"You have a lot going on," he said in a faraway voice. "Are you saying the trip is contributing to that feeling?"

"No, sorry. It's the opposite. What I mean is that the trip is something I can count on. It's one of the only things right now that I know I can, like, expect to happen, you know? I sort of know what's happening. I know what I'm doing. I know when I'm doing it."

We moved along steadily, our feet crunching into the gravel.

"I get that. So it's more than just something you're looking forward to."

"Right," I said.

The run to the end of Paradise Highway required only twenty minutes. We both agreed that we hadn't waited long enough after eating and our stomachs complained accordingly.

"Let's stop," Mikey concluded, halting at the crest of a small ridge in the trail, where the highway was capped off to the left. "Look. It's our little pathway."

I nodded. "Not so scary this time, right?"

"No," he said, whipping his sweatshirt toward me in retaliation. "I'll even lead the way."

He did so in his own relentlessly charming manner, pretending to hack away at intervening branches with an invisible machete, conjuring the associated sounds with his mouth.

"You're in my way," I whined, bumping playfully into him, letting my cheek thud softly against the cotton covering his sweaty shoulder blade.

"Stay behind me," he said. "It's not fit for you out here."

I forced my way past, laughing, tearing down the remainder of the pathway with Mikey close behind.

Out on the sand there was evidence of a small gathering that had occurred the night before. A ring of rocks, their inside surfaces blackened, sheltered a pile of soot and embers that still barely smoldered. The exposed fuselage of a half-burned beer can lay near the edge. I had wanted to believe that no one else knew of this location; I couldn't remember encountering a single soul when my dad would bring me here years ago. My naive glorification of the place felt silly to me now and fell quietly away, without feeling. At least we were alone today.

"People are such slobs," said Mikey, collecting a few un-burned cans that lay scattered and chucking them into the pit.

I felt hot and let my sweatshirt fall onto the dry, gritty sand. I took off my t-shirt and drank about half of the water in my bottle. "We didn't bring sunscreen," I said. "But I can't believe I'm even talking about it in March."

Mikey shrugged. "To tell you the truth, I want to get some sun. Maybe even a little burn."

I pretended to gasp. "Never let my mom hear you say that. She's like sunscreen's ambassador to the world. Cancer will consume us all."

He grinned. "She's probably right. But what can be done?" He stole a quick glance down at my bare chest and stripped off his own t-shirt. He lifted his water bottle to his mouth and tossed his head back, taking in a good amount. "Jesus," he said, "is it actually hot out today? Can we call this hot?"

"It's partly the running, I think. But I'll take what I can get. Let's call it hot."

"That means we can swim," he reasoned, stepping over to the edge of the water and allowing the tiny tide to rush over his feet. "Fuck, it's a little cold."

I came to his side, testing it for myself. "It's not so bad."

Mikey took down his shorts and cast them back behind him. His black briefs were snugged against the tops of his thighs. He looked over at me. "Are you a good swimmer?"

"Not especially. I can get by, though." I paused. "I'm sure you were on swim team or something."

"I was, actually."

I laughed. "You're such a jock."

"Maybe," he admitted. "Not a dumb jock, though." He then dashed into the ocean, finding himself immediately up to his chest. "Oh, fuck. It's definitely cold. And deep. Fuck."

"The shore's not very gradual here," I explained, tentatively taking down my own shorts.

"No shit," he said. He went out a little farther, to where he could no longer touch the bottom, then bobbed silently, expectantly, in the few still seconds before I threw myself in.

"It is cold," I said, splashing my way out to him. "But I was so hot."

"I was, too. It actually feels pretty nice. And I'm adjusting to it." He swam out away from shore.

I trailed him. For a while we splashed at each other, laughing and playing around. Mikey dove under for several seconds and then resurfaced with a hulking piece of seaweed draped over his neck. At first he howled in surprise, unsure of what it was, then yelled, "Get it off," and flung it in my direction. I ducked under to avoid it.

"There's a little current here," he said. "Can you feel it? It's moving north. Look." He pointed to our beach, which had shifted a small distance south of us.

I told him I could feel it.

"You're not a bad swimmer at all," he said.

The sun beat down on us, reaching even the tanned surface of his scalp, visible only as a thin line in the parting of his soaked black hair.

I said nothing and continued out toward the unreachable enormity of a container ship. It was a frozen black wall, below which a massive band of red rose just above the level of the water. I kept swimming for a short time, caught up in the notion that I was, in my own minuscule way, bringing myself closer to it.

Mikey came out almost to me. He suspended himself about fifteen feet closer to shore and perhaps one-tenth the distance to the beach, which now lay decidedly southeast. "You and your ships," he said.

I just smiled back at him.

"I'm cold now," he said. "Are you ready to go in?"

"Sure."

As we began to make our way, the distance between us quickly lengthened. Unquestionably, Mikey was a much stronger swimmer than I was. I identified a new challenge in that the current moved not only steadily north, but also slowly out, away from shore. It was enough to noticeably burden my forward progress. I wondered if my considerable distance from land had increased the strength of this outward pull. In fact, I couldn't tell if I had moved closer at all, and was astonished by how quickly Mikey pulled ahead.

I knew suddenly, with a terrifying sense of inevitability, that the shore grew more distant. I swam harder. This was, I thought, exactly the kind of thing I read about on my phone, in the morning at the back of the 40A. People just floated out like driftwood and didn't come back. The water looks safe, but it's not. Stay out of the water. I assumed they referred to the frigid gray soup along the north wall, close to the harbor. Was it true here, too? This far from shore, it probably was.

Achieving the requisite deep breaths became almost impossible to me now; several times, I drew in only a small amount of air before panic clamped my throat shut. Was he even capable of coming back for me? What if he only had enough strength left to get himself to shore? Finally I yelled out his name. "I can't make it," I told him, finding it painfully difficult to speak. Another few seconds passed before I could say, "Mikey, this is bad."

He said nothing and swam immediately back toward me. I heard myself make odd, new struggling sounds as I waited, just trying to hold my place in the water. Mikey's body cut like a blade through it. He reached me more quickly than I would have ever thought possible.

"It's okay," he said. "Don't worry. This isn't a big deal. Just hold my hand and swim with me, okay?"

I nodded silently and his hand tightened around my own. We swam together but I felt like little more than dead weight behind him.

"Let's just go with the north current, okay? We'll walk back down the shore."

"Okay," came my shaky voice. In that moment, Mikey was a force. It seemed I was dragged along by something much more massive, more powerful than his own body. But it was him, and in relation, I felt very small.

Through frustratingly little effort of my own, the distance to shore gradually diminished by half, and then half again.

"You've got this," Mikey said. He let go of my hand. "You're doing great."

I moved alongside him now. He held back, waiting for me; I could tell. I would have preferred it if he hadn't. He had told me he was cold, that he had wanted to return to land. I was disgusted with myself. Why should he have to remain longer in the water just because of my stupidity?

As we picked our way along the shore, occasionally stepping back into the shallows to circumvent batches of foliage, I told Mikey I was sorry.

He turned to me in genuine surprise. "What the hell are you sorry for?"

"You shouldn't have to watch over me like that."

He was quiet for a second, and then said, "We both kind of watch over each other. It's fine."

We arrived back at the beach in little time and sat close in the sand, still in our underwear. Not yet quite at rest, we breathed steadily together, in and out.

I felt more grateful for the sun in that moment than I had been in a very long time. But my gratitude for the unconcerned monument sitting next to me was something else. At first, after I had calmed down a bit, I couldn't think of a single thing to say to him. Eventually I said, "I guess I won't apologize. But you don't know how lucky I am that you were there. If I had been alone…I can't think about it." I turned to him. "Thank you."

He spread his knees slightly apart and smiled down at the sandy earth between them. "You would've made it."

I paused. "I really don't think so, Mikey."

"You were panicking," he said. "It's okay."

"Yeah, I was. And what if you hadn't been there?"

"You don't have to worry about it," he said. "That's just not how it happened."

Something about the way he stated this—maybe it was his shoulders lifting slightly, or his voice's stony descent—told me that every part of him was confident in this answer. Even if his logic had been unsound, I would have left it alone.

I scooted myself closer to him. Our shoulders pressed together. "Would you like to stay over at my place tonight?"

"I was hoping you would ask," he said.

"I thought so. I saw you put your toothbrush in your bag."

He laughed. "I just like to be prepared. Got any good movies?"

"A few," I said.

As we trudged back north along the trail, Mikey situated his blue jacket over his shoulders and zipped it to his neck. "Damn. It's not quite summer yet." A strong breeze had kicked up, and blew directly south.

"No," I said, putting on my own. "Not even close."

"Have you done any writing lately?"

"What do you think?" I asked.

He laughed. "That's exactly what you said last time I asked."

I didn't doubt it. He seemed never to lose interest in the topic, and by now I owed him something better than brief shreds of compliance. "If I were to start again," I asked, "what do you think I should write about?"

He dedicated himself to a careful response, not speaking for a while as we continued along. "Honestly?" he said. "I would want you to pick up right where you left off. With Cheryl, or whoever."

I laughed. "Charlotte."

"Exactly. Charlotte's got a big choice, right?"

"Yeah," I said. "She does."

We walked the remaining distance to the car without saying much. However, the car ride back livened things; we brought our windows down and Mikey turned up the stereo. As usual he drove quickly, which I had grown accustomed to and presently found exciting. By the time he pulled along the curb outside my building, I felt much lighter.

Sunlight filtered in through broken-out sections in the blinds behind my couch. The slivery shafts of light grasped for the surface of the coffee table, and swam with bits of dust. I tilted the blinds open and drew them to the ceiling, then slid open the broad glass pane. I did the same with the smaller window across the room, close to my bed. My home became suddenly brighter, fresher than it had been in a long time. For the first time since setting a move-out date with the landlord, I felt like I might miss it, just a little.

"This place feels different," said Mikey. "I can't believe it's the same place I came to that first night. I don't know why…it just feels different now."

We sat together on the couch.

"I can't believe it was only a month ago," I said.

"Wow, yeah," he said. "I wish I could say it's been…I don't know. I guess I want to believe I've known you longer than that."

"I know what you mean. I feel that way, too."

He propped his feet up on the table and frowned at them. "We don't have a lot of memories together. It feels like we do sometimes, but we don't."

"No," I said. "I know."

"Maybe it's because I remember you from before we ever talked."

"You do?"

"Yes," he said. His voice retreated a little. "Many times, before you ever talked to me. I just thought you were attractive. I wondered what you were like. And that first day you sat next to me, I thought, 'This is it. Here he is.'"

"No way," I said. That was my experience, not Mikey's. It couldn't have been his.

"I'm dead serious," he continued. "And when you spoke to me, that's when I decided maybe you had noticed me before, too."

"I had, Mikey. So many times."

"See?" he said. "I knew it. That counts for something, right?"

"I think it does."

He glanced around the apartment. "I don't know if you could tell, but I was pretty terrified that first night here."

"I had no idea."

He nodded. "It's true. I didn't know what you were expecting. And I didn't know what the fuck I was looking for."

I laughed. "I wish you could have known how lucky I felt. I had really built you up in my mind. Then suddenly you were sitting here in my shitty apartment."

He looked at me. "Have I lived up to your expectations?"

"I don't know," I said playfully. "Time will tell, I guess."

"Well, shit, I don't have much longer to convince you." He slid himself closer to me and pushed me over onto my side.

I let it happen. He came crawling over me until his face was level with mine. He lowered himself and began to kiss me. I felt his hair fall lightly against my forehead. Our mouths did not open fully; his tongue prodded gently into mine as I felt at his chest through his shirt. After a moment he stopped, lifting himself a little. "Want to shower off together?" he asked.

I made to take off my shirt and he sat up. We stripped off our clothes until we were once again down to our underwear, which was still damp with saltwater. We moved quietly to the bathroom, where I tore back the curtain and got the water running. We stepped out of our underwear, watching one another. Mikey was becoming hard, and moved toward me. He kissed me once more, pulling me close to him at the waist before we parted and ducked under the hot stream, closing ourselves in behind the curtain. He let it cascade over his hair, which stuck out at odd angles like frayed black wires after having dried freely in the wind and sun. It flatted quickly, after which the water came streaming down over his face and his stretched, grinning lips. I put a hand on each side of his head, over his ears, and brought him to me, kissing him gently. The water ran satisfyingly hot, tumbling over and between us. Mikey kissed me harder, pulling me very tightly against him, as if something were at stake in this moment, as if I might disappear if he didn't.

Once he let up, we stepped slightly out of the stream. We were both completely hard, and reached down together, feeling ourselves, and then each other. One slid his length repeatedly against the other's. Mikey seemed to enjoy this in particular. He took both of us into his grasp so that we were one doubled mass, then began stroking. A new kind of elation moved through me, and I had to ask him to slow down after only a short time.

"Okay," he said, and we worked separately on ourselves. We began to kiss again. I knew that Mikey was not far from his release. I built myself up so that I wasn't, either. He emitted a long, soft moan and I felt him spray in forceful bursts against my stomach. I came immediately after him, diffusing hard against his thigh. These traces of us washed quickly away, slipping between our feet and into the drain.

Afterward we changed into fresh clothes. Mikey made light of my barren refrigerator by suggesting we order takeout. Awhile later we settled into a movie, armed with clean plates and forks; various unopened boxes of American-style Chinese food formed a small city, perched at the edge of the coffee table.

Before the sun went down we walked around the neighborhood. We didn't discuss anything of consequence, but Mikey stuck close to my side as our shadows grew long. Every so often he would take my hand into his, hold it for a few seconds, then let it go.

We went to bed early. It was not overtly communicated, but I think we both felt we hadn't slept long enough the night before. We lay facing the living room and he brought his body back to fit neatly within my embrace.

"Are you still sore?" he asked.

He did not see me smile in response, and I saw little besides his thick heap of hair. "Yeah, but I like it," I said, and his quiet laugh drummed through his back. He felt big to me, superimposed. "Mikey, I have to tell you, because I'm having trouble letting it go. Out in the water today—I really did think I might not make it."

He took in a long breath. "I can see how you would feel that way. I know it must have been scary."

"I understand that things happen the way they do, and we have to let them go. I shouldn't be concerned with the disaster that didn't happen. But for some reason I can't shake it. If you weren't such a strong swimmer, you wouldn't have been able to come back for me. Or maybe you would have tried and we both would have drowned. I don't know."

"I think if that were the case, I would've known it was too far for me. I would've swam back to my phone and called 911. They would get to you in time."

"You're sure?"

I felt him nod. "It's okay, Chickadee. I know it seems scary now, but it'll pass."

I slept deeply through the night and well into the morning. I did sense, in a delirious and far-off way, our bodies shifting through positions during the small hours, sometimes twisted into one another, sometimes separated entirely.

We drifted passively through much of the next day, carefree and uninterested in planning our next given move. We went outside, ate, came back in to watch television, went out again, and in the late afternoon, Mikey mentioned that he hadn't felt so comfortable in Corbin in a long time.

The sun became low once again and we stood beside his car. I assured him he was welcome to join me for dinner with my parents, or that I could call and cancel. After all, Stephanie could not make it this week, either.

He told me I should go, and that maybe he would go the following Sunday. "I'll drop you off, though," he said.

"Actually, we're going out this week, so they'll be picking me up. Sure you don't want to come along?"

He shook his head. "Don't worry about me. I should probably call Sophie about work tomorrow, anyway."

"Back to the grind. Have fun."

He gave me a wry smile and opened his door. Before ducking down into his seat, he leaned me against the back door of the car and kissed me. "See you tomorrow, okay?" he said. "You'd better not start avoiding me now."

The thought was inconceivable, although I suspected he was only playing around. "Of course I'll see you tomorrow. I might even show up tonight."

"Yes, do that," he said. "That's better. Now we don't have to say goodbye." He got into his car and started the engine. "Ask your parents if it's okay. You know, about next week. I don't want to come by unannounced."

I told him I would and he drove away. I lay down in the grass and pulled out my phone, staring into the black screen for a few seconds before tossing it out of reach. I closed my eyes, pressed my neck deeper into the blades and waited for my parents.

17

Nostalgic feelings came easily to me these days, brought on by encounters with everyday minutia like the sun-dried black leather of my mom's rumbly old Legend, which crackled underneath me as I shifted my weight in the back seat. I surmised that like any other car, this Acura must have rolled paint-glittering-new off a lot once, but that was before I was around, and long before my mom owned it. It was the first car I ever drove, and because bus transit to my high school had been impractical, I shared it with her for a couple years before leaving for college.

"Twist your keys up so they don't jingle like that," she said to my dad as he steered onto the highway. When he couldn't manage it she reached over and did it for him. She moved halfway around in her seat and said, "Wyatt, thanks for making time for us. I know you must have a lot to do before you leave."

"Not that much," I said.

"Still. It's nice."

"I got the money for the moving van credited to my stipend," I told my dad, "so we can just use the truck."

"Great," he said. "I'm glad that worked out."

"When is your last day of work in the city?" my mom asked.

"Next Wednesday." I paused. "Can Mikey come to dinner next week?"

"That's your new friend, right? Of course he can come."

I watched as she exchanged a look with my dad; they were at it again, ever-superseding, assuming to know exactly what was going on. I hadn't seen it in a while, actually. Back when I lived at home, the condescending pageantry of it all would have left me fuming, but now I just laughed it off inside my head. Whatever conjecture they had assembled probably wasn't far off.

"Just so you know," I added after a pause, "his parents passed away a few years ago." My decision to bring it up beforehand was policed by a wish to prevent rehashing the brief awkwardness we had slogged through with Marie and Sloan. With this in mind I had also bothered to text Stephanie about it the day before, somewhat out of the blue.

"Oh no," my mom said. "That's terrible." She kept silent for another moment as this new, unfathomable detail sank in.

"Sorry to hear that, bud," said my dad.

"Don't worry," she said, making up her mind. "We'll just leave the subject alone."

Awhile later I sat facing my parents in an old booth near the front of a Vietnamese restaurant. We had been here many times; my dad maintained a rapport with the owner who, as a ritual, would bring around the most recent pictures of his young children each time we visited.

To rid them of imaginary splinters, my mom rubbed her disposable chopsticks against one another as we waited for our food. "So," she said, "should we treat Mikey just as we would any of your other friends? Or is he more than just a friend?"

"I don't know," I said. "You can treat him however you want."

"Do you think you guys will stay in contact after you move?"

"I don't know," I said again. I wanted to leave it at that, but worried she would think I was being short with her, which I was not. I lifted my head a little and added, "I hope so."

Dinner carried on without incident and my parents dropped me off after dark. I texted Mikey to let him know I would be over.

"See you soon," he replied.

I packed a bag to sustain me for the better part of the week. I wasn't sure where I would end up. The day before we had discussed spending multiple nights at his place in order to make the most of my time left in the city. We would commute together each day into work. Mikey said nothing about the swollen state of my duffel and garment-bag as I entered, nor did he question the worn gray Toms I carried in my left hand, to replace my work shoes in the evenings should the weather remain warm and dry.

"I have to go back to Boise," he told me late in the evening, as we lay in bed.

"When?"

"The 30th. That's after you move, right?"

"The day after."

"That's what I thought. I just bought the tickets tonight after talking it over with Sophie. They're looking to be our biggest client, so they need some special attention."

"That makes sense," I said.

Over the next couple of days, warm weather made its tentative home throughout the area, not as much in the mild gusts that swept through busy downtown trenches, but especially in a sprawling city park north of Mikey's neighborhood, and of course, along the balmy trail atop the levee. We visited these places daily, and I did not spend a single night away from his home. We showered together each night before bed, ate breakfast early in the morning, then left in his car for work. "It makes it feel like our own private world," he had told me on Monday morning, as if to justify his sudden and thorough abandonment of the bus. Every morning he would ask if I wanted to drive, convinced that I would take up the standard transmission without drama. By Wednesday I opened myself to negotiation, suggesting we try the lonely farm roads east of Corbin. I told him I needed a few days to mentally prepare. He laughed, and then when he saw that I was serious, said we could go early the following week.

With surprising ease, as I no longer stayed with him under the constant clause of my next departure, his apartment came to feel like a second home. I sat beside him at his desk and watched him sketch a rather ornamental version of our beach and the surrounding landscape. The clouds moved in at night and held in a small amount of the day's warmth, so we stepped out onto his tiny balcony and stood at the rail, balancing a piping-hot box of pizza on the corner, laughing and lunging for it as it threatened to fall. A group of kids passed by—probably students at the nearby high school—and one yelled up, asking if we could spare any weed. ("I wouldn't waste it on you," Mikey shouted down cheerfully, eliciting the finger from more than one of them.)

On Thursday night we had intercourse again, after I had accompanied him to his gym on a guest voucher. I did not ask Mikey if he was ready for me to put myself inside of him. I knew he wasn't. But each of us was more than eager to relive the night after the club. Again, I refrained from cautioning him to begin slowly. The pain was more acute this time, due probably to my sobriety, but I preferred it this way. The room was brighter; Mikey saw my face plainly in the bedside lamplight and came to know the nuances in each wince and grit of my teeth. Although I fought hard and won against the threat of returning tears, he had already made up his mind that I should straddle him from on top, so that I could control the rate of his intrusion. It was just as well, as the pleasure it brought him was clear each time I would lower my body down on him, lift it slowly, then sink down again. He put up his own battle against climaxing and fought well, but in the end I wouldn't back down, and he surrendered himself deep inside me. I released in direct response, straight up his stomach and chest to his neck.

For most of the week, Mikey and I did not talk much about our work. To some extent we both may have felt that it only disrupted the precious, numbered days we had left together—at least I felt this way. Still, by Friday morning, after an impromptu return to the bus, Mikey did not try to hide his excitement at the awaiting events precipitated from a recent breakthrough, which he described to me presently over a flurry of hand gestures.

"It will totally change our approach to their restructuring," he said. "Our time investment is cut in half. It's incredible. We've reduced our package cost with them, but I mean, we were already undercutting whoever they're cross-shopping us with. They told us that from the beginning." He sat back and folded his arms. "The best part is, we can adapt the method to some of our other clients' systems. Everybody wins. I fucking live for this stuff."

I grinned, reached out and rocked him back and forth. "I love seeing you like this. And I'm so glad your company is doing well."

He turned to me. "It's you. You're part of this."

"What?"

"Sorry," he continued, "I mean, without you, I'd be sliding back toward workaholic stuff. I can feel it. You've helped show me I can live outside of work. And now I'm seeing that good things just keep happening. The company evolves, kind of in spite of me. I put my best foot forward as a leader, do my time, then leave it at work just like everyone else. I go home and I live separately."

"It's not me," I told him. "You cut back on work before you ever met me."

"That's true. But it wouldn't have lasted. I know how I am."

"You also have drawing to keep you occupied," I said. "And what about your friend in Seattle?"

"He's just a guy I ran track with in high school. He's one of those people from your past, where all you can talk about is the way things used to be…what used to happen. And I hate doing that."

I smiled a little. "I just think when I'm not around anymore, you'll find something else to fill your time, other than work."

"I guess I hope you're right. But you're not, like, a thing, okay? That's the difference. You're a person, not an activity."

"I know, I know. Alright…what about someone else then?"

He closed his eyes. "Please don't say that."

I touched him on the leg. "I'm sorry, Mikey. I don't mean it like that." I wasn't sure what I had meant.

"Do you really think of yourself that way? Like someone could just replace you?"

I didn't know how to answer him. He sighed and fell silent for a minute. I tried to read him during this time. His face flooded not with agitation, just sadness.

"No. I'm sorry," he said finally. "I know you didn't mean anything by it, Chickadee. I know you're just trying to reassure me. It's not your problem anyway. It's mine."

I told him it wasn't his problem, or that maybe it was both of ours. He said it was shaping up to be a beautiful day, and that we didn't need to talk about it anymore.

I worked relentlessly over the course of the day—typical me in the face of actual issues to deal with. A small part of me wanted to cycle through them in some corner of my mind, like a background process running on a phone, allowing me to continue my external functions uninterrupted. And maybe I had unwittingly done so; unexpectedly, I came up with something definitive to say to Mikey on the ride home.

I turned to face him, once seated on the worn, hard seat next to his. "I don't like my job. I don't like the career path I've chosen."

He raised his eyebrows. "That sounds like something we should talk about."

"It is," I insisted. "The way you talk about your work...I mean, you light up, like it's the only thing you could possibly be doing. I can't relate to that. I don't feel that way at all. I've never felt like that, and I'm pretty sure I never will."

He looked at me, then past me, through the windows on the other side of the bus. "Sometimes I think I got lucky. Most people probably feel pretty lukewarm about their job. I'm not saying that's right. It just seems like it's a common feeling."

"I don't think you're wrong about that," I said. I wondered if my feelings toward my job fell in categorically with the people he described—people like my own parents, working their fingers to the bone in positions of which nobody in their right mind would be envious. How many times had they felt the way I did? Was theirs even the same feeling? It must have been.

"Maybe I'll give it a little more thought," I told him.

He nodded and I cast my doubts temporarily aside. We laughed and joked our way through the rest of the ride. On the walk back to his apartment I asked him how his day at work had panned out.

He explained that a new contract had been presented to and signed by the client, establishing a shorter timeline for the project. "You should've seen it, Chickadee. They were ecstatic."

I suspected that he dialed back his excitement on the surface to some degree, perhaps in deference to our earlier discussion. I wished he wouldn't, and could sense it continuing to bubble underneath his casual stride.

"My parents also do jobs they don't like," I determined awhile later, seated on his couch, staring blankly at the wall.

He sat next to me with his feet up on the coffee table. "I don't think that should be a factor, though. They've led different lives than you have."

That was certainly true. I sighed and said, "It's almost like my feelings are worse than lukewarm, if I'm honest with myself. I'm really good at convincing myself that I'm into something. But it's like...part of me will always know the difference between that and what comes naturally, you know? The idea of doing this for the rest of my life or, fuck, maybe just another few years—it isn't playing through in my mind. It doesn't feel right. Something about it just seems wrong."

He paused for a moment. "If you don't feel like the job is worth moving for, then you shouldn't do it."

I didn't know what to say. Even the notion of discussing it terrified me.

"I hope I'm not letting my own feelings into this," he continued. "I'm trying to be objective. That's just how I see it. Objectively, at least."

"I appreciate that," I said in a very quiet voice. "And part of me..." I trailed off momentarily, quivering a little, then drew in a breath. "Part of me is worried that you're right."

I knew suddenly that I was going to cry. It would be brief

and contained, but nonetheless it rushed, unyielding, to the surface. I leaned myself against him, making it clear what was happening. Already I shriveled with embarrassment.

"Hey." He set his feet down to the floor and put his arms around me. "Hold on, hold on," he said calmly, "you're okay." He held my head against his chest, running his hand over my hair. "You're okay," he said again. "Part-of-me-this, part-of-me-that. Man, you've got a lot of parts, you know that?"

I managed to laugh a little, still shuddering against him. "You don't even know."

"It's okay," he said. "Look, you don't have to make up your mind yet. You still have time."

I sat up and groaned, holding my head in my hands. "I'm so tired of not knowing what the hell is going on. I feel like I'm going crazy. Jesus, I'm the last person who should be making this decision, really. Can't you just decide for me?"

He laughed. "No. But if what you told me earlier—how you feel about your job—is true, then I can give you my objective opinion, which I did."

"I know. It's totally valid."

"So," he began slowly, after a pause, "is that really how you feel?"

I sat back and composed myself. "I think so."

One of Mikey's strongest assets, which I had gradually come to know, was his uncanny ability to shift the mood toward something lighter. He reached out, placed his thumb at the corner of my eye and wiped away the wet glaze from my skin. "You need good food," he said, and announced that he was taking me out. We were on our way out the door just a short time later. I slipped one shoe on and reached for the second, but he snatched it up and held it to his chest.

"Come and get it," he said.

251

I swore at him and wrestled him to the floor.

"No," he shouted, reaching up and anchoring himself to the handle of the front door, wrenching it open. We spilled out onto the murky emerald carpet of the fourth-floor hallway, our laugher bounding down its entire length.

Sunday evening came circling around once again, after what amounted to a weekend of simple activities, joy and detachment. As I texted my mom to confirm, Mikey pondered aspects of the evening which were unknown to him.

"Will anyone be dressed up?"

I laughed. "No. That's a good one."

"Isn't this your last dinner before the move? If it's a family thing then I—"

"They don't care. I promise. Come on, you said you would go this week. You'll have fun."

He gave in without any additional reluctance and we left in a hurry, as it was already almost six.

Completely out of character, my mom met us right at the door. "Come in, please," she said, introducing herself before I could open my mouth to speak.

Suddenly I understood why she had asked if Mikey was just a friend, and realized that my response should have been far less ambiguous. I had brought this upon myself.

My dad heaved himself up from his chair, adding, with a grin, that it was about damn time Mikey showed his face around here.

For his part, Mikey didn't seem to mind. "Nice to finally meet both of you," he assured them. "Can I help out with anything?"

"Oh, how kind of you to offer. Maybe some of that courtesy will rub off on Wyatt."

I rolled my eyes. "What's that supposed to mean?"

"No," she continued, "the table's set and the food is nearly done. Just make yourself at home. We'll be eating soon."

She left for the kitchen and Mikey and I ventured into the living room with my dad.

Stephanie stumbled in just as we sat down. "Oh, he's here after all," she confirmed. "Mikey. Welcome. My mom wouldn't say for sure that you were coming."

"That's because I wasn't sure," she countered through the wall.

"Maybe she had to see it to believe it," suggested Mikey.

Stephanie beckoned him into a hug. "Aww, so glad you made it. Jesus Christ, you're tall."

Mikey laughed. "It's a really nice place you have," he said after sitting back down and turning to my dad.

"Thanks. Keeps us busy. As you can see, there are quite a few unfinished projects."

"I like it," said Mikey.

"Unfinished or completely abandoned?" Stephanie muttered in my direction.

My dad either ignored this or did not hear it.

Mikey sat to my right as we took our places in the dining room, at a fifth table setting along the length of the oak table.

"Mikey, we really don't eat western food all that often," said my mom, indicating toward the serving plates of steak and baked potatoes, "but I hope you like it."

I winced a little.

"I like all food," said Mikey. "Makes things easier, being from around here."

"Wyatt tells us you grew up in Corbin, too," my dad said.

He nodded. "Right. And now I live just south of midtown."

"Are you close to St. Augustine's-Midtown?" asked my mom. "It's where I work."

"Sort of. Maybe a fifteen-minute drive."

"That's a nice Honda you have out there," said my dad. Is it a lease?"

"I bought it, actually."

"Good for you. It's nice when you're paying each month towards actually owning the thing. That is, if you're planning on keeping it a long time."

Mikey had bought the car all at once with cash, but of course he wasn't about to announce this to my dad. Decidedly, he said, "I'd like to run it into the ground."

"Well, you picked a good one. The way they're building them now…it'll be around long after they put me to rest."

My mom sat up suddenly. "The wine." She stood, bumping the table, and shuffled toward the kitchen. "Mikey, will you have a glass?"

"Yes please. Let me help you."

She delighted at this. "You are just too polite," she told him.

Together they poured glasses for all of us. Mikey returned with three in his clutches, placing one in front of my dad and handing the second off to me.

Once we had settled well into the meal, my dad pointed his fork toward Mikey and asked, "You're in software, right? I hear you run the place?"

Mikey nodded, sipping from his wine. "I run it with my cousin."

"Good for you," he said for the second time. "And business is doing well?"

"Business is booming," he said, his enthusiasm bleeding through. "I think we've got a really effective team put together."

"How many?" asked my mom.

"All of us make seventeen."

"That's wonderful," she said.

Stephanie remained unusually quiet as the conversation continued, tuning in politely (and probably in genuine interest) as Mikey offered his replies. Perhaps she had decided that all of this stitched-together questioning was overwhelming enough. I thought it was, too, although I did smile to myself once or twice at how artfully they avoided the subject of his parents.

"Give him a rest," my mom said finally as my dad had begun fashioning, with some difficulty, an inquiry into the specifics of his business.

"Fine," he said, smiling and gesturing dismissively at Mikey. "You're off the hook."

Mikey did look a bit relieved.

Near the end of the meal my mom tipped her glass directly up, finished, placed it down next to her plate and said, "I really hope you two don't lose contact when Wyatt moves away."

I swallowed my bite a little too early and said, "Mom. We won't."

"Don't worry," Mikey added quietly, "we won't."

She brought a hand to her mouth, as if she had spoken out of turn. "Just ignore me, both of you. I don't mean to meddle."

Later on, everyone collected in the living room, traipsing together through the second half of *Cloud Atlas* (we had missed most of the first half, but had all seen it before). I sat next to Mikey on the couch, a calculated several inches hovering between us. Stephanie tucked her knees to her chest at my right, engrossed in the final scenes, and my mom squeezed in with my dad between the arms of his giant old chair. We had passed around a bowl of popcorn, now leveled to reveal the pearl-slick amber of un-popped kernels.

"Mikey, it was a pleasure meeting you," said my mom, standing and stretching as the film ended. "I think we're off to

255

bed, but please stay as long as you like."

"Thanks for having me. And for dinner," he said.

We all stood and my mom pulled Mikey into a hug. Unthinkably, my dad did the same and said, "Hope we get to see you again soon." I noticed now that even Mikey did not surpass my dad's imposing stature.

Once they had disappeared down the hallway, Stephanie announced that she had an early morning and should be going to bed soon, too.

"We'll walk you out to your car, if you're ready," I said.

As we made our way across the lawn I reached up, letting my fingers sift through the young, milky-white blossoms of the cherry tree.

"Mikey, I'm proud of you for weathering that interrogation earlier," said Stephanie.

"It really wasn't that bad."

"My mom...she worries about things, and she has a habit of prying. Especially when a situation confuses her. She needs to have everything worked out in her mind."

He shrugged. "It's okay. I don't blame her. Our situation is very confusing."

Stephanie smiled. "I'm sure you guys will work everything out."

"I'm still debating even going," I said suddenly. "Please don't tell Mom and Dad, though."

"I figured you still weren't sure."

"I guess it's mostly that I'm not sure if I want to keep doing what I'm doing, as a career."

She paused, folded her arms and leaned slowly against the sealed passenger window of her Camry. She looked briefly at Mikey, then back to me. "I might have guessed that, too. Look, Wyatt, I know that in the end, you'll do what's best for you.

You'll look inside of yourself and figure out what that is. And you'll do it because you listen to all the valuable advice your big sister gives you."

Mikey laughed quietly.

"Thanks," I said.

Before driving away, she hugged both of us and said to Mikey, "Don't let my brother make you crazy."

He smiled a bit sheepishly.

Her car disappeared and Mikey and I stood alone in the mist above the front lawn. "I could go for a walk before we leave," he said.

"Sure."

We made our way down the middle of the street, wandering to the edge occasionally as cars glided past. We skirted a cul-de-sac inside the next block, where I had once sweated away summer days playing roller hockey with other kids from around the neighborhood. I pointed out a few scars still visible in the pavement. I showed him a well-tended hedge farther down the street, into which I once wedged the Acura on a rare snowy night during my senior year of high school.

"It had to be towed out," I said. "You can still see where it hasn't quite grown back, right there."

He laughed. "I did worse, back in the day."

We didn't speak for a while. I could tell that everything about the evening with my parents had been a lot for Mikey— not more than he could handle, I guessed, but a lot.

"Anything you want to talk about?" I asked him finally.

He hesitated before saying, "Just feeling a little strange, I guess."

"Yeah. I understand. Thanks for braving my family to-night."

"It was okay. Honestly, it's just hard not to, you know, feel like I'm your boyfriend when I'm around them."

"That's mostly my fault," I told him. "My mom asked, and I didn't say you were, but I also didn't really tell her you weren't."

"It's alright. Maybe you didn't know how to answer."

"I mean, I did. Before you met Marie and Sloan we made it clear, remember?"

He paused. "I don't expect you to feel that way forever."

I didn't know how to respond.

"I'm sorry," he continued, "it's just that, even after all this time, I don't feel like I'm ready to have a—" He stopped himself, drawing in a breath. "I'm just not ready to call you my boyfriend."

I looked over at him. "It hasn't been that long," I said. "You shouldn't feel bad at all. Look how far you've come already."

We had long since circled back and I began to make out his car through the mist, huddled under the streetlamp at the edge of my parents' yard.

"I feel relieved now," he said, "and I hate it."

I asked him what he meant. He said he didn't know.

18

I crawled into bed later that night back at my apartment, tired and alone. Earlier in the day we had agreed that a break—even for just one night—was a healthy move. For a while I had half-expected Mikey to later succumb, to turn to me in the car, for instance, and tell me that he wanted to stay over after all. I knew later, certainly after our walk down the streets of my childhood, that the basis for this outcome was entirely my invention; it bore no resemblance to the reality of our situation.

I also knew, as I considered it rather heavily now left to my own thoughts, that our situation marched its way steadily toward calamity. I realized that no matter the outcome, it would carry with it a fair amount of drama. Troubled by the certainty of this, and perhaps even more by the uncertainty over which outcome it would be, I did not sleep particularly well.

"I'm a little offended that you didn't bring anything with you to stay over tonight," said Mikey the next morning at the bus stop. "I'll get over it, though. Don't worry."

"You expect me to carry it around all day?" I asked, flashing a grin. I found it alarmingly easy to drop all concern as I nestled back into his presence.

"No. I mean, you could've texted ahead and dropped it off at my place. Come on, Chickadee, a little prior coordinating never hurt anyone."

"Hey, you have to do that all the time, for work. It doesn't come as easily to me."

"Hmmm. Maybe so," he said. "How about we pick up your stuff on our way through Corbin after work? You're not getting out of learning to drive a manual."

"Oh yeah. I forgot about that."

"I'm sure you did," he said. "Anyway, I could stay at your place tonight if you prefer."

"I don't prefer. It's not even my home for much longer."

"I see."

"No matter what I decide," I added. "Someone's already signed to take my place on the first."

"Fuck," he said, casting a strange look down at the sidewalk. "It's scary how fast things like that can move."

I just nodded.

The bus approached with a deep, descending moan and we climbed on amid a small line of people.

That evening, my role as passenger became decidedly studious as Mikey drove us to my apartment after a quick dinner at his place, and only more so as we departed for open farm roads to the east. I viewed this desperate, last-ditch attentiveness as my only hope of avoiding catastrophe once seated behind the wheel.

"Do you always have to put in the clutch between gears?" I asked as he started south down the highway.

"Always." Mikey's driving had become correspondingly de-monstrative. "Otherwise you're forcing the engine to change its speed immediately, which is very hard on the transmission—and the clutch, which is sort of a means of diplomacy between the two."

"Okay, I'm already not following you."

"Don't worry. You don't need to understand it like that. But yes, the clutch must be in when changing gears. It disengages the transmission from the engine, which is necessary when changing from one drive ratio to another. When you let the clutch slowly out, it facilitates the gradual reconnection."

I paused. "And why does the clutch need to be in when you're just sitting at a stop light?"

"Actually, you can let the clutch out at a stop light if you put the shifter in neutral, or turn off the engine. Obviously turning the car off doesn't make sense, but I use neutral all the time, when my foot needs a rest. But, assuming the car is in first, the clutch must be in because the engine is turning and the wheels are not. So the car is in gear, and the engine is turning at, say, seven-hundred times each minute. If the clutch is let out, then the wheels need to also be turning a certain number of times a minute, correlating to the drive ratio determined by first gear. When you're stopped, the wheels aren't turning at all, so letting out the clutch would force the engine to stop turning, too—unless you let out the clutch carefully, and with a measured amount of throttle, which is exactly how you start moving from a stop."

I sighed. "This is what happens when an engineer teaches you to drive a manual, isn't it?"

He laughed. "I wouldn't know. I'm not an engineer. Close enough, though, maybe." After a pause he said, "But you're right, this isn't the way to learn. There's no other way besides just doing it."

Awhile later Mikey turned down a fairly narrow agricultural access road, elevated slightly above the surrounding fields and also paved, but so unburdened by traffic that no painted line existed to divide the two lanes. He stopped square in the middle and turned off the car. We switched positions. Only after finding my place in the driver's seat did I wonder, in amazement, how long it had been since I'd driven at all. Was it four months? Or maybe even five? I had dropped off Stephanie at the airport one morning in late-November. That was it.

"There. You're starting from nothing," said Mikey. "The clutch needs to be held in to turn on the car."

I did so and then turned the key. The engine trembled back to life.

"Keep your foot on the brake. Now try putting the shifter in neutral. There you go. Now you can let out the clutch if you want."

I let it out slowly.

"Perfect. Now, if you want to put it back into first gear, the clutch has to be in. Do you remember why?"

I thought a moment. "Because the engine is turning and the wheels are not?"

"Right, and the clutch connects the engine to the wheels through the transmission. Man, you're a fast learner," he said with a grin. "Go ahead and put it back in first. You can look at that little diagram on the top of the shifter." He waited as I did as told. "Great, now you're ready to get the car moving. Take your foot off the brake. Now press lightly on the gas. Bring the engine speed up to around three thousand, okay?"

"That's the three?" I began adding gas and heard the engine's pitch whine upward.

"Yes, that's the three. Perfect, keep it there. Now you're going to very slowly let the clutch out."

I did so and we began to roll forward. Thinking the clutch had finished engaging, I removed my foot completely from it. Mikey's car—not small by any means—bucked forward, the tires chirping hard against the pavement. But we were still moving, and I was driving. The needle kept climbing, nearing four thousand.

"Awesome job," he said. "And now you can see how the car isn't shifting itself like an automatic would. But we'll get to that later. Let your foot off the gas and put in the clutch...good, now keep the clutch in and use the brake to stop the car, just like you normally would."

Once the car was stopped again, he said, "So, obviously you can't run the engine way up like that every time you start moving from a stop. You have to work the gas and clutch at the same time, keeping the engine speed fairly low until you get the car going."

"Okay."

"Go ahead and try. Give it some gas and slowly let out the clutch at the same time."

As I attempted this, the car pitched suddenly forward, then stopped dead with a massive lurch. "That's it," I said. "I'm done. This is hurting your car."

Mikey just laughed. "The car's fine. It's made to handle a lot worse. This is the hardest part of the whole process. I think you'll find actual shifting between the gears much easier. We can do that next; you just need to get it moving again."

My second attempt failed, too, indistinguishable from the first. But by the fourth try, just as I thought the car would stall again, it made a second lunge ahead and our forward movement smoothed out. I gripped the wheel hard in my left hand as Mikey guided me through the forward gears. I had reached fourth and was approaching highway speed.

"Chickadee, you're doing incredibly well...although," he added casually, "we are running short of road."

I braked suddenly, frantically, in order to stop short of landing the car in a muddy field, which lay just past an approaching intersection. The brake pedal pulsed, the tires skidded in quick bursts along the pavement, my bag thudded against the back of my seat and then everything fell silent.

Mikey laughed harder than ever, pounding his fist into the armrest.

"Stop that," I said. "Why is the car off?"

"You forgot to put in the clutch. Look, the shifter's still in fourth gear."

I insisted that he turn the (fucking) thing around so I could try again in the other direction.

"That's the attitude I'm looking for," he said, clamping his hand down on my shoulder.

We made our way back to his apartment as it became dark. Twice Mikey had assured me that I'd already progressed enough to drive us home, but I kept refusing and he gave up.

As he drove and I relaxed, back at home in the passenger seat, I said, "That was actually a ton of fun. Sorry for almost crashing your car."

"Think nothing of it. You learned that even though you're adding new responsibilities, the old rules still apply."

"Right, like not driving off the road."

"Yes," he said, "that is certainly an old rule."

After we had stepped into his apartment and kicked off our shoes, I returned my duffel to its now familiar spot by the bed.

"Where's your suit?" he asked.

"Unlike you, I do not enjoy dressing up all that much. I've only got two days left at the office and I'm going to make them a little more casual."

"Wow, dream big," he said.

I landed my fist lightly against his arm.

"Hey," he said, surrounding me tightly from behind, pinning my arms against my sides, "you tried something new today, so I was thinking...it's only fair if I try something new, too. Something that makes me just as nervous."

I wriggled myself out of his grasp and turned to face him. "If it's what I think it is…"

"It is," he said, nodding eagerly.

"Mikey, that's not quite the same. Don't do it just because you think it's fair."

He shook his head. "That's not why I brought it up. I want to know what it is…having you do that to me. I want to feel it. I'm ready."

"You're sure?"

"I'm sure," he said. "That's my decision, as long as you're willing to…you know."

"Jesus, I'm more than willing. I'm getting hard already just thinking about it."

"And I think I'm—you know—ready down there, too. Just in case you were wondering."

"I'm sure it will be fine," I said.

Calmly, slowly, we began to remove our clothes, first throwing our jackets over onto the couch, then peeling away our shirts. I stepped slightly away from him, just as the dark skin and hair below his navel emerged from under white cotton; I sought a more complete view of his body before we were brought together. Next his pants came down, as did mine, and we faced each other in our black briefs, already swollen in silent but frenzied anticipation of the new, reciprocal exchange in which we were about to engage.

Mikey stayed still so I stepped up to him, took his hand in mine, pressed my other against his chest and then let it trail slowly down his abdomen. "Are you okay?" I asked him.

"Yes," he said, in a hollow, timid voice I hadn't heard since the first night we had walked down the trail to the beach. "Do you mind leading the way? I don't know what I'm doing."

We removed our underwear and I brought him over to the

bed. He lay down on his back on top of the covers. The room was very warm. He laughed a little. "It's going to hurt, isn't it?"

I retrieved the small, slick bottle from his nightstand drawer. "It will at first," I said to him. "We'll take it very slowly, okay?"

He nodded. "Okay."

Mikey spread his legs apart. He granted me complete access; it required an encounter with immense, new vulnerability on his part, a truly sacrificial act which I did not take for granted. He looked me straight in the eyes, then moved his gaze down to the attentive, rigid presence between my legs. "You," he said. "I want that part of you. I need to know how it feels."

"Do you want me to use my finger to relax you a little first?"

"No," he told me. "I'm ready for it now. Just take it slow."

I told him not to worry as I arrived between his legs. I placed my hands behind his knees and opened him further to me. "You're sure you don't want to be on top of me?"

"No, I want it like this," he said.

I pressed myself against him, noticing the minute change in his face once he accepted that it was only seconds from happening. Finally I felt a small extent of me open him up. His eyes squeezed shut. I asked if I should stop, but he said no, that he wanted more, so I stayed within him and pressed on. I could tell he had not yet relaxed and the warm space he had offered up remained snug and restricted. This stubbornness was not him; it was his body, which had never before known such an encroachment.

"Remember when you didn't want to hurt me?" I asked. "You made me get on top so that I could be in control."

He clenched his teeth and nodded stiffly. "I'm sorry. Now I understand. You wanted me, even though it hurt. Well, now I want you. I want you to stay on top. I want you to fuck me."

I slid the rest of myself steadily in. Mikey exhaled, kept his eyes shut, and a broad smile spread across his face. I pulled out to half my length, then sank myself back into him. He actually laughed. "Fuck, Chickadee. I knew you were big, but…this is something else."

I smiled down at him. "It's going to feel pretty big."

"Oh my god. No fucking shit."

"Are you doing okay?"

He paused. "Give it to me again."

I drew myself out, and then plunged deep into him.

He gasped. "Fuck…hurts like fucking hell. But it feels so good. Please, just keep letting me have it."

I gave him what he asked for, removing and then reinserting myself over and over. He had relaxed somewhat, though his accommodation remained fresh and favorably constricted. Mikey was still new, he was tight, and I was concerned that in my excitement, if I continued to offer him what he desired, I would lose control of myself too soon. I decided not to care. He moaned softly as we kept at it, touching himself intermittently from one moment to the next, unquestionably hard as stone. I spoke his name as a warning and he told me to let it go inside of him, that he was ready to let himself go, too.

"Here it comes," he said. "Can't stop." His abdominal muscles tightened and he curled forward, adorning his dark stomach in pearl-white.

As this occurred I felt the inside of him swell and tighten around me. I began to climax with the sensation of a warm and welcome current plummeting from the base of my neck, down my spine, extrapolating into rhythmic gushes of release from my center, where our bodies were joined. As I finally tapered away I was reacquainted, after a long time, with the inimitable feeling of having left a small part of myself in very special place.

As my eyes fell to meet with Mikey's, his blurry, wondering expression communicated a sense of understanding for exactly what I felt in that moment. Releasing into me, he, too, must have recently come to know its graces.

I cautioned him that I would remove myself, and that it might feel strange. He nodded and then I did so, very slowly. I went over to the hamper and found him some underwear so that he could clean himself.

He propped himself up on his elbows. "Chickadee, that was incredible. I feel indebted to you now."

I handed him the underwear and he began to wipe himself down. "Don't say that," I told him. "We gave something to each other."

He nodded, focused somewhat on removing the mess. "Now, if you don't mind, I'll excuse myself. Then would you like to join me in the shower?"

I told him I would.

Later on we curled together in his bed, beneath the open window, waiting for sleep to take us over.

Mikey pressed his lips into the back of my neck, then drew back just enough to say, "I suppose I'll be sore tomorrow."

I laughed quietly. "Yes, I suppose you will."

"There's a satisfaction that goes along with doing something you know you'll never regret."

"Is that how you feel?"

I felt him nod. "Yes. I'll always know that you were the right one to do that to me."

His arm was slung over me, hand held gently to my chest. I squeezed it tightly against me.

The next morning I lay awake, half an hour before the alarm was set to go off. Mikey awoke, too, not long after me. It was not yet light outside.

"Can't sleep?" he asked.

I turned to him. "I have a lot to prepare for. Tomorrow's my last day of work downtown. I should text Jennifer and find out what furniture she'll be contributing to the apartment. I haven't even started to pack. Fuck. There's just a lot to do."

"So you decided to go."

I paused. "Yeah, looks like I did."

"'Looks like'? What the fuck does that mean?"

I moved myself away from him. This was new. "Yeah, I mean, I didn't decide not to go. That's kind of the point."

He frowned. "I don't think that's the point," he said slowly. "It seems like you're being very passive about this decision."

I didn't say anything right away. I lifted myself, sitting up against the headboard. I pretended to itch my cheek with my hand in order to obscure my face. "Mikey, when I think about what it's taken for me to process all of this, 'passive' is the absolute last word that comes to mind."

He nodded. "Okay. I just don't like to hear that it 'looks like' anything. Not with something that has such an impact on whether or not we get to hang out anymore. I want to know that you've really thought this over."

Maybe he was on to something; maybe in some way I hadn't. But in another way, I felt like I had considered and reconsidered the decision to death, and now just continued beating at its lifeless body. To Mikey I said, "Actually, I'm exhausted from thinking it over. And now I know that I will go. I have actively, consciously made that decision. Is that okay?"

He didn't answer right away. He closed his eyes, pulled the comforter up over his mouth and muttered, "Yes, that's okay." He paused for a long time. Finally, he continued, "The other day. You told me you didn't like your job, that it felt wrong to keep doing it. What about all that?"

"I felt very strongly at that point. I'm more collected now." I paused. My throat tightened. "What about when you said you would always support my decision, no matter what?" I could feel my emotions threaten to spill over.

Mikey's face was entirely hidden now. "That was before I knew you hated your job."

"I don't hate my job," I said. I had begun tearing up. "And are you sure that's all it is? Are you sure you haven't developed real feelings for me, and you can't own up to them? God forbid that would be even some small part of the problem. Fuck, it certainly is for me."

He tore away the blankets, rose up and walked across the apartment. His footsteps landed heavily as they departed and I knelt on the bed, peering over the half wall. He stood in the middle of the kitchen in just his underwear. His back was to me. He was crying. "Well, fuck. I fucking knew this shit would happen."

I knew it, too. And now, in a way, it felt like I had always known. But it had hit so suddenly, and with such force that I felt acutely the sensation of staggering uncontrollably backward, even as I sat motionless.

He held still, seemed to calm himself a little and then said, "I just thought...I mean, given what we have...I thought it might sway your decision."

"Mikey, what exactly do we have? We've known each other for hardly more than a month. You're a really fun guy to hang around. It seems like we make really good friends. In another life we could be...something...I don't know. What else is there to say about it?"

He lifted his arms and clasped his hands on top of his head. "There's nothing else to say, I guess."

Unlike him, for whatever reason, I did not feel the urge to

cry as I continued speaking. "This whole thing is fucking insane. I mean, think about it—we don't even know each other. Not really. It was impossible for us to have gotten to know each other well enough in that span of time. You know, for me to know if I…" I took a breath and lowered myself back down to sit on the bed. No longer could I see him over the wall. "And even if it had been enough time, you yourself said that you're not ready to call me your boyfriend."

"I'm not," I heard him say. "I'm just…not."

"Of course you're not. And I don't think I'm ready for that, either. Fuck, neither of us should be. This is exactly what I'm trying to say. We don't have a history at all. I think we tried to make it seem like we did, but we don't—I mean, my god, you don't even call me by my own name."

I heard him approach, feet pounding across the wood floor. He came to stand—to tower—over me at the foot of the bed. "Wyatt. Your name is Wyatt. Hello, Wyatt. Please don't move away, Wyatt. See? I know your fucking name."

I buried my face in my hands. "Stop it," I said. "I hate it. It doesn't sound right at all."

He sat down on the end of the bed, his back to me once again. "I can't win, then."

"No, you can't. Neither of us can." I stopped and thought for a moment. "You know how I know that moving is the right thing to do? Because if I'd never met you, I would be going for sure. Yeah, it would have upset me and all that, but in the end, I still would have gone. That's how I know now that if I stay, it would only be because of you. Which is a bad idea. Remember what you told me? That you don't expect me to put my life on hold for you?"

"I wasn't talking about this," he said. A bitterness had crept into his voice. "You've made up your mind already. Don't use my own words against me just to leverage your side of things."

He sounded angry, and I quaked with the knowledge that I had made him feel that way. "Sorry," I said, just above a whisper. I held my body firm against this new, stronger swell of anguish.

He began slowly. "Chickadee, I just don't think you're being true to yourself right now. You told me you're not headed down the right path with your job. You said it so clearly, and I can't let that go."

That was it; he knew exactly where I remained weak, and now he spun the wheel freely, steering everything in that direction. A part of me was so willing to listen to this talk that I gathered myself up, instead interpreting it as a signal to hold my ground. "Please look at me right now," I said. "I don't want to talk to the back of your head."

"Come work for my company," he blurted out. He twisted around to look me in the eyes. "There's a place for you there. There always has been."

We were both very quiet. Mikey was speaking out of desperation now; he knew it just as the words came out. There was a reason this had never come up before. Somehow, without ever saying a word on the subject, we had sustained an understanding that mixing business arrangements into our relationship was never, would never be right.

His mouth was shut tight for a few seconds. Perhaps in defiance, he turned away again. "Okay, fine," he mumbled. "I know I can't keep making it like it's all about you. The truth is that I can't do this without you. I think you know that. I still spend so much time feeling scared. You know I still have some things that I'm very scared of. You're the only person who knows everything, and who I've given everything to. I'm so terrified to think about what it will be like when you're not around anymore. I just can't face it all on my own."

I turned to him. "But you can do it alone—in fact you need experience processing it on your own. You'll never believe you're capable of it until I'm gone. Then you'll see. Right now you think you need me. You don't see yourself as strong enough. You've come to understand so much about yourself… your attraction…but you're convinced that it's been me doing all the work for you. Well, I haven't done anything. All I've ever been is a guy you find attractive enough to make yourself reconsider things. Fuck. If I ever needed another reason to go—"

"God, I can't stand that you're putting it that way. This is exactly what I suspected about you. You constantly undervalue yourself. Just listen to what you're saying. You honestly believe that's all you are in this. Look, I'm explaining to you that yes, I know my problems are a part of this—and yes, I do feel like I need you. But I'm not about to apologize for that. I don't even think it's wrong for me to feel that way." He paused. "It's not just that, though. It's, like, simpler than that. I'm so unbelievably happy when I'm around you. I really, really don't want it to stop. I know you've made up your mind. I know I should believe that in the end, only you know what's best for you. But I just can't respect it. I don't want to. I don't think you're right. That's selfish, I know. I'm very selfish. There. Now you're finally getting to know me."

Since I had met him, with a sureness that had come to feel unbreakable, I counted on Mikey's support in my final decision, no matter what it would turn out to be. He withdrew himself from this assurance so cleanly now, so easily—as if it had been nothing at all to him, like it had never carried any real weight. He was right; it was completely selfish. This wasn't him—it couldn't be. Yet he did not back away from it.

I began to feel very strange, like something inside me would rupture if I continued to stay still, so I bolted to my feet and began, naked, to gather my clothes off the floor beside the bed.

He looked over his shoulder. "What are you doing?"

"I'm packing," I said. "I'm going home to shower. I'll be late for work—fuck it. We shouldn't be around each other anymore. It will make things much harder. If you have any respect for me and what I need right now, you'll commute by car, today and tomorrow."

He sat hunched over. He didn't let me see his face. "Okay," he said. Any anger or bitterness was gone from his voice. "I just didn't ever think it would end up like this," he said. "I am so sad." He cried, curling further into himself as I dressed.

I knew that if I didn't hurry, he would see me cry, too, which certainly would not make anything easier. I thought I heard him say something more and couldn't help myself from asking him to repeat it.

"Nothing," he said. "It's just so cold in here."

I looked more closely at his body and saw that he was shivering. His shoulders shook as he continued to cry quietly into his hands.

"Just leave," he said.

I lifted my bag from the floor and left him, quickly putting on my shoes by the front door. The deadbolt released with a heavy clack. In the next moment the door shut behind me and I was alone out in the hall.

I walked briskly in the cold morning air over to Stratham, arriving at the stop for the 40B just as it came roaring down from the north, headlamps still blazing in the twilight. I had never ridden the southbound route so early in the day; it arrived empty and I sat at the very back, against the window, setting my bag down on the seat beside me.

Whatever imminent event I had been expecting, this morning had exploded into something worse than I could ever have foreseen. My left hand clutched my stomach. Reality was in the building: My body, the seat cushion below me, the windows of the bus—everything around me lay awash in a burning, clarifying chemical bath of reality. Gradually, still shaking, I peered back toward the place from which I had come, no longer able to imagine how else it could have played out.

19

My phone didn't make a sound all day, which was not entirely out of the ordinary. I didn't know whether to expect anything from Mikey. At work, I pushed back against this silence with indifference; already during the early-morning bus ride home I had cried at length, the front of my shirt no less than soaked in my sorrow. A meager assortment of riders had climbed on along the southbound stops, and I felt relief only because none came to sit near me.

It had been enough to carry me through the day. I made cheerful conversation with Jennifer about whose couch would be better-suited to our new living area. I slotted into my familiar productive groove and began clearing my desk of personal effects toward the end of the day.

I came home to a still, silent apartment and lay on my bed, the few items I had removed from the office spilling out around me. I looked at my phone, then placed it screen-down and scooted it across the blanket, over the edge. I heard it thud on the carpet below.

Mikey had fully respected my wish to be left alone, and maybe he wouldn't have tried to contact me anyway. If he was upset then he probably wanted to be left alone, too.

I lacked the self-control necessary to keep memories at a distance, and they flooded me now—most of all: his bare feet out on the sand, t-shirt clinging to the taut skin of his chest, black hair kicking up in the warm wind. I thought of the way his smile, in that moment, offered up the slightest amount of vacancy, awaiting fulfillment by wonders soon to arrive. This behavior was innocent. It did not calculate. He waited like a child would wait, because he understood that he could not know what mysteries these wonders would hold before their time.

With my head against the pillow, I looked up at the ceiling and started to cry again for the first time since early that morning. I imagined him alone now, wishing he could contact me but believing it to be something I didn't want. I remembered his plea, about how happy being together made him, and how he didn't want it to stop. He had described the feeling as a simple one, and he had been right.

But it didn't matter. I knew myself, and I knew what it would take for me to stay. Mikey was quick to admit to (and could probably have listed, had I asked) the things that scared him. I was frightened at least as much by other things, but they were more difficult to lay to paper, and whereas his fears were cause for me to stay, my own were the driving force in my departure.

The radio silence would last through the rest of the night. I got along by cooking dinner, then throwing myself into packing the apartment, chiseling out a significant portion of the job before I realized that if I continued at this rate, there would be nothing left to distract me on Thursday and Friday. I wanted to go to bed, but the hour was not suitably late and I knew I wouldn't sleep. I read until I could not focus anymore.

Whatever experience Mikey and I had shared, I stood just barely outside of it now. I had minimally but effectively decoupled myself from it. For a precious couple of minutes, I saw our relationship for that to which it amounted; it did not feel like a lifetime now, nor could it be compressed down to a single whirlwind day. Several weeks brought together two compatible people, each interested in the other, interesting to the other, to a decidedly extreme degree.

Objectivity was helpful now in a way, but I did not feel especially comforted by it, and I got the sense that it wasn't accessing something important—some overarching essence of what it was to be in the same place as him. After preparing for sleep I lay on my side, slightly off to the right portion of the bed. There was room left over for Mikey to lay facing me, and it was not hard to imagine it now. The feeling of assurance as his eyes looked deeply into mine from the other pillow, as our fingers fluttered lightly against one another's between us, was powerful and complete.

His absence and his silence now dug into me. I had no less than demanded it, and I knew with some amount of incredulity that if I did nothing, Mikey would be gone, silenced forever. I had asked for it, and there was no doubt in my mind that he would honor it. This truth rattled me; I tucked up my knees, pulling my feet close to the rest of my body, and remembered nothing else besides crying in prolonged, wrenching sobs until I fell asleep.

I rode the bus into the city the next morning, imagining what it was like for Mikey to be driving alone in his car for yet another day. I wondered how quickly he would return to this groaning, shuddering beast once he knew for sure that I was gone. I hoped it would be easy for him to come back to it, to sit alone, smiling to himself from time to time, content in his quiet productivity, just as he had been before we ever met. I hoped he would soon feel calm and happy, back on his own, more aware of his own identity, and free.

By the end of the day, the thought of returning to my small, upended home was not yet bearable, so I did not text or call ahead, just departed from the 40 as usual and then crossed under the highway toward my parents' house. It would occur to me later that I had not showed up unannounced at their home in some time, and at first I could not comprehend my mom's surprise when I walked through the front door and began removing my shoes.

"How's packing going? Oh, and this was your last day downtown," she said. "Are you feeling overwhelmed at all?"

I took long enough to respond, stepping slowly over to the couch and resting my chin on my hands, that I was certain she sensed something was amiss already. "It's not the packing, Mom, or work. How is work going for you?"

She cleared her throat and said, "It's pretty good." She then came over and sat next to me. "Tell me what's wrong, sweetie."

I leaned against her, feeling very much like I needed to cry again, but holding it back. "It's been hard saying goodbye. Actually…it just didn't work. It fell apart. I think it's done."

She knew whom I referred to without asking and said nothing in response; she knew, too, that I would continue on my own after enough time. Her hair tickled my neck and I felt a thin curtain of safety rise up around me, blocking everything out except for her and the sunlight pouring in through the front window.

"When I left his place yesterday morning," I began slowly, "he didn't say much. He was crying, and he said something about how he didn't think it would ever end up like this. He said some things that I don't understand, and some things I don't agree with. But I agreed with him when he said that."

"Oh no. Did the two of you argue?"

I nodded. "He wants me to stay, Mom. He wants it so bad,

and I kept thinking that it was so selfish of him. He always said he would support my decision to go. But when I was leaving, he just looked so sad that I couldn't see anything else—not selfishness, and nothing else he would be playing at. I don't think he operates that way. All I could see was his sadness. He was, like, shivering, Mom. It was very cold in the room. And he even said it—he said, 'I am so sad,' like that was the only thing he had left to say."

Her body shifted against me. "Wyatt, has he committed himself to you?"

"No." I paused. "Well, sometimes it feels like he kind of already did, in a way, but he can't say it. I don't think he could promise me anything like that, even if I wanted him to."

"You don't want him to?"

"I don't know," I said. "I don't think so. It's been a month, Mom. I'm not sure it's right to even be asking for any kind of promises." After saying this I waited for her response, but she offered none, and although she had turned toward me, I could not tell how she felt from her expression. "What do you think about that?" I asked.

"A lot of people say this," she started. "I think it's true, though. Every situation is different. Everyone is an individual. I can't tell you if a month is long enough, or too short a time for anything. I haven't lived in your experience with him. I don't know."

I waited to continue, gathering an inclination together in my mind which seemed simple in a way, but was difficult for me to articulate. "I think it kills me just as much to leave him as it kills him that I'm going…but still, we came up with two different decisions about it."

She nodded. "It's weird how things like that happen some-times, isn't it?" She hesitated for a moment. "And there's no chance you could keep seeing him while you live up there?"

I took a long time to answer her, finally lowering my head and muttering, "I just can't have it that way. I don't want it. I don't know why."

"Some people just aren't built for that, and it's okay. I certainly don't think I could do it."

"In my last relationship, I was willing to try it." I paused and looked up at her. "Remember that?"

"I do. Maybe you've changed. I'm tempted to say change like that is more common at your age, but people can change at any time in their life. Or maybe it's just that you see it differently with Mikey. Maybe it's all or nothing with him."

"I guess so," I said. I thought for a moment. "Part of what bothered him was me letting on that I had some serious doubts about my career, then deciding to go through with the move anyway." I glanced over at her, anticipating her surprise—I rarely ever really talked to her about my job—but she barely reacted at all. "On top of everything," I continued, "he believes I'm not being true to myself if I go."

"He can't really say if you are or you aren't. Only you will know that."

"Yeah, I know. But it doesn't mean he shouldn't have brought it up, if it's how he feels."

"Alright, yes, I see that, too. Look, sweetie, I got a particular feeling from the two of you the other night. It seemed like you were awfully close...and it seemed like a good thing to me." She stopped and looked me in the eyes. "I'm just wondering if it's going to make you incredibly sad not to be around him. I believe in the potential for another person's presence to affect how happy you are. I know you probably already know that, but please consider it as you make your decision."

"I did consider it. And I think I have already," I said.

"Wyatt, I need you to tell me this, because I'm worried you're holding it back from me. Are you missing him as much as I would imagine you are?"

"I'm not sure that it's had time to sink in yet," I said. This was mostly a lie and there was no reason for me to have said it. "Everything just feels so quiet and empty right now."

I stopped talking, aware that I had shared more of myself with her in this one conversation than in all of the weeks leading to it. She was right; I missed Mikey so much that I felt ill. I nearly rejected the thought of having said goodbye to him forever. I began to consider the full gravity of it again, took one more look at my mom and started to cry.

She brought me into her arms, hugging me tightly and said, "I know." I believe she began to cry then as well. "I know, I know," she kept saying, aware, as some people are in these situations, that sometimes there is nothing else to say.

After a moment, when we had both calmed down a bit, she gripped my arm within her small hands and said, "Wyatt, I have something I need to tell you. But first I need to say that I know I haven't been very emotionally available."

"Come on, Mom, you've been—"

"No, just let me say this now. There have been times when you've wanted to talk about something and I've been distant with you, because whatever you brought up was making me encounter my own problems and I didn't like it. You want an example of selfishness—well that's it. All I can tell you is that I'm sorry."

"You don't have to be sorry for that, Mom."

She shook her head. "Yes I do. You won't change my mind. Wyatt, the last time we talked about your career was before it ever started—your senior year of college, over the winter break. You had some considerable doubts, and I told you to stick to it.

I don't think I really said anything else. It destroys me because…" She paused and looked for a moment like she was about to cry again. She let go of me and straightened herself up. "It destroys me now because I had doubts about my own career back then, but made up my mind to ignore them. My only way to hold onto that conviction was to tell you to do the same. I feel responsible in that way, and it's very painful for me."

"It's not that simple," I told her. "I respected what you told me then. I still do. And besides, you aren't the only factor when I make those decisions. You must know that."

"I do know that. But I still feel responsible. I'll get over it eventually, but right now I just need you to know that I'm sorry. I put myself before you at that time. It's the worst thing a parent can do to their child."

"That's overdoing it a little. You gave me advice, that's all."

"I gave you self-interested, and therefore bad advice."

I managed a laugh. "Fine. If that's how you really feel, then I accept your apology."

She smiled at me. "Okay, well I'll keep this brief, because it's not about me right now, but next week will be my last at the hospital. I'm taking your advice and pursuing my passion. I'm doing it for me, and no one else."

"Oh my god. Are you kidding me? That is such good news, Mom."

"I wanted to tell you right away, yesterday, when I finally went through with it, but I figured with everything you have going on that I should wait."

"No you shouldn't," I said. "I'm so happy for you."

"Well, thanks, sweetie." She gave me a hug and then sat back. "I can't believe I actually did it. Your little old mom takes care of business." She laughed, but before long some of the excitement had faded from her face. "You know, I really don't like to see you cry, Wyatt. Not like you did today. I just can't stand it."

"I know. This makes me feel better, though."

"So, will you think about it?"

"Think about what?"

She paused, laying her hands in her lap. "Think about what I did to make myself happy, and be sure that whatever you choose is going to make you happy."

I sat very still, staring at her for a moment. "Alright, Mom, I can try to do that."

She begged me to stay for dinner, but I insisted that I wasn't hungry.

"You're just like me," she said. "Your appetite vanishes when you're stressed. It's okay."

I promised her I would eat something later on.

That night I didn't cry. I didn't feel much of anything. I packed meticulously, tetrising over half of my belongings with great care into boxes and milk crates, following a methodical order of importance which would aid future retrieval.

"Do you own a television?" Jennifer texted around nine.

"Yes. I'll bring it up," I replied.

I left for a nearby corner store, where I purchased a small dinner and one felt-tipped marker. After eating, I slowly, carefully labeled the containers with general respect to their contents. By ten o'clock I forced myself to stop everything, concerned that there would be nothing left to do the next day.

Before falling asleep, I attempted to clear my mind of all thoughts, but settled for new imaginings of my mom, upstairs in my old bedroom—now her sewing room—smiling and working away.

The next day I realized I would have been much better off

working through Friday. I tried to slow myself down as I continued boxing and labeling, to become even more methodical, more meticulous, but I could only take it so far. I had too much time on my hands, and pounced on my phone once I noticed Marie had texted. She had just finished up at work and asked if I needed help packing, or at least some company.

"I could use some company," I replied. "I'll borrow my mom's car and pick you up at Southgate if you want."

She didn't respond to this, which was her customary way of deflecting offers. She showed up at the door an hour later.

We hugged and she began poking around the apartment like a cat in a newly-discovered room. "Oh, wow," she said. "I haven't been here in too long. I'm a little sad to see it in this state."

I sat on the edge of my bed and listened to her remark at the packed containers, as well as a few larger items that would be carried out individually.

"Oh, Wyatt, remember this couch? Remember your record player?" she asked, lifting the transparent lid on its hinge and then setting it back down.

"Yes, I remember them," I said with a small smile. "I live here."

"I just can't believe you won't be in the city anymore."

"Me neither, Marie."

She regarded me in complete silence for a moment and then sat down on the edge of the couch nearest me, crossing her legs. "Please tell me how things are."

I sighed. "I let myself feel it all, Marie. I did what you said."

"And what happened?"

I invoked a miniature explosion with my hands. "The battle. Like you told me. It happened two days ago. And in the end, moving away won out." My voice quivered now. "I think I lost him, Marie. I don't know if I'll ever see him again."

"Oh no. That's not good. I told you to give each a fair shot."

"I tried, Marie. I really think I did."

"I take it you're not talking to him now? Have you been thinking about him?"

"I've been trying not to."

"Stop that," she said. "It's not giving him a fair shot."

"I know. You keep saying that. But he's not ready for a relationship with me. He won't call me his boyfriend, and I don't know how to feel secure in him sticking around. The only way he could ever be worth...you know, not leaving, is if I knew for certain that things with him would last."

She smirked. "Well, let's ignore the fact that you can't know that yet, and maybe not ever, no matter what he says. Do you really need him to say he'll be your boyfriend to feel secure with him? Do you actually think he won't get there? The guy seems to like you an awful lot—I mean, this bleeds with irony right now. You're worried about commitment from him, when he's the one begging you to stay."

I frowned at this, then drew in a slow breath. "In a way, I just wish he could put aside the raw feeling of wanting me to stay, and stop to consider that I'll be losing my job. I'll have nothing. What does he want me to do—go back to my summer job? And where the fuck will I live? I can't get it out of my head that it's a selfish point of view on his part, and I didn't know he could be that way."

She paused. "Maybe it's not so much about whether he's worth it, or not worth it, or whether he's selfish or not. I think it has more to do with you and your personal needs. Take a look at your job. If you move to keep it, who are you doing that for? I really hope you're doing it for yourself, and no one else. I'm a little skeptical about that part, to be perfectly honest with you. Now, if you stay to be with Mikey, I'm pretty sure you'd be doing it at least as much for yourself as for him. Probably more."

"Oh god, Marie. How do I even figure that out for sure? Jesus, maybe you're right. I don't know."

"Maybe I'm not," she said. "Maybe this is just the disturbing form my eleventh-hour pleading has chosen to take on. See? Everybody's fighting to get what they want. We're all selfish, Wyatt. I think it's doable to just accept that about people, and chase after what you want. Keep others in mind, but most of all, look out for number one."

I smiled a little. "Right. Riding two buses clear across the city to help a friend in his time of need—that's really selfish, Marie."

She stayed silent, smiling and shrugging. I went over to the couch, sat down next to her and pulled her into a long hug. She patted my shoulder and said, "Everything will be okay, Wyatt."

"Marie," I said shakily, "I mean, if I...fuck. If I actually don't go, then every second passing right now is just pointless torture for him. How can I live with myself knowing that?"

She hugged me more tightly. "Stop. Just take the time you need. It's yours to take. He'll handle himself. Wyatt, I'm telling you that if you do change your mind, he won't resent you for the number of days it required."

I let her go and lay back against the cushion. "Fuck me, I don't want to talk about this anymore. I want to know about someone else's life. What do you have for me?"

She searched her mind. "Hmmm, not too much. I suppose I'm really starting to think I need someone. I don't like being alone at all." She laughed. "That's probably another way I'm biased when you ask for my advice."

"Do you have any prospects?"

"Plenty. Or no, not really. Depends on my expectations, which pretty much rise and fall with the tide."

"If you had to pick a number-one right now, who would it be?"

"It would be me, Wyatt," she said, smiling. "I thought we already discussed this." She paused. "No, but really, it's so hard to imagine any of them. Dating has been a true horror. Fuck, I don't know. Maybe I'll just date Sloan. Who the fuck knows?"

I gasped. "Is Sloan really on the table?"

Her eyes narrowed as she attempted to read my face. "What would be your response if he was?"

"I don't know. I'm still in shock, Marie." I was smiling, I'm sure. "Since when has this been a possibility?"

She hesitated, intensely thoughtful. Looking past me she said, "You only need a man to take care of you once...to help you walk home after you've embarrassed yourself with alcohol ...to hold his coat over you when it starts to rain. He looked right into my eyes, Wyatt. He said if I needed anything at all, to call him right away. There's no question in my mind that he wanted to kiss me then. I can tell those things. But he didn't do it, because I wasn't in a good state."

"Sloan's a complete gentleman," I said.

She sighed. "I know. It's taken me a long time to notice him, Wyatt. Oh, it had nothing to do with what he looks like with his clothes off—I got over that a long time ago. In fact, I don't think it ever would have mattered. I think it's that we're primarily good friends, Sloan and I. You don't always notice people like that."

"Follow your dreams, Marie."

She crossed her arms. "Well, who the hell knows if it'll go anywhere? No one, that's who. We'll just have to wait and see."

"We will," I said.

Marie stayed with me long into the evening. The intensity of our discussion diminished; we put on a movie and she helped me with what little packing I had left. I thought back to what my mom had said, about how people can change, no matter their age. I believed she was right, but I also believed that some aspects of a person never change, which was why that evening with Marie flooded with the same warming light as our evenings spent together years earlier. In fact, nothing of substance had been lost from that first day when, in the middle of the commons lawn, before the weather turned cold, she appeared out of nowhere—complimenting my shirt, of all things—and asked me if I was looking for a friend.

20

The sky illuminated in a colorless haze, though the sun was not yet up. I stood still in the middle of the room, where the coffee table had been, just staring at the couch for a couple of minutes. Something settled in one of the moving boxes and my feet left the floor. I sighed, bit my lip and went over to the right side of the white mammoth, gripped underneath its bottom edge, lifted it a few inches and set it back down on its stubby metal legs. My eyes swept the room. I swiveled around, scanning wide-open kitchen cabinets, all empty. Thank god there was still cleaning left to do.

By eleven, basically everything was done. My appetite soared, so I put on a jacket and left. It was about time, too, as the now-bare walls of my apartment had begun closing in on me. Down at the corner I ordered banh mi to dine in and waited longer than usual in a small booth by the window as it was prepared. My phone vibrated an inch across the table. I did not recognize the number and held my breath as I opened the text.

"Hello Wyatt. This is Sophie. I got your number from Mikey's phone. I'm aware that it's not my place to be sending you this, but I just don't care anymore. Mikey is destroyed right now. I understand that you have already decided to go, but don't let your doubt of his commitment be the reason. Please let it be anything else. Just not that. No matter what was said, you should know that he cares very deeply for you. We're at work right now and I know he would never forgive me if he found out what I've done. Don't reply to this message. Hope to see you again sometime."

I put my phone in my pocket. My order was announced so I went to the counter, retrieved it and returned to the booth to eat. Just outside, a woman stood on the sidewalk, guiding someone who reversed a large car incrementally into a narrow parking space. She put up her hand for the driver to stop but the car continued to roll back, so she shouted and waved her arms until it halted suddenly, just an inch or two from a metal post.

This text offended my present sensibilities. Fearful of the conclusion at which I would certainly arrive and variety of conceivable subsequent actions, I had suspended any estimation of Mikey's wellbeing (or lack thereof) so much that I became aware of my own mastery of the task. This text offered me more than conclusion; it was confirmation, and I ingested it as such, along with my sandwich, which I ate now with great effort as a practical means to sustenance, and no longer to satisfy any actual hunger.

With nothing left to do at the apartment and no wish to return there, I stood in the parking lot ten minutes later and considered my options. There were many, it occurred to me suddenly and with a fantastic feeling of immensity. It struck me that my behavior must become different from how it had recently been. It seemed as good an idea as anything else to walk to a nearby branch of the public library, sit down at a terminal and type a third chapter to the story.

I labored over it for the entire rest of the day. I wrote slowly and carefully, occasionally turning to my phone and scrolling through the previous two chapters for reference. I was grateful for the library's generous hours of operation as it became dark and a fourth digit now prepended the time at the top of the screen. I made up my mind that I was finished not long after and left for home, reacquainting myself with the charms of the nighttime by virtue of its ambassador, the warm, familiar and abiding wind which both dispatched through and inspired the trees, and came to brush itself against my hands and lips.

I sat at home, finishing off a few leftovers from the refrigerator, content with my use of the day. Before bed I double-checked that everything was ready for my parents' arrival in the morning, then looked over what I had written, correcting a fair number of objective errors but otherwise not interested in changing it. If it still felt like the right thing to do, I decided, I would send it to Mikey the next morning.

I slept deeply and woke up without much time to spare before my parents were supposed to show up, although I was all but certain they would be late.

"I hope you enjoy the third chapter, if you still want to read it," I texted Mikey. "I want to meet with you. If that's okay with you, please let me know. It will have to be in the evening or tomorrow because my parents are helping me pack today." I attached the file and then sent it.

The Acura droned noisily up the hill and my mom emerged alone from it. Her footsteps pounded their way up the stairwell, impossibly energized. "Morning, sweetie," she said after I let her in. "I can take off my shoes if you like, or is that no longer a thing?"

"Just leave them on," I told her. "I think Dad and I will be able to get the couch. I want it out of the way. You can guide us down."

"He's on his way. I had to use a pry bar to get him out of bed this morning." She laughed, and then stared at me for a moment. "Is something on your mind?"

I looked at her. "Didn't have breakfast. Hungry, I guess." I drew the final bagel from a clear bag by the sink and began to gnaw at its cold, unsliced flesh.

"Did you talk to Mikey?"

"Sort of."

She paused. "Okay, well that's good." It was clear she was not satisfied with my answer.

"I sent him a text."

"When? Did he reply?"

"No. It was only half an hour ago. And I wasn't really asking for a response."

"I bet he'll answer you anyway," she said, glancing around the room. "Christ, Wyatt, I should have you come clean up the house. Did you do all of this yourself?"

"Marie came by the other night," I said.

"You've hardly left anything for us."

A deep rumbling sound buzzed through the front windows.

"That'll be your dad with the pickup. He put the trailer on it last night. I think we'll get everything in. Stephanie said she'd come by later, but I'm not sure there will be anything left."

My dad showed up at the door not long after and the three of us began the long journey downward with the couch, resting on each landing, giggling endlessly at the array of absurd maneuvers necessitated by the awkward confines of the stairwell.

After moving the bed, coffee table and drop-leaf table, as well as several of the boxes, my dad suggested that we break for lunch. We drove back to the house and made sandwiches. I knew I had been brought in for questioning once they had finished arranging themselves across from me at the table in the dining room. I looked from one of them to the other with a mouth full of deli turkey.

"You're absolutely sure about this move, sweetie?" asked my mom.

I continued to chew. "I'm as sure as I'll ever be."

My dad cleared his throat, peered into his sandwich and then closed it again. "Wyatt, if you were really trying to convince someone, I think you would put it differently than that."

"I guess I'm not trying to convince anybody." I swallowed the bite. "I mean, come on, both of you know I have no idea what the fuck I'm doing. I've made a decision but honestly I have no clue whether it was built on the hard rock or the sand —isn't that how you always said it, Mom?"

"The wet marshes," she corrected. "And Fitzgerald said it. I took it from him."

"Yeah, that's right, the wet marshes—look, I've fallen in love with him. That's my fault. It was bad timing. If it weren't for him, I'd be going. That's why part of me still thinks I should go."

"But you can do whatever you want, sweetie," she said. Her expression was strained.

My dad touched her arm. "Just let him do what he decides is right."

"I'm sorry for the way this is happening," I said. "I didn't mean to bring everything down to the wire like this."

"It's how things happen sometimes," said my mom.

"It's okay," said my dad.

Stephanie showed up as we returned to my apartment to finish loading boxes and smaller items.

"I don't like this day," she said, pulling me close to her, not letting go for several seconds. She looked up at my building. "Will you miss the place?"

"In a strange way, yeah."

She didn't ask me what I meant. She probably knew already, in her own way.

After another two hours spent toiling at the relaxed pace to which my family was accustomed, the last of everything was packed into the truck. My dad chugged away, one arm out the window, waving back at us as he left for home. We stayed behind to do some final cleaning.

"Jesus, Wyatt, did you ever mop this floor?" Stephanie was down on her hands and knees scrubbing at a dark spot in the linoleum close to the stove.

"Once or twice," I said. "I didn't ask you to do that, by the way. Keep in mind that it wasn't perfect when I moved in."

"When was this place last renovated?"

"Once in the 80s, I think."

She stopped scrubbing. "Oh my god, it's older than me."

My mom laughed from the bathroom.

All the while I checked my phone for an answer from Mikey. I only half-expected something. Based on the text I'd received from Sophie, I figured he would want to see me, too, but I didn't know for sure. Nothing had come by the time we were ready to leave around four, so I tucked it back into my pocket and left both copies of the apartment key on the kitchen counter. Carrying my vacuum under one arm, I locked the door from the inside and closed it behind me for the last time. I followed my mom and sister, who made their way down the steps.

My phone wouldn't make a sound until after we'd finished dinner, once Stephanie had left and my mom and I had cleaned up after a game of Scrabble. I had denied myself any real hope that a reply would ever come at all, but that's exactly what it was.

"Sorry," it read, "had to go into work today to prepare for being gone again. I got home and decided I should wait to text you until after I'd read it. Beautiful. I don't know if you're trying to say anything by having it go down the way it did. I'm worried I'm reading into things. I want to see you so bad. Please come over tonight if you can."

"Mom," I said. "Mikey texted me back. He wants to see me tonight."

She looked up from her tablet. "Well Jesus Christ, Wyatt, go see him then."

I went down the hall to the bedroom, where my dad lay on the bed reading. I thanked him for all his help and he smiled back at me.

"Wyatt," my mom said quietly as I put on my shoes, "all your things are safe here in the garage."

I looked up at her. "Thank you, Mom."

"What I mean to say is, if we're not bringing it up to Fern Hill tomorrow...no matter what we end up doing with it all ...it's safe here for the time being." Her eyes returned to the screen.

"I understand," I said as I straightened up. "What you're saying means a lot to me. I'll let you know what happens."

I left the house and waited for about ten minutes at the side of the highway for the next bus. Once I had boarded, I began crafting a text to Jennifer. I struggled with it, keenly aware of the full impact of my actions. Finally I came up with something I could live with. I looked it over once more, removed the middle of three apologies and sent it.

Her reply came back quickly, as if she had already prepared herself for this outcome. "Aww, Wyatt, I know you. You wouldn't be doing this without a lot of thought. No hard feelings. We can work out the details later. I'll miss you up there.

Proud of you for following your heart."

As I turned down Mikey's street I saw where light spilled out of the window by his bed, just barely illuminating the rails of his balcony. I entered the lobby, where I was wordlessly buzzed in, and began making my way up to the fourth floor.

I knocked, the door swung open, and there he was, taller and broader than I remembered, his hair wild as ever. "Hey, Chickadee," he said softly.

I had wanted to say something to him in that moment but couldn't, instead stepping forward and putting my arms around him. He started crying, and so did I. We stood in the doorway like that for a minute or two before parting and stepping back into his apartment.

We sat down together and I said, "I'm so sorry. I've handled this whole thing in weird ways that are so hard to understand. You're good at letting your emotions guide your decisions—at keeping things simple in that way. I should have trusted you."

"Did you change your mind?" he asked. "I need to know that now."

"Yes, Mikey. I'm not moving. You're right, I don't like my job anymore, but mostly it's that I've realized I'm in love with you. And I don't need you to tell me how you feel about me. It's not important for me to hear it."

He looked straight into my eyes. "Well, I'm going to tell you anyway. I should have said that I was in love with you, too, because I am. You were right. I was very afraid to say it. And now that I know you're staying, I want to start calling you my boyfriend."

"You don't have to do it for me."

"I'm not," he assured me. "And if you're worried at all about whether or not I would make a good boyfriend, please know that I will honor you every day. I'm not going to hide who you are to anyone. You'll see that I will be very good to you."

"You've already been good to me," I said.

He looked away. "I realize what you're giving up by not going."

"I know you do," I said, looking down at our hands, which were pressed into the cushion with just an inch separating them, "but it's the right decision, for so many reasons."

I looked up to see his face just as his massive grin made its return. "Well, fuck, that's true," he said.

"God, Mikey, I missed everything about you."

He stood up. "You really missed all this, huh?" He gestured back at himself with both hands, up and down his body. "If you say so." He came over to me, knelt down on the couch, straddling me where I sat, and kissed me. He kept it brief, sat back with his hands on my shoulders and said, "I missed you, too, Chickadee." He stood up and looked around the room.

"Are you packing already?" I asked, coming to stand next to him. His suitcase lay open and mostly full near the foot of his bed.

"Yes. I'm leaving tonight. So...the thing is, I decided I didn't want to be here when you left town. I thought it would be, you know, just that much harder for me. So I canceled my plane ticket. I figured I could make it past Seattle tonight and find a hotel somewhere."

"Oh. Okay," I said. "Yeah, I understand."

"Is there any way I could convince you to go with me?"

"Are you serious?"

"Yes," he said. "I planned it so I would have some downtime. I promise you, it's nice there. And I'm only going for a few days."

"Of course I'll go with you."

"Okay," he said. "Alright."

"I won't be in the way?"

"Are you kidding?" He began moving excitedly about the room, straightening up his Playstation controllers and finishing his packing. "I can't believe this is happening." He stopped and turned to me. "We'll go by your place so you can pack a bag."

I shook my head. "There's nothing left there. All moved out. I've got a bag already packed, though, at my parents' place."

"Wow, I completely forgot," he said. He closed his suitcase. "I'm going to miss your apartment."

I shrugged. "I only ever liked it when you were there with me."

We left in a hurry. The ride to my parents' house flashed by; I remember the heat from the palm of his hand against my fingertips. He kept glancing over at me, flashing his smile, telling me he was just so happy I was coming with him.

The light was off in the living room. I had left my bag just inside the door. Having begun at whatever age such noiseless discretion becomes relevant to a young person's life, my years of practice served me well now. I leaned inside, lifted the bag and was gone.

As I crept back across the lawn, I picked a cherry blossom from the tree and then looked and saw his earnest face through the passenger window. I stepped toward the car, holding the flower up for him to see. He smiled, incredulous, like he still couldn't believe I had come back to him. I wanted to cry one last time, but I didn't. I opened the door and told him I was ready for the trip.

ABOUT THE AUTHOR

Kid Boise was born and raised in Boise, Idaho and now lives in Vancouver, British Columbia. He hasn't quite settled down yet.

CPSIA information can be obtained at www.ICGtesting.com
Printed in the USA
LVOW11s1241090516

487358LV00006B/427/P